I0738988

Breaking Steele

H.B. Tyler

BURKWOOD
Media Group

This book is a work of fiction. Names (except as stated in the Acknowledgements), characters, places, and incidents either are the product of the author's imagination or are used fictitiously, and any resemblance to actual persons, living or dead, business establishments, events, or locales is entirely coincidental.

Copyright ©2018 by H.B. Tyler

All rights reserved. In accordance with the U.S. Copyright Act of 1976, no part of this publication may be reproduced, distributed, transmitted, or retransmitted in any form or by any means, including scanning, recording, uploading, or other electronic or mechanical methods, without the prior expressed written permission of the author, except in the case of brief quotations embodied in critical reviews and other noncommercial uses permitted by copyright law. Thank you for your support of the author's rights.

Printed in the United Sates

For information or permission contact:
Burkwood Media Group
P O Box 29448
Charlotte, NC 28229

ISBN: 978-0-692-10069-1

Acknowledgments

I would like to begin by thanking Cris Steele and Jeff Bolton for the use of their names, as the fictitious characters share some of their real and amazing attributes. I had these nameless characters in my head for a few years. Once I got to know Cris & Jeff (who in real life don't know each other) and saw how their qualities matched those of my characters, I knew I had the names which were previously eluding me. Cris and Jeff are both strong, good hearted, caring people who are willing to sacrifice and go out of their way to help others and put others before themselves. I consider myself fortunate to know them both.

There are also many people I would like to thank for their expertise and help in writing of this book.

Special thanks to Debra Funderburk for guiding and putting up with me and especially all her tireless help and patience throughout the entire publishing process.

Also, in no particular order, an additional thank you to those who helped me along the way: Georgia, Cindy, Stephanie, Paula, & Dr. J. And, of course, my family who stood by me as I locked myself away to write or walked around musing about another world that was entirely in my head.

If I've missed anyone with my sleep deprived brain, please accept my sincerest apologies.

No doubt, there are some errors in the book, and they are all mine.

For Georgia, my right hand.

"Knowing your own darkness
is the best method for dealing
with the darknesses of other people."
~ Carl Jung

Chapter 1

Detective Cris Steele looked up as she was sitting against the old Live Oak tree. As the sun fought through the branches and split the Spanish moss that appeared to be stretching and trying to reach the ground, a big white egret swooped through looking for its next meal, its shadow in the sun like a plane gliding over. The birds were loudly singing and swooning, many chasing each other like they were playing a game of tag.

"Hey, earth to Cris!" Luke's melodic voice drifted in and broke her concentration of nothingness.

Cris looked over at him and couldn't help but smile. While they had only been married a short time, they have been best friends and inseparable for 18 years now. It didn't seem possible, but she would swear she loved him more every day.

She gave a slight shake of her head. "Sorry, did I seem like I was lost?"

"Yeah, you scared me, you seemed so peaceful and still. It's not like you to just sit and relax, you're always going 100 mph and so serious; no-nonsense. I was wondering if you were having a stroke or something." Luke shot her his signature crooked smile, knowing she would revel in the round-about compliment.

Cris couldn't help but return a smirk. "You're such an ass. Did you think to bring your calendar with you? You need to mark this down. I was just sitting, doing nothing, thinking of nothing except the beauty of this day and this spot. Listen. Do you hear those birds all around us, singing, chirping, doing whatever the hell it is they do? I'm being present in the moment and it's bizarre and beautiful."

"Holy horse shit, you *are* having some kind of medical emergency. Where's your phone? I know it's glued to you somewhere, I need to call 911, get you to the hospital."

Cris found a nearby stick, reached over and grabbed it and pitched it in his direction, again she was not able to hide her smirk as she threw it. This was their way of showing affection, sarcasm and razzing each other.

"I'm sorry. If it's any consolation, I'm sure it won't happen again. This is a first for me; to not have an active case to think about. No doubt this is an isolated incident."

Cris saw Luke scowl at the mention of a case. She knew he loved and supported her completely, he always had; but he would never stop worrying about her with this line of work and career she seemed to be destined for. Every time her phone rang, Luke cringed, wondering what latest psycho she would have to find next. Cris knew he didn't mean to be so crude, that's not who or how he was, but when it came to her it was gloves off, a whole new ball game.

"Well, amen to this isolated incident, I'll take what I can get! So, I guess then we can both concede that my, I mean this, idea to come relax here for the day was a good one?"

"Have I mentioned that you're an ass?" Cris again saw that crooked smile that she absolutely loved, it melted her heart every time. "I'm not sure I'm ready to admit it was a good idea, but I will say I am relaxed for the first time in a long time."

Luke rolled his eyes and teased at her, "Ugh, would it kill you to admit I had a good idea?"

"Probably not, but it might hurt my alter ego immensely." Cris couldn't help but snicker at that one.

With a big exaggerated eye roll she kept going. "I'm sure your students lavish you with compliments about how wonderful and smart you are and about how your ideas and teachings are *so* great because you teach them differently than the other teachers with hands on experiments instead of book and rote learning and blah, blah, blah, blah, blah." Cris flapped her fingers like people were blabbing away.

She paused, saw the look of implied boredom on Luke's face and decided to continue on. "And, I'm sure the girls on your soccer team think you're just the best coach there is since you do all the warm-ups and cool-downs with them and you can demonstrate to them the exact play you're trying to teach them. And the big bonus; you're so young and hot and fit." She knew she was really getting him now.

Luke gave her his crooked smile again, knowing it would crush her heart. "Yes, of course I hear that from my students and my team pretty much every day, but I want to hear it from my beautiful, smart, extremely stubborn wife."

As hard as it was, Cris was not taking the bait. "I want to know how we went from me being relaxed to this?"

Luke conceded. "You are good. No wonder you graduated best in your class and quickly became one of the two lead detectives in your department, shit in the whole county for that matter! It scares the hell out of me, quite frankly, but I'm so proud of you and love you for it."

"Well, we both busted our butt's and sacrificed to get where we are right now."

No truer words were spoken. They did fight their way, together, through childhood as well as college, with no support and no one to lean on but each other. Nothing was handed to them, and in exchange, they took nothing for granted.

They seemed to be the only ones here. There were dirt trails winding throughout the preserve which were mostly covered in pine straw from the tall pines that swayed and loomed all around. There were some small ponds and as you got closer they had some wooden walkways and decks over-looking the water here and there. They were great places to come watch the beautiful sunrises and sunsets. It was frequented by both hunters and nature lovers throughout the year. It was more of a "locals" place, off a back road and not known to the tourists. It was normally a relatively quiet and secluded area, but today is was empty, which was a special rarity and treat. They were relaxing in the thick shadows under the huge tree and to Cris, it felt like they were the only ones left on the planet after an apocalypse, besides the loud abounding wildlife of course.

She looked around lazily, again noticing the peacefulness, serenity and beauty in the day. "You know, I think it's the beauty of this area that helps me get through all the excrements I have to see and deal with every day. There's not a single day I don't drive to work or over a bridge and not be taken away by the beauty of it all, even on the few cloudy or rainy days it's still beautiful in its own way. The sunrises and sunsets are the most beautiful I've ever seen."

She now looked Luke in the eyes. "I still can't believe you were born here and I'm so sorry you had to leave and end up in my little Podunk town; but wanting to come back here to settle our lives and start our family was the best idea."

Cris realized she was rambling. She knew it was because she didn't have an active case to be distracted by, idol time was not usually good for her. This was one of the first times she could just sit and relax and have nothing important to think about. It was making the flood gates open and she needed to stop. She kept the touchy-feely stuff tucked away inside, buried where no one could find it, even herself most of the time.

She quickly added "Anyway, don't let that go to your head," and gave him a cool smirk.

Luke knew her way too well by now. "Don't worry I won't hold it over your head that you actually broke your inner steel wall and showed some slight personal emotion. I, on the other hand, have no problem showing my soft, warm underbelly to you. Don't you ever apologize for me having to come to your little "Podunk town". He made little air quotation marks with his fingers. "You know I believe everything happens for a reason. As much as it hurt and still haunts me to have seen my parents' lifeless bodies and empty eyes staring at me after the car accident, if it hadn't happened we wouldn't have met. Okay, so I'd have grown up in this beautiful little paradise, but it would not be with you, so I would not be truly happy. This, *you*, were my destiny. This is what was supposed to happen, I'll never be sorry for that!"

Luke had no problems telling her how he felt. Cris was so envious of that, she couldn't imagine not having all her thoughts and feelings locked inside. Of course, the psychology degree in her knew she had many deep seeded issues which caused this, and she should work on them instead of continuing to keep them buried. No time for that.

Cris knew Luke believed everything happened for a reason, hell she did too. Sometimes it was hard to remember when all the bad stuff in life happens. Being honest with herself though, looking back, that same belief is what helped pull her through the tough times. Knowing somehow at the end she would be better and stronger for what she went through. She also knew that you'll tell yourself whatever you need to in order to get through when life keeps pelting you with snowballs made of shit.

Luke was laying on his belly, propped up on his arms at the edge of the blanket, his sandy brown hair all tousled from the slight breeze. His green eyes were staring at her, boring holes into her soul.

"Are you trying to find my soul in there or what Steele Appeal?"

It was a stupid nick name Cris gave Luke as kids and she never stopped using it. It was her little private pet name for him and because of that he never complained about it. They both knew it was another one of her back-door ways of showing affection.

"If that's what you're looking for good luck. You know I have no soul."

Luke lifted himself to his knees and started crawling slowly towards her. "Oh, I know it's in there and I will find it."

He was trying to have a very serious face as he crawled her way, but she could tell he was struggling with it. He was almost on top of her and she knew he was coming in for a kiss. She started to lean forward when she heard an all too familiar crack. In the split second it took her to realize what it was, it was too late. Luke collapsed on top of her, blood pouring from his lifeless head.

Chapter 2

Chief Jeff Bolton closed the latest case file just as his door burst open and hit the wall knocking one of his pictures crooked.

"Sir, I'm sorry to interrupt you but we just got a call!"

Chief snapped his head up from behind the neatly stacked mountains of paperwork and files to see Melinda, the dispatcher, standing, wide eyed and out of breath with beads of sweat sticking her dark hair to her brow. The dispatchers just dispatched, pretty cut and dry, never did they run back here to his office to personally tell him. *What the hell?* No sooner were her words gasped out before Chief's cell phone started vibrating and dancing, adding to the sudden chaos.

"What the fuck?" He held a finger up to Melinda, quickly glanced at the flitting phone and saw it was Detective Pete Bryan.

Chief snatched the phone and hit the answer button, not allowing Pete to speak, "Bryan, hang on just a second!"

Chief looked back up to Melinda. "We get calls all day, what the hell is going on Mel?"

His booming voice showed his impatience. He didn't mind her coming to his office but obviously something serious was going on and he wanted to know now!

"I'm sorry to barge in here like this, but I knew you would want to know right away and I felt I had to tell you in person! It's Detective Steele, Sir!" Mel was getting choked up, her cheeks turning red, and she was really having a hard time getting the words out.

"Not Cris!" "What about her? What's wrong?" It just intensified, his haunches were up.

It was Steele's day off, she just finished up a long case and Bolton knew she was looking forward to some relaxation and quality time with Luke.

"It's not her, it's her husband. Luke was just shot and killed, right in front of her!"

At having said it out loud, the tears spilled over and silently rolled down her cheeks. It always hit home when it was one of your own.

Bolton's head started to spin, this couldn't be happening, there had to be some mistake! He struggled to get his wits about him and strength in his voice.

"Mel, who called this in?"

"Detective Steele did herself, Sir. I'm so sorry!"

With that acknowledgment Mel walked out the door, shoulders drooped, head down. Bolton watched her walk away and close the door, everything moving slow.

He still couldn't believe it; no way was this really happening. He looked down at the old coffee stains on his desk. It felt like those stains were swirling and that his head was swaying the way it does after just getting off a ship. Chief felt utterly lost and numb. He had to call Cris himself to hear it. He looked at his phone and was surprised that it was already in his hand for some reason. *Shit! Bryan is waiting for me, I completely forgot!* Bolton took a drink of cold stale coffee trying to get some moisture back in his mouth which was now like cotton. It only made it worse.

"Pete! Hey man I'm sorry, Melinda from dispatch was just in here to personally deliver some shocking news."

"Yes, I heard her through the phone. This is why I'm calling myself, to tell you too." Pete sounded almost breathless.

No! If Bryan was called about it too then it probably was true. This can't be happening to Cris, can't she just catch one frigging break? Can't something good in her life stick for once? No one deserved happiness more than Cris and for some reason she seemed to be cursed, everything good and worth a damn ripped from her hands.

Chief shook his head and returned his attention to Pete. "Yes. Apparently, Luke was shot and killed right in front of her?"

"Worse than that Sir, apparently Luke was so close in front of her he actually collapsed on her."

At hearing those words Chief's mouth went even drier, which he didn't think was possible previously. Bolton looked up towards the ceiling, imagining the sky above. *Seriously? Watching her husband get murdered wasn't bad enough, he had to actually fall on her? Why does this have to happen to her?* His only answer was the rattling of the old air conditioning blowing luke warm air and more dust particles through the vents. Nothing divine or profound was answering him, not that he expected it to. He took another swig of the stale coffee, getting the same nasty, non-existent results as before. Slamming the cup down harder than he intended, he watched some drops jump out onto his desk.

"Where the hell did this happen?"

"About a mile into the nature trail next to their house. There's a big Live Oak just a little ways off the trail, that's where they were sitting." Bryan's voice was low and cracking, it was obvious it was hitting him hard.

Pete was friends with Cris and Luke. He had watched their dog a few times and hung out with them a little on the rare occasions they both had down time simultaneously. This was personal for him too.

"Right near her fucking house? How is this possible? It is not the type of area where this would happen! Are you sure about this? They weren't visiting the city or something?" He knew he was reaching, that Bryan would have accurate information, but it just didn't seem right.

"Yes, Sir, I'm positive. I know it's bizarre and even worse since it is not a well-known or popular place there are no security cameras there. It is not exactly on the town's list of priorities for surveillance. I've been in there before; another obstacle is the trails are hard compact dirt and mostly covered by pine straw. Getting tracks from anyplace in there is going to be near impossible." Both the pressure and defeat already bearing down on him was evident.

Leave it to Bryan to already be thinking about the evidence and nailing this son of a bitch, good for him! Bolton had to get a grip and get his own head in the game.

"Bloody hell, that's right! This could be insurmountable in obtaining evidence. Damn it!"

Bryan still had a shaky voice but thankfully appeared to be keeping his typical cool head about him. "We've got the road patrol, M.E., forensics, everyone on the way already. I'm on my way right now too, I'm only about five minutes out. Of course, Steele has already assessed where the shot must have come from. She's sure it came from the other side of the trail straight ahead of where she was sitting. She figures she would have been looking right towards that direction. She says the bullet went straight through and is stuck in the tree. We will at least have that evidence going for us."

"Of course, she goes right into detective mode, right down to business. Thankfully she stayed put and didn't run off half-cocked trying to get him, and potentially ruin any evidence. So, you actually spoke to her? It wasn't a call from the department?" Bolton still couldn't wrap his head around all this.

"Yes, Cris called me right after she called dispatch, asked me to come out to help her process the scene, get a jump start on it until she would be able to help. Like it would even be a question! I'm sure it will be awhile until the forensics team is done enough to move the body for her to get up."

The thought of that made the coffee churn in Chief's stomach and he could feel it starting to make its way up his esophagus. *Better grab a quick antacid.* He had to get there to be with her, to let her know she was not alone and try to comfort her, somehow.

"I'm heading out the door now, I'll meet you there in less than 10!" Chief gave a slight pause and quietly added before hanging up, "Pete, as much as she will let you, please stay with her until I get there. This has got to be a nightmare for her!" At that he ended the call, unable to say anymore without breaking down.

He was rounding the corner of his desk heading for the door and the burning in his throat reminded him he needed those antacids. He quickly turned back and grabbed them out of the desk drawer. Righting himself to head for the door again he dropped his keys as he tried to snag them off the desk. As they fell to the floor Bolton realized how frazzled he was. He spent his whole adult career being cool, calm and making life altering decisions under extreme pressure in a matter of seconds; and it had paid dividends in his current career as a Chief. But this, this had him all shook up. He had a few miles to get his head and composure together. He had to be strong, the Chief in control for his team, but more than anything, for Cris.

Chapter 3

Detective Pete Bryan peeled into Steele's driveway slamming on the brakes lurching his Chevy pickup, and himself, forward. In one swift swoop he yanked the keys from the ignition, stuffed them in his pocket, grabbed his cell phone and locked the door as he slammed it shut and bolted to the tree line. At that moment he was thankful for both being in shape and that he had been on the trails before, Pete knew right where he needed to go. On his mad dash to get to the location, he was also looking and scanning for evidence, and as improbable as he knew it was, he was looking for the perpetrator to be hiding in the shadows somewhere. There was nobody in sight, it was deserted the whole way in except those damn black birds circling around overhead, cawing obnoxiously. Those bastards always reminded him of death, and this memory now forever ingrained in his brain.

Coming up onto the scene, Pete realized he was arriving just behind the rest of the crew. The yellow "do not cross" tape was just beginning to get put up to quarantine off the area. Inside the local PD, medical examiner, crime scene techs and forensics were busy writing notes, searching the grounds for any evidence and taking pictures of the body and surrounding area. Steele was sitting right next to Luke's body, leaning against the tree. He flashed his badge at the lackey rolling out the tape, not even looking at him or saying a word as he walked through.

Rushing over towards the tree where Cris was sitting, Pete saw more details of the scene. The blood all over the blanket they had laid out, the shattered, lifeless body of somebody he knew and cared for. As he got closer Steele's face became clearer. Blood spattered and smeared all over it, but the worst was her eyes. Those normally beautiful bright blue eyes were dull, unblinking, lost and empty. Cris had obviously mentally checked out, she didn't even see him running towards her. Knowing the techs were done with her physically, there was no way he was going to even try to restrain himself as he reached her.

Pete knelt down in front of her, touching her hand, gently calling her. "Cris, hey I'm here for you."

At hearing his voice, Cris came out of her trance and looking relieved, stood up. "Pete, thank God you're here! We've gotta go check out the rest of the area, see if that piece of shit is still around, find some evidence to nail this guy's nuts to his ass..."

Pete cut her off there and pulled her into him. He held her tight and caressed the back of her blood ridden head. "We will Cris, we will, I promise. For right now, I'm here, just breathe."

Seeing everything up close now, holy hell the blood was everywhere! Her jeans, t-shirt and sneakers were spattered and smeared matching her face. Then he made the mistake of looking at Luke, his face and head half gone. Pete squeezed Cris even tighter. For the first time in his career he had a hard time not throwing up. A huge lump formed in his throat and he knew he couldn't speak without having much more than words coming out of his mouth. This was one image and entire scene that would haunt him for the rest of his life.

Cris pulled back from him. "You know as well as I do we have to get moving. The more time that passes the lesser our chances of finding him or any viable evidence. The shot must have come from that direction" she pointed across the way "based on the impact point. Maybe something was dropped or left there we can use. Maybe a casing from the bullet will have some prints on it. If it's something small, like a piece of paper, a slight breeze could blow it away. It could be too late since there has been a breeze."

"Yes, I do know that, but look, there are teams already out there scoping. We are going to join them, but nothing will blow away before we get there, they would have already picked it up and bagged it. I need to know you're okay. You are not alone, I'm here now and Chief will be here any minute. We are going to get this son of a bitch, but right now you need to try and begin processing all of this." Pete's eyes were pleading with her.

He realized by the surprised look on her face as she was scanning the perimeter that she never even noticed there were already teams out searching the area for evidence and the killer. Pete didn't know how else to stop her from running out into the forest searching. He knew she was in no condition to be looking for anything, most importantly, but there wasn't a snowball's chance in hell Chief Bolton was going to allow her to be a part of this investigation in any way shape or form. Besides the fact it was too personal, any evidence she found would be torn to shreds by the defense in court saying she planted it or something stupid like that. Pete could tell Cris was hell bent on getting to work right now, like an M-80 ready to explode, and he had no idea how to put out the match she had ignited to light that fuse.

Pete saw Cris had paused and was looking him in the eyes, but differently, softly. He wondered if his crystal blue eyes were betraying him, if they were actually showing the sorrow he was trying to hide and how difficult this was for him. They were more than just colleagues. Cris gave a heavy sigh.

"Thank you for coming Pete, I don't think I could get through this without you. We are more than just occasional partners, I consider you a friend. I know you're trying to help me right now and I really appreciate it, more than you know. That being said though, I, *we*, need to get moving to find this asshole." With that she started to turn away.

Pete still held onto Cris' arm, searching for something to say to stall her. Looking around, he thought he saw the familiar shape of the Chief in the distance lumbering in. At 6 foot nothing Bolton was a decent sized man to say the least. With increased age and the sedentary lifestyle of most of his time now being spent at a desk job he had gotten a little paunch, but overall, he was still in good shape. As the figure loomed closer, Pete could make out the salt and pepper hair and knew Chief Bolton was finally here to save him.

"Cris wait. I see Chief is coming in right over there." Pete pointed his finger in Chief's direction, thankful the boss was finally here. It had only been a few minutes, but it seemed like an eternity.

"He will want to see you, he sounded really shaken up when I was talking to him on my way here."

Cris turned her head in that direction as Pete slowly let go of her arm. They both walked brusquely over towards Chief to meet him. Pete was trying his best to give Bolton a look to warn him that Steele was on fire to get moving. No doubt Chief got the picture when she started in before he could even speak.

"Chief, good, glad you're here, we could use all the help we can get! I think we should start over there where the shot must have come from."

Chief was staring at her wide eyed and jaw dropped as he came upon her, the disbelief at the sight of her with all the blood covering her was evident. He closed his mouth and took a deep breath to gain his composure and Pete was sure Bolton understood the message he had been trying to convey.

Chief spoke slowly, obviously a tactic to try to calm her. "Cris, I can't believe this has happened, I really can't. I know words are useless in times like this, but I really am so sorry!" He swiftly glanced wide eyed at Pete, then looked at Cris. "Listen, I know you want to help us catch this prick, but you know you can't be involved in this investigation. The court and defense attorney would tear us apart and have the case thrown out."

Pete could see the anxiety turn to anger in Cris' face and body. Her eyes narrowed and brow furrowed, her body got real stiff and rigid, arms crossed over her chest, she was ready for a fight.

"I understand protocol Chief, but with all due respect, this is different and you fucking know it! It wouldn't be official, nobody would know. I would hope the rules would be bent a little in this case." Even under the dark smears of blood it was obvious her cheeks were turning red, her blood boiling.

Chief expelled a sigh. Pete could see he was trying his damnedest to stay calm, cool headed and find the right words to make her understand. Pete felt bad for him, he would not want to be in those shoes right now!

"Do you want to nail this guy?" Chief calmly and quietly asked.

Cris was seething, "What kind of asinine question is that? Of course I do!"

Chief moved a little closer to Cris and lowered his voice even more. "Then please understand, I am doing everything in my power to make that happen, to make sure this bastard rots in jail for the rest of his life before he rots in hell. You know the defense would have any piece of evidence thrown out you had anything to do with, say it was tampered with, planted evidence, anything they can come up with. I know you think you can do it incognito, but we can't afford any screw ups on this Cris."

He gave a slight pause, stole another clump of oxygen, probably trying to inhale some courage and quietly told her "I'm putting Bryan on this."

Pete inwardly groaned as Chief looked over at him. They looked each other in the eye, giving a mutual nod of agreement and understanding before Chief looked back at Cris.

"You know he's the best there is, he will get the job done."

Pete wanted nothing to do with investigating this case, but he did his best to hide his thoughts as he placed his arms around Cris' shoulders and pulled her into him. She immediately stiffened, obviously still livid.

"You know I'll do everything I can and I'll do it right, no evidence will be tossed out on my watch." Pete hoped he sounded more confident than he felt.

Cris was still standing there, quietly now. Pete knew her silence was not necessarily a good thing, that she was still rip roaring pissed.

Chief spoke up again "Let me walk you home, please. You probably don't realize it, but you're a mess. I really think it will do you good to take a shower and get cleaned up."

She cut him off with an icy glare at that comment. Pete knew exactly what she was thinking, no shower was going to wash this nightmare away.

Cris looked down at her hands and clothes, apparently for the first time judging by the shock on her face. She picked her head up, squared her shoulders and dug her heels in, her eyes boring into Bolton's.

"No need to walk me home, I know the way. It would make me feel better if you stayed and helped with the investigation. I've got my big girl panties on today, I'll survive."

Pete noticed Cris said she'll survive, not the typical response of I'll be okay.

Apparently Chief noticed it too. "I have no doubt you'll survive. But look at all the people here already searching, and Bryan will be jumping in there too, I'm not needed here. Make me feel better and let me walk home with you please? Afterwards I will come back here and check in and help if it's needed."

Pete could see the resign in Cris' eyes, her brow less furrowed and a slight rounding in her shoulders. He knew she was going to allow Chief to walk home with her. He also knew Chief would not leave her unless he was completely sure she would be alright.

Pete gave her a quick, but strong hug as he whispered in her ear "I've got this Cris, go home and do what you've gotta do, even if it's drowning yourself into a bottle for today. Go curl up with Stormy and hold her tight, she's going to be real confused and need you too. You know to call me if you need me for yourself or the dog, I'm here for you."

To stop himself from saying anymore, Pete let her go and turned his back on her to walk away and begin what he knew would be the worst investigation of his life.

Chapter 4

Cris was still steaming hot and chewing on the fact she was excluded from the investigation and Pete was the lead. She knew he was good, hell Chief was right, Pete was the best, but it didn't take away the sting she was feeling. She wanted the rules bent, this was a special situation, the defense attorneys would never find out she was involved, no matter how irrational it may be she wanted to believe it.

She watched Pete as he walked away, noticing he was in jeans and a t-shirt instead of his normal work attire of khaki pants and a polo shirt. This made her realize it was his day off too. He took her call and came running to help, not even taking time to change. His day off was abruptly ended, he wouldn't be going home anytime soon and certainly wouldn't have a day off until he solved this case. He was sacrificing himself for her and she knew he wouldn't give up. Being honest with herself, she knew he was the best one for the job and would get it done better than she could, especially given the circumstances. But still...

She felt Chief Bolton grab her under the arm, gently trying to coax her to the trail to leave. She took another look around. The sun was still shining in the bright blue cloudless sky, but it didn't hold the same beauty and wonder it did just an hour ago. The birds seemed to be in mourning too, they had all gone into hiding and stopped singing their songs and talking to each other. Just the black birds were whirling and stalking above like they were celebrating and gaining life by the death and darkness below. The Spanish Moss sagging from the old Live Oak now looked like it was weeping instead of reaching for the ground. Everything now appeared so dark and foreboding, despite the brightness of the day. Not only her life, but the whole forest forever changed. Looking away from the old tree and Luke's body being bagged, the zipper just closing up, she swallowed the cement that had formed in her throat and blinked from the burning of tears welling up in her eyes. She would not cry in front of anyone, would not let them see a crack in her facade. She would stay strong, had to in order to solve this and get revenge for Luke's murder. Cris gave an exasperated sigh, raised her head and straightened her shoulders again then turned towards the trail.

"Let's go Chief." She hoped he hadn't heard the crackling that was trying to break through in her voice.

The mile walk out was filled with some kind of conversation, Cris couldn't remember what. She also couldn't remember the walk itself, not what any of the scenery looked like, if they passed any other team members, nothing, it was all blocked out, a complete blur. She simply responded to whatever Bolton was saying while her mind was racing. He didn't seem to be looking at her sideways so Cris assumed she must have had coherent responses. She had a lot of work to do. She had to get a list going of potential suspects, which she had none right now, she also wanted go back to the scene later after everyone else had gone and see what she could find; and shit, she didn't even want to think of the funeral arrangements. Before she knew it they were reaching the edge of the tree line, her house in site.

"Thanks for walking with me Chief, you know you really didn't have to but thank you."

It was a very weak, automatic halfhearted response. She knew Bolton probably realized it, but quite frankly she didn't give a damn at this point.

"Thank you for allowing me to. If you don't mind I'll just continue to the door with you, make sure you get in and settled alright."

Trying to gain the strength and composure she really didn't feel was left in her, Cris conceded. "I'm not going to fight you on it, but just to remind you I am a grown ass woman; and just so you know I have fought through the depths of hell to get through life and where I am today. I *am* going to survive this too."

She started in the direction of home and heard Chief take a deep breath, about to say something. She turned to looked at him and she could read the sadness in his eyes. He looked like he was trying to form some words, words that pained him, but what she couldn't imagine. He exhaled deeply, clearly releasing those words and thoughts, unspoken. Obviously, he had thought better of it. Instead he responded softly and low. "Yes Cris, I understand. Thank you for appeasing me."

This was not the first time she had felt like Chief treated her a little differently than everyone else. He was always softer and gentler with her it seemed. Not that she wasn't held to the same standards and regulations as anyone else, she was, and not like he was uncaring to anyone because he wasn't. He was a kind and caring person to everyone, especially his team. He just seemed to genuinely care more about her, it almost felt like he was watching over her, protective. She really didn't understand why, but also didn't have any more time or energy to think about it. As they weaved in and out through all the vehicles parked in and around her driveway she tossed those thoughts aside thinking for some reason, they must just click and dismissed them at that.

Now realizing all the vehicles were scattered around her house like a jagged parking lot she knew her neighbors must be wondering what was going on. There were county vehicles and personal vehicles crammed in at all kinds of angles. Looking around the road of the small community Cris did notice more people out walking their dogs and doing more yard work than normal. Trying to be inconspicuous, many averted eyes looking her direction as she came walking through. Chief must have noticed them too.

"C'mon, we need to get you inside. This is not something you see in these parts. Besides all the obvious police activity near your house, here you come walking home with another man; and all covered in blood. The rumor is probably already started that you went crazy and killed someone.”

At the word “crazy” Cris flipped a switch looking out into her neighborhood. “It certainly wouldn't be the first time I've been called crazy. Fuck them, I don't care what they say. Let them think I'm crazy, keep them the hell away from me that way. I'm sure my Pitbull and I are just the vicious crazy ones in the neighborhood, better watch out for us!”

Her voice getting louder as she went on, almost like she wanted them to hear. Cris was trying to continue, but Bolton put his arms around her shoulders and steered her towards the front door.

“Let's get inside. You get along with your neighbors, no need to start something which isn't there to need starting.” His voice calm and quiet, trying to cool her down.

“Whatever, nosy ass fucking looky-loo’s!” Bolton was practically shoving her through the door now.

At hearing the voices outside and the door opening, Stormy had run towards the door to greet them. Cris gave a smile as the white and brown dog came barreling around the corner. Her ears flapping, tongue hanging out and tail wagging, she quickly skid to a halt upon getting closer. Her butt going low to the floor, tail between her legs, eyes wide as her nose was assaulted with the metallic scent in the air.

“Damn it! She smells the blood.” Cris crouched down slapping her hands on her thighs. “Come here Storm, come here girl. Come see mommy. C'mon sweetie, you're a good girl!”

The dog got on her belly, slowly, cautiously crawling over. Bolton slowly walked over to her and knelt down to pet her. Stormy nudged his hand, then timidly started licking it. As the dog calmed down more, Cris walked over too. Stormy looked up at her, not sure what to do.

"It's okay girl, momma's okay." The dog looked at her but would not give her the normal arrival kisses or excitement.

"I think a shower will do you good and make Stormy a heck of a lot happier too. She's scared. I can stay with her until you get out of the shower. I don't think it would be good to leave her alone right now, not until after the smell is gone. She knows something is wrong, she is already an anxious dog, no need to make it worse."

Cris knew Chief was right. The poor girl had been through enough before they got her from the shelter. No matter what the true reason was for her going to the shelter, one thing was for sure, something bad happened because she now had high separation anxiety.

Cris stood up to quick, the room giving a starry swirl. "Yeah, I think you're right. If you don't mind sitting with her, I'd really appreciate it. I promise I'll be quick."

"Of course I don't mind! Take your time, let the hot water wash away some of the stress. We will be fine together."

Like hot water or anything else could get rid of some of the stress, but she knew Bolton was trying, his heart in the right place. Doing the best he could with something he couldn't possibly understand on such a personal level.

"Always a comedian aren't you Chief? Her blankets are probably on the couch. If you want to go in there with her she will probably lay down and suck on her blankets, that will calm her down. I'll be out before you know it."

He rolled his eyes at the latter part but didn't say a word, just walked with the dog towards the living room. She peeked around the corner as they walked in and Stormy jumped up onto the couch, bunched her blanket until it was just right, then crossed her paws over it and started sucking on the blanket. The self-soothing already evident as her eyes were half-mast and she started her little whine.

As satisfied as she could be at the moment, Cris continued on to her bedroom to get clean clothes. She was struck with the onslaught of memories as she entered the bedroom. The paintings on the wall they had painted together at one of those franchise painting studios. She remembered how much Luke enjoyed the experience, how much genuine fun it was for him and how serious she had been, her OCD and perfectionism driving her nuts and not letting her have fun with it like he had. The bed where they had just enjoyed a playful night, celebrating the anticipation of a few days off together. His dirty clothes laying at the side of the bed where he had stripped them off. His nightstand with their wedding picture, a bottle of empty beer and a glass of unfinished water. She would have bitched at him to pick up his clothes, beer bottle and water glass when they got home today. He was very good about picking up after himself, it would've only been her smart-ass way of showing affection, but now she had to wonder, did *he* know that? Thinking back on the smart-ass sarcastic responses of his own, *he must have known, right?* How stupid all that seemed now!

Entering the master closet to get her clothes was a whole new ambush of emotions. The sight and smell of his clothes almost dropped her to her knees. Seeing the work clothes on one rod, the weekend clothes on another, his dirty clothes still smelling like him; it was all more than she could take. She could "see" him everywhere. How in the hell was she going to do this? She realized tears were silently dropping off her cheeks.

You have to stop, suck it up. If you don't you will not be able to make sure this worthless, life sucking, piece of shit rots in jail. I promise you Luke, I will make this bastard pay! With that she wiped her cheeks and picked out her workout clothes. After getting rid of Chief and comforting Stormy she was going to go for a run, kick her ass, then get down to business of solving his case on her own, she didn't need Chief Bolton, Bryan or anyone else.

As Cris paraded into the master bathroom she was further invaded by all Luke's toiletries around the sink and shower. Cris lifted her head a little as she set her clothes down. *I've got this baby, I know*

you're here with me and I swear you can count on me, I will do this!
Cris could almost see Luke standing there, nodding, agreeing with her and having complete confidence. She turned on the shower and got undressed. Then Cris made the mistake of looking at herself in the mirror. Her jaw dropped.

"Holy shit!"

Chapter 5

Cris had to admit, the shower and cleansing of the body had also helped cleanse her mind, just a little. She would take what she could get. Putting on her workout clothes she looked in the mirror. How could she not have some kind of mark? It seems this deep of a hurt should show battle wounds of some sort on the outside. Grabbing a band she gathered her long red hair up and snapped it into a high pony tail. Her crystal blue eyes accentuated now with the hair away from her face; so were the dark bags under her eyes. Her eyes moved to Luke's toothbrush and cologne. She gently touched the bristles on his brush, picked up and smelled his cologne. Quickly setting it down she brought her attention back to her new reality. She reached for her clothes, then realized they were covered in blood. What to do with them? She didn't have the heart to wash them, not yet. They also couldn't be where Stormy could smell them and really go nuts. She decided the garage would be the best place for now, and by tonight Cris was sure she would be ready to wash or throw them away.

After depositing the clothing in the garage, she walked into the living room where Stormy was all calmed down still sucking her blankets. Chief was staring out her front window. Cris silently approached and stood next to him. She noticed there were less cars parked out there now. That couldn't be good, so many leaving the scene this quickly meant they were done and didn't find much. Of course, Pete's truck was amongst some of the few remaining.

"Looks like quite a few have left already."

Cris was expecting to have startled Chief, for him to flinch in some way. He didn't, there was no sneaking up on him, he always knew when someone was there. It was like he had supersonic hearing or some sixth sense. She knew the more logical reason was his nerve endings were shot at this point and not much made him jump, something she understood all too well.

"Yeah, some of the primary responders whose jobs are done and are no longer needed for the investigative part have left." He looked down at her now. "Well, you look much better and more comfortable now."

"Thanks, I guess. I decided I am going to go for a run. Pound out some of my anger and try to come to some kind of reasoning and direction of where to go from here, how to best live with just Stormy and me."

Keep it simple. Don't let on you're going to work on this yourself, or that this will hold you back personally or professionally in any way. Life goes on which is exactly what you are going to make it look like you're doing.

"You need time to grieve too. Don't forget it's okay, and shit even healthy, to be human. Mourn, go through the process, then get back on that horse and beat life like the bitch she is, just like I know you will." Bolton had put his arm around Cris and yanked her towards him, her head tossing back and forth and her pony tail swaying as he pulled.

"Yes, Sir, I'll do the best I can." Cris broke free and meandered over to the couch where Stormy was half asleep, her eyes beyond half-mast. "She seems much calmer now."

At hearing her momma's voice right next to her, Stormy stopped sucking the blanket and popped her head up. The tail beating on the couch playing its own melodic drum solo. She lifted her muzzle to Cris' neck and began to nuzzle with her. Getting more excited, Stormy got up and put her paws on Cris' shoulders as she began licking her face, tail swinging full force. Cris couldn't resist the laugh that busted out as she was pulling her head back and swinging it side to side.

"Hey Storm, I'm happy to see you too girl!" Stormy was not letting up on her kissing assault. "Alright, that's enough!"

She looked up at Chief to see him watching them with a smile. "There's nothing like a dog to help you get through life. They are there to distract, comfort and love you, no matter what is going on."

Chief paused, took his glasses off and mopped his brow. "I know I have overstayed my welcome, I'm going to go check in with Bryan and see how he's doing. I can see Stormy has got things under control here."

At the mention of her name, Stormy stopped her attack and looked at him then gave him a little "woof", like she completely agreed she had it under control. Cris took that opportunity to get up. Placing her hand on Chief's arm, she let him know she agreed, it was time for him to go.

"Thank you for being here for me Chief, your support means a lot to me! I'll see you at the office tomorrow." She pulled her hand away and started walking towards the door to show him out.

Bolton reluctantly followed, giving Stormy a quick pet to the ears as he walked by, who of course decided to join them.

"You will have time off for bereavement. I will not see you at the office tomorrow, but I promise I will get in touch with you if anything breaking comes up in this case." He was trying his best to sound stern to end any argument that would have otherwise ensued.

Cris knew damn well she was going to the office tomorrow, but for the sake of getting him out without a further fight she decided not to even respond to his statement. At least by not acknowledging it one way or another she wasn't lying when she showed up tomorrow.

She grabbed a hold of Stormy and opened the front door for him. "Thanks again, Chief."

Bolton shook his head as he walked out the door. She knew he understood her response, or lack thereof, but he must have felt the same way, not going to argue about it right now.

As the door softly clicked shut, she quickly realized how silent the house was. Even Stormy, who was sitting at her feet, seemed to be holding her breath, there were no sounds emerging from her either. She looked around, seeing Luke everywhere. His recliner he loved to sit in, his magazines and books he liked to read stacked on the stand next to it and his favorite coaster sitting on top. Pictures on the mantel from some little mini vacations they took on long weekends. Her stomach started to churn.

She looked down at the dog who was quietly staring at her. "C'mon Storm, let's go out and go potty. I feel like a caged animal in here, I need to go run."

At the words out and potty, Stormy was prancing around and started nudging her leash. Cris walked her around for a few minutes, making sure she had enough time to stretch her legs before being left home alone again. She kept her eyes averted from Luke's truck as they walked past. Time to get her head in the game.

Typically, Cris' runs were to the beach about a mile from their house, then run a few miles down the beach before heading back. She wasn't feeling in a beachy mood today, but she had no idea where she was going to run. It was totally unlike her, she always had a plan of where she was going to go before she even left the house.

She put an earbud in one ear, always leaving the other ear to listen for her surroundings, hit shuffle on her "workout" playlist and at the front yard decided to head left out of her quiet little community. As each foot hit the pavement and each inhale expanded her lungs a little more, she began to feel more strength, mentally and physically. She was on auto pilot and still didn't know where she was running to, but just turned onto roads she felt the urge to once she arrived at them. Glancing around, suddenly coming into the moment, she realized she was on Main St. Just ahead on the left was her church, St. Michael the Archangel Roman Catholic Church. *Damn it Luke, everything happens for a reason, right? I didn't think I knew where I was going, but obviously someplace deep inside of me did. Well that's just craptastic!*

Cris entered the empty narthex, noticing the faint smell of frankincense which always seemed to be lingering, and immediately went to the font of holy water, dipped her fingers into it and blessed herself, genuflecting towards the tabernacle. *In the name of the Father, Son and Holy Spirit.* She timidly began heading through the nave and started approaching the altar.

What the hell am I doing? My faith right now is a real struggle. I do believe everything happens for a reason, but what could possibly be the justification for taking this young, vibrant, amazing human being who makes such a positive impact in the lives of so many youth? Who fought so hard, for what? An early death? She realized she was almost at the altar and tears were slipping down her cheeks, she never even felt them coming or falling until now. She knelt at the bottom of the carpeted steps and folded her hands.

Please help me! This is the first time in my life I don't know what to say to you. I'm sorry, but I'm so angry right now. How could you let this happen? Why make him fight for a better life only to rip it away once he gets it? What could the reason for this possibly be? Please help me to understand this insanity and give me the strength to do what needs to be done.

Cris was suddenly distracted by the sound of footsteps in the otherwise silent church. She quickly snapped her head up to see Father Tony approaching from the sacristy. He was still a little ways away, but close enough that he must be able to see her tear-soaked face.

"Oh, hi Cris! I'm sorry didn't mean to interrupt, I didn't even see you there. I'm used to people kneeling in the pews, not at the sanctuary, not that there is a problem with it..."

He stopped walking towards her, obviously seeing the distress in her face. Just as abruptly as he had stopped, he now quickly hurried over to her. "What's wrong? Can I help you with something?"

Cris wiped her cheeks on her shoulders and stood up to face him. "Forgive me Father, but it's been a piss of a day!"

Chapter 6

Pete was wrapping up the physical part of the investigation and was beginning to take down the yellow crime scene tape when he saw Chief Bolton coming off from the trail and onto the grass, heading his way. Some of the tall grass licking the bottom of Bolton's pant legs.

"Hey, Chief! How did everything go at the house?"

At Pete's raised voice in the otherwise silence, the previously still air became busy with scared off birds fleeing from a nearby tree.

Chief made it to where Pete was raveling up the tape and blew out a snort. "Shit, you know how hard-headed Steele is! It went as well as could be expected I guess. She went off on her neighbors from the front porch when we first got there. I think I managed to get her inside before too much damage was done though."

Pete had to crack a smile at that image. He could completely picture all 5'2 and 110 pounds of Cris telling her neighbors in no uncertain terms where they could go.

"If someone pissed her off, I can just imagine her going off like a pyrotechnic, all wiry and ready to take on the world."

Bolton chuckled. "Yes, I agree, I think that sums her up pretty well. I stayed with the dog, who was less than pleased at the smell of all the blood, while she got cleaned up. Afterwards she seemed more like her normal, hard assed self. I felt more confident leaving her at that point. So, how have things been coming here? I see everyone else has already left, if that's any indication."

"Yeah, unfortunately it is an indication. Evidence is pretty much non-existent, just like we feared it would be." Pete knew this case was going to be a nightmare on so many levels.

Chief shook his head. "You know, after her shower Cris saw me looking out the front window and came over. She noticed how many cars had already cleared out. I tried to play it off saying it was the first responders and non-essential to the investigation teams. She's not stupid, I know she knew it was because they hadn't found much of anything. Thankfully at least she didn't say anything, I'm not sure how I would have responded honestly." Chief looked down at the trampled grass and shuffled his feet slightly.

"Well, one thing is, it appears Steele was right about the direction and location in which the shot came from, not that I'm surprised. Right across the path over there behind those bushes there is a little spot of matted down grass. It is a pretty good guess that is where the shooter was crouched. Angle and trajectory seem to match."

What Pete had left out was the rest of his suspicions of why the shooting occurred. No need to go into it now, there was still the questioning and interrogation line of the investigation to get through. He didn't even want to think of it since his primary, and right now *only*, witness and person to question was Cris.

"What else have we got?" Bolton looked simultaneously hopeful and hopeless. Pete understood the complexity completely.

"I have a few leads I want to follow up on before I make any preliminary guesses. Really the next step I need to take is to interview Cris on Luke's history and any potential threats, you know the usual." Pete paused and gave a little head shake. "Except it won't be the usual with her. After I finish conducting her interview I can follow up on any new leads and have more solid answers. All I'm willing to say is the suspicion going on in my head right now is not good. I don't want you to form an opinion based on my suspicions which very well could be wrong. I want to show you all the facts at the end for you to give me your unbiased opinion."

Normally they would share facts and brainstorm their ideas together. This case was different, he wanted to have as much information together as possible before they sat down to digest it all.

"Understood. I don't like feeling left out right now, but I appreciate your honesty and thought process on this one and I will go along with it, at least for now. This case is fucked two ways to sideways, some of our normal methods are going to be different this time."

"Thank you, Sir for trusting me on this. I gotta say, this is one case I wish I wasn't assigned to, but of course I will do my best."

"I know you will, it goes without saying." Bolton paused, obviously thinking about what he wanted to say.

He placed his hand firmly on Pete's shoulder, gave a good hard squeeze and held it there. "Listen Pete, I want to be there when you interview Cris. This is probably going to go into some sensitive territory she will not want to answer or even think about. I want to be sure you have a witness to the answers and I also want to be there for her, so she knows she has a friend and support and I need to be sure she is okay."

He couldn't help but notice Chief's use of the word "need" instead of "want" to be sure she's okay. He dismissed the thought as soon as it entered his brain. *Let it go, you're over thinking things Bryan!*

"Of course, I agree. In fact, I feel better about it already, knowing you will be in there with me."

Pete had a soft spot for Cris and he was worried about keeping up the strength to ask her the tough questions he knew he was going to have to ask. Having Chief there to help Cris stay calm would help him have the strength he needed to get through the interview.

Chief released him and took a few steps back, almost tripping on a rut peeking through the ground, his head slightly brushing the limb the frantic birds had recently flown from. Bolton brought his hand up, instinctively, but calmly swatting at the limb.

"Good. Let me know when you schedule it with her."

He started to turn to walk away, then spun back around on his boot heel. "Oh, and Bryan, go home and take a shower. I didn't realize before that you had blood all over you." Bolton turned around smartly as he headed back towards the trail.

Pete looked down at himself, he hadn't realized there was blood all over him either, but sure as shit, he did. It must've happened when he was hugging Cris when he first got there. No doubt much of the blood on her was still wet, or at least moist. *Ah hell, I might as well just throw these away. I doubt it will wash out now, it's way too dried on. I don't think I could ever wear them again anyways. Damn.*

He finished untangling the caution tape from the trees. Nothing left here for him to do. Forensics already took the few bags of potential evidence they had gathered. From an investigative stand point, this was no longer a crime scene. The thought sickened him. This would always be a crime scene. Besides the hole remaining in the tree from the bullet, that probably nobody would notice in the massive tree unless they were looking for it, and the blood still stained here and there, which would be washed away after a good strong storm, there would be no indication anything ever happened here. Of course, anytime Cris came through, it would forever be a bloody, heart wrenching, murder scene. It didn't seem right. It felt like there should be some kind of symbol or memorial it happened and people's lives are forever changed because of it.

Pete looked at the yellow tape wadded up in his hand. He folded it in half hoping to make the black words as least visible through the other side as possible. He then wrapped it around the enormous tree trunk a few times and made a huge bow at the end. It was the closest attempt he could do to have a giant yellow ribbon tied around the tree. It would have to suffice for now.

As satisfied as he could be given the circumstances, Pete himself headed for the trail out now as well. He watched the shadows of the tall pines swaying in the breeze, almost mesmerized by the slow melodic rhythm. He heard the breeze whispering through, like a freight train ushering him towards the way out. The palm fronds on the palm trees were also making their rough rattling noise when the breeze picked up. The death ridden black birds seemed to be gone now and the normal sounds of the other birds singing and chattering away had resumed. Almost like nothing had happened here today; all was back to status quo.

Pete kicked at some pine straw covering the trail. Would it ever go back to status quo? He didn't think so. How different would Cris be, and more importantly, what would this do to their relationship? He mostly knew Cris as a colleague, a damn good one. They had worked on several cases together and he really enjoyed not only her intelligence for solving the cases, but also her determination, wit and sarcasm to get them through the struggles each one presented. She would not let her emotions get the best of her, or hell even show. Pete had gone to their house a few times, very few, and Cris seemed to have the same personality outside of work as well. He liked that. Luke also seemed like a fun guy, with a great sense of humor. And of course, Pete was their go-to dog sitter when they went away for a few long weekends, so he knew and loved their dog too. He could certainly imagine his dog sitting days would be done now, no more long weekends. Cris was going to need Stormy's companionship at all times. Pete hoped maybe she would still let him visit, make sure she was okay and get to see the dog for a while. No, nothing would ever go back to status quo, for him or for her.

Pete realized he had already arrived back at the truck, either those tall pine shadows really had mesmerized him, or he was lost in his thoughts of Cris the whole walk out. He noticed the car and truck were both there so he figured she should be home. He glanced quickly at the house, trying to appear nonchalant, to see if she was anywhere in sight. All he saw was Stormy in the window, tongue hanging out of the side of her mouth panting while she was looking out at him. He could go in and see if Stormy needed to go out, make sure Cris and everything else was okay while he was in there. He had the house key since he was the dog sitter, it never left his key chain. *No better not, she's probably very fragile right now, no need to push anything!*

Damn, what he wouldn't do to get closer to that girl!

Chapter 7

Cris jogged next door to Luke's house. Another school day was over and the sun was still shining brightly in the blue sky, which tended to be a rarity these days. She leapt up the porch stairs and gave a quick knock on the storm door before letting herself into the front room. The ancient wall paper that seemed original to the old house covered the room with the same repeating image of a tree and waterfall all the way around the room. The small tube television with rabbit ears on the back was sitting kitty corner on an antique stand and had the early evening news going. About two feet away from the television was Luke's grandmother, sitting in her beloved rocking chair. She looked over at Cris when she walked in.

"Oh, well look at who's here!" It was the same greeting each time.

Cris smiled genuinely and wide. "Hi Grammie." She greeted Luke's frail little grandmother with a hug, as always.

Luke came strutting around the corner from the parlor which housed the same ancient wallpaper, "My turn!"

She spun and put her arms around Luke's neck giving him a big squeeze. Then, making sure Grammie couldn't see, she quickly gave him a swift, loving smack on the ass. In response, Luke gave his crooked smile, knowing she couldn't resist it and kissed her on the cheek.

As she stepped back, she gave him a playful little punch to his bicep. "C'mon Steele Appeal, let's go out and enjoy the sun and warmth while it lasts!"

Luke leaned against the antique brown furnace, which was currently off. It always looked like it had a face on the front of it and looked really mean when the mouth had the fire going in it.

"I have a bunch of homework to get done, as I'm sure you do too." Luke's eyes lowered, he looked genuinely disappointed.

"I do, but we will sit down and do it together when we get back. We don't need to be out long, it will probably be getting cold soon anyways."

She was pleading with her eyes and rubbing his free arm. She knew he wouldn't refuse.

Luke glanced up at the comparatively new clock on the wall behind his grandmother. "I never could quite say no to you. Let's go for a little bit."

He bent over to his Grammie and gave her a kiss on the cheek. "Be back a little later, love you!"

Grammie smiled up to both of them. "You kids go have fun but stay out of trouble."

That was also usually the same send off every time. She was the kindest and sweetest lady, but unfortunately signs of dementia were creeping in.

As they headed towards the door Cris gave a wave and called back "Bye Grammie!"

A wave was given in kind just before she returned her attention back to the evening news.

They lazily walked down the street hand in hand and turned onto the neighboring street. Just a short distance ahead they crossed over the old rail road tracks that housed grease spots on the railroad ties, the rocks around the ties, and the spikes on the outsides of the rails. There was also a flattened penny on a rail someone must have recently placed there to get squished by the train. As they crossed over the tracks, they decided to sit on the huge pile of white concrete chunks remaining from a building which had collapsed many years before. It was fairly secluded as the enormous blocks sat back off the road and many trees, mostly sumac, had grown throughout them. She sat between his legs, leaning back on his chest. They were both looking at the sky and its white billowy clouds. Nothing else to look at besides the cars periodically going down the back street or the chain link fence going around the empty lot where an old building had burned down.

Cris broke the silence. "I can't believe graduation is almost here! We will be leaving for college soon and not have to be stuck here anymore!"

Luke pulled her in closer, wrapping his arms tight around her. "I know, we did it! We showed all those cliquey has-beens who picked on us all these years because we didn't have their perfect, fake, lives. We are graduating on the honor roll, got accepted to the same university and both got scholarships to boot. But, the best part is, we are still rock solid, more than any single one of them can say!" He kissed Cris on top of her head.

She began rubbing his strong forearms that were wrapped around the front of her. "Hell yes! Let them have their fancy cars and parties and everything handed to them. We know what it's like to bust our butt for what we want, we know the value of a dollar and we know the value of true love. We are humble, compassionate and determined. Those are things they will never learn, we are so much richer than them when it comes to the important things in life. We have to remember that."

"Damn straight! I know neither of us will ever forget where we came from and the heartaches we have had to overcome."

Luke leaned forward and began softly kissing her neck, she responded by wrapping her hands around the back of his neck pulling him closer and resting her head on his shoulder. She loved him so much! Through everything they had each other and she knew even though they were both broken, they were also the luckiest people in the world!

It was already starting to get cool, a light but constant breeze making it worse and reminding them it still wasn't summer quite yet. The newly budded leaves rustled as the branches danced and the birds sang their evening songs. As much as Cris didn't want to leave this pile of old cement blocks, she was starting to get a little chilled and knew they should go get their work done.

She turned and gave him a gentle bite on his bottom lip. "C'mon Steele Appeal, let's go get our work done."

"Yes ma'am!" Luke gave her a little salute, then broke out that damn crooked smile, his green eyes glistening.

They got up and stretched then intertwined their fingers as they clasped hands. As they headed back to the street they heard the whistle of an oncoming train.

Cris looked up at Luke with a sly grin across her lips. "Hey, we could hop on and ride it home for old times' sake!"

Luke chuckled. "Ha, we haven't done that in a few years! Let's walk over to the crossing like we would be anyways. If the caboose isn't at the end, why not? This might be our last chance before we leave for college."

Still holding hands, they walked down the street and reached the crossing just as the red and white striped gate was coming down and the red lights started flashing on top. The engine sporting gray, blue and gold, gradually appeared and went past. The train was moving slow but it was still loud; the cars swaying from side to side, always looking like they would get a stiff breeze and topple over while singing their "clickity clack" theme song. There were a few coal cars and tankers, but mostly box cars. Looking down to the end of the swaying box car parade, it didn't appear to have the caboose attached tonight.

Luke yelled to Cris "I don't see the caboose, I take that as a sign, get ready!"

They started to walk briskly alongside the moving boxcars, heart rate increasing along with the adrenaline. When the last one reached them, they began to jog onto the track right behind it. Luke leapt up and grabbed the wrung on the ladder and pulled himself up further, then he wrapped his arm around the rung and turned and held his hand out in case Cris needed his arm for balance. Of course, she ran and jumped right up and grabbed the rung. They both started laughing. It had been so long since they did this. Their hair blowing in the breeze, each had one arm slung around the wrung and the other hand they held together again, then they leaned out and kissed. It didn't last long; their short ride was over. At the sight of their houses they both jumped off to the side of the tracks, landing on their feet for the most part and giving a simultaneous jog to the trail that went through the bushes and led to their yards. They should be professionals at tuck and roll. They looked at each other and just laughed, it felt good!

Luke put his arm around her trying to contain his laughter "That is so juvenile, but damn was it fun and brought back memories!"

He blew out a little sigh, like he was realizing they are grown up now, those old days are long gone. "Is your mom home?"

She let out one last chuckle, then Serious Cris already back to business. "No, she's working, as usual."

"Okay, cool. Let me run in and grab my bag and I'll meet you at your house. Maybe after we get our homework done, we can reward ourselves in the bedroom!"

Luke gave her a little wink accompanied by his signature crooked smile, then paid her back with her own, much harder, smack on the ass and raised his eyebrows as he ran for his house laughing.

Chapter 8

 ris bolted awake to tear soaked cheeks. She swore she could
still feel the sting from Luke's smack on her ass and smell
the grease from the rail road tracks. She wiped her face with
the inside of her arm and propped herself up on her elbow. The
headache was immediate, and the room had a slight spin to it. She
looked around and realized she was on the couch, with an empty
bottle of wine on the floor, and no wine glass in sight.

She slapped her palm to her forehead. "Ah, shit!"

Reality hit again like a freight train with broken brakes. Inside she
was dead on impact.

At the sound of movement, Stormy came slinking up from Cris'
feet where she was laying. She pushed her way through, making
room for herself. Once reaching her destination Stormy began to
lick the salt off Cris' face. She pet Stormy's ears, trying to soothe
herself more than the dog right now. It was still dark outside; the
sun had not yet come up. She grabbed her cell phone off the end
stand, 5:15 am. *What happened last night? I can't even remember.
I do remember being at the church, but not going there or coming
home.* Looking down at herself she saw she had comfortable
clothes on, but not her running clothes. *Okay, so I took a shower at
some point after I got home, that's good at least.*

She looked at Stormy with her nose in her face. "Stormy, did I at
least take you out girl? I'm sorry I was such a mess last night!"

She tried thinking back. She couldn't distinguish reality from
imagination, but she had a sense of Father Tony bringing her home.
If this was true, it was probably a bad thing. *What did I say to him*

or what did I look like to make him feel like I needed a ride?! She continued to pet Stormy, trying to think. *Did I go back to the trail, back to the tree, or try to? That would explain the empty bottle of wine which was obviously drunk straight from the bottle. Maybe I lost it in the bedroom again? That would explain the couch.*

"Damn it, this can't happen! This is not acceptable! I am not going to go through life wondering what happened because I am missing chunks of my time and memory. I am not Crazy Cris and this stops now!"

With the final yell she heaved the empty wine bottle across the room. It hit the wall and shattered, dark green glass raining chunks and shards all over the beach gray polished hardwood floor. Stormy got scared and jumped down off the couch, her brown and white tail tucked between her legs, nails scraping on the floor trying to get some grip as she went running towards the bedroom.

"Aw, Stormy, it's okay girl, I'm sorry!" Stormy didn't come bounding back out.

That's good, I must clean this mess up anyways before she steps on it! As she walked down the slightly spinning hall towards the broom closet she noticed the office looked different. *I should clean this glass up first, then deal with why this room looks different.*

She made quick work of sweeping up all the glass, then vacuuming over it just to be sure she got it all. Upon walking the dust pan out to the kitchen to throw away the debris, she noticed a bunch of scattered papers all over the table. *What the hell? I would never leave a mess like this!* Emptying the dust pan, then setting it down on the floor, she walked around the breakfast bar over to the dining room table. There were several pieces of paper sketched with notes, pictures and diagrams, all pertaining to solving Luke's case. Glancing over them, she realized some of it was actually pretty damn good, thinking outside of the box, getting creative. *Guess the wine got my mind going in areas it might not have gone otherwise!*

She remembered the office seeming off as she looked at the clock on the stove. Ugh, 5:45. *I gotta get moving to be at work by 8. Quick check of the office!* Cris quickly padded back down to the office and walked in. She immediately noticed it was her desk area that was different. The wall above her desk was completely cleared off. Apparently last night she had removed her calendar, pictures and inspirational quotes which were hanging there.

"Well, I'm not sure exactly what my intoxicated brain had in mind, but apparently there was some kind of mission in place. Hopefully it will come to me, but for right now, time to go kick my ass and clear my head, time to get focused!"

She shuffled back out to the kitchen and grabbed some ibuprofen out of the cabinet, kicking them back with her caffeine concoction. Grabbing her protein powder, she quickly mixed up a shake.

"Alright, that's a good start to clearing my head. Stormy, come on girl, let's go out!"

Obviously feeling it was safe to come out now, or she really needed to pee, Stormy now came prancing out. Cris brought her shaker bottle out with them, finished shaking it up and chugged it down quick as they walked, still refusing to look over at Luke's truck. Trying to reel herself in, telling herself she was not going to think about what happened, only focus on moving forward and solving this case.

In this spirit, she decided to pay attention to and enjoy her surroundings while she waited for Stormy to finish. The sky was starting to get a little brightness to it, the sun would be rising soon, even though the moon was still fighting to continue its own bleak brightness. The owls were hooting nearby, and the rooster was crowing from somewhere. She had no idea where the roosters were. Birds were already fluttering around, looking for food and singing their morning praises.

Stormy finished up as indicated by her flinging dirt all around the yard and then took off like a cannon back towards the house, sounding like a galloping horse. Yup, she was good and ready to roll now.

Cris quickly got changed into her running clothes, snapped her hair up in a pony tail and grabbed her phone and ear buds without looking around or thinking about Luke's belongings all over the place. Proud of herself for reigning in that laser focus she is known for, she threw Stormy a treat, gave her a kiss and locked the front door as she went out.

She released a huge breath. "I can do this!"

Today was going to be a beach run, although maybe a shorter distance because she was getting a late start, but she knew where she was going today, laser focused! She pushed the ear bud into her right ear, shuffled her playlist and hit the pavement. The sky was getting a little brighter, she was going to miss the sunrise if she didn't move it. Fueled by both her pain and determination to find this killer no matter what, Cris was lost in thought. Thinking about the papers on her table this morning, her mind going to possible leads to investigate. She didn't know what songs were playing or even remember running this far, she was completely consumed in her thoughts.

She was approaching the small wooden bridge at the end of her little community that she took to go towards the beach when she noticed a man standing there, staring at her. Even though it was still a little dark, she was wearing her sun glasses, knowing she would need them soon and also keeping the bugs out of her eyes. She didn't think he could see her eyes through the dark glasses. If he could he would see the interrogating eyes boring through him. *Who the hell is this? Why is he just standing there staring at me? Could this be Luke's killer? Am I being paranoid and suspecting everyone?* No doubt she noticeably slowed. This was a safe and friendly neighborhood where strangers wave and smile to each other, or at least that's what she thought up until yesterday. Not wanting to give him the satisfaction of knowing he startled her, Cris held her head up high, picked up just a little speed and ran right past him. She waited a few seconds before she looked back. He was still there but walking slowly away as he had his head turned, still watching her.

At the rate she was going she was on the beach in less than five minutes. The last sliver of the sunrise touching the water, she hadn't completely missed it, probably due in large part to kicking it into over drive after being surprised by the stranger. Cris couldn't get him out of her mind and she was very upset with herself for not seeing him sooner. That was not like her. She was always hyper vigilant and alert. It was very unnerving not seeing him until she was right on top of him. *Gotta pull it together if you're going to find this killer!* That thought gave her the kick in the ass she needed and she pounded the hard compact sand right next to the crashing waves, the sun now fully blazing down as the sea gulls and pelicans soared in searched of their morning meals.

Deciding to make it a little harder, she ran up in the soft sand on the return trip. Her calves and thighs were starting to scream. *Good, feel the pain and keep pushing through damn it, this is nothing!* Waves in one ear, music in the other and nothing but pure hatred driving her, Cris made the best time ever for that distance, even better than when Luke was there with her pushing her to keep up.

Other than her thoughts and the singing, swooping birds, thankfully the return trip was uneventful. As Cris poured herself through the front door she felt like she was going to throw up.

"That was for you baby, I will avenge you I swear. The son of a bitch will regret ever messing with us!"

Panting, she strode down the hall to the shower. The streaming water pounding her aching muscles felt good and soon her breathing stabilized, her churning stomach would take a little longer. Quickly getting on her work attire of fitted black pants with multiple pockets throughout, including one to conceal her Smith and Wesson, and a plain fitted t-shirt, she glanced at the clock. 7:30!

One more quick walk for Stormy, then grab whatever she could find in the fridge for lunch and she had to fly.

Still feeling the effects of not enough sleep and too much wine last night, she was at least feeling invigorated after the run, but mostly had the fuel of revenge running through her veins as she got into her car. Pushing in the clutch and firing up the horses, Cris had the feeling today was going to be another piss of a day, but she was ready!

Chapter 9

Cruising into her unofficial designated parking spot and taking a quick glance in the rear-view mirror, staring back at her Cris saw dark puffy eyes, her normal crystal blue eyes not so bright today, a little dull; but otherwise all looked normal. Some make up would help but that was not her style.

She looked away from the mirror. "Never did care what people thought about me, sure as hell not gonna start now."

Inhaling a deep breath of strength and courage, she shut the car off and meandered out, exhaling her weakness. She knew Chief was not going to be happy to see her, but she wasn't leaving, and she was ready for the argument today. Shoulders back and head up she marched to the back door, swiped her badge and went in.

The first hallway was empty and quiet, far enough away from the hub of the office there was not much activity here unless you were coming or going. Continuing ahead, around the corner the busyness became more evident. The smell of the typical thick, burnt coffee was the first thing to assault her nostrils. The constant buzz from both the phones and mouths of the department running, along with the clicking of keys and cell phones buzzing, vibrating, chirping and singing with the latest sounds and tones were the familiar sounds she lived by.

Might as well jump right in and go get some coffee. It was the department's equivalent of the stereotypical office's water cooler. *Let's see what trash is being talked this morning.* Stealing a breath, she quietly walked through the open door of the break room and overheard a man's voice.

"... I heard he was laying right on top of her!"

Moretti stopped short, apparently, he saw Reed's eyes go wide at something behind his back. He quickly turned as Cris was walking in.

His jaw dropped, and he began to stammer, "Steele, hey! What are you doing here? I thought you were off for a few days. I was just telling Reed here about the latest rumored love affair going on, but it's a mutual friend of ours, nobody you would know. I don't want to embarrass you with that kind of conversation."

Moretti was rambling, and his face was bright red. Reed was just standing there. She could tell he was watching his friend trying to cover his ass, quite poorly, and he had no intentions of getting involved.

Cris rolled her eyes and stopped the bleeding. "Shut the fuck up Moretti. You have never been ashamed to say anything in front of me before, you sure as hell aren't going to start now. And of course, it's nobody I know because you have no names off the top of your head for your fabricated story, you're not bright enough to think that fast. The only thing you should be embarrassed of is your tiny pencil dick you keep trying to spread around the department. You know you really outta keep that itty-bitty thing in your pants so the rest of us don't have to keep hearing about it, we're embarrassed for you."

At this point Reed's smirk had turned into a full-blown snicker. Moretti thought he was the original Italian Stallion, *this oughta knock him down a few pegs.*

Moretti did not appear amused; his scalding red face had now spread to his ears. "Screw you, Steele."

"Oh, careful Moretti, I might take that as a come on. You're not equipped enough to handle me!"

She pushed her way past him, hitting his arm with her shoulder on the way through as she went to the coffee station.

Reed looked over at her, still grinning. "It's good to see you Steele, and to see you're in your usual rare form."

"Thanks Reed. Good to see you too."

As she looked back at Reed she saw beyond him, several other officers and comrades were on the other side of the tiny room, all with sneers on their faces. *Well I guess the word should spread quick that I'm here and I'm completely normal.* Cris turned back around and mixed her lousy coffee in the paper cup. She knew she probably wouldn't drink the shit anyway, it was more to keep her hands busy. She turned on her heel with the thick motor oil and headed out the door. *Time to go face the music. Big inhale of strength and courage and exhale out the weakness.*

Cris walked the short distance down the depressing gray hall to the chaos of the office. She strutted straight over to her little office area, that really wasn't much more than a glorified cubicle. She didn't even have a door she could shut. She noticed Chief's door was shut as she passed, but she saw his vehicle outside in his officially designated parking spot, so she knew he was here. Pete had a similar glorified cubicle right across from her, and unfortunately, he was sitting in his. *Well no time like the present. Let's see if I can keep the roll I'm on going!*

As she turned to walk over to Pete she took a small swig of the grimy coffee and winced. *Damn this stuff is nasty, how can these guys drink this all day, no wonder they all had heartburn and stomach issues. It isn't the things they see on the daily basis, it's this crap!* Pete looked up as she hissed from the drink, his eyes grew a little wide.

"Steele, hey!" He seemed not quite surprised, more like uncomfortable to see her. "Ah, shit! You know Bolton is not going to be happy when he sees you here! How are you feeling?"

"I'm feeling pretty good except this bitter shit in the cup. I swear it gets worse every day! And don't worry, I'll deal with Bolton."

He gave a nervous little chuckle. "Yeah, I think they have some kind of additive they put in to see how much worse they can make it, but yet we still tolerate. A little science experiment or something."

His smile faded, and he furrowed his eyes. "Are you sure you're okay? With me, with us, after last night?"

Last night! The night she couldn't remember! What in blue blazes was he talking about?! Fear struck in her for a moment, her stomach immediately sinking, the one sip of coffee now churning it's way upward. Pete was sexy as hell, buzzed black hair, amazing blue eyes, a chiseled body in which she didn't even want to think about, and his ass.... But she was not interested in him that way, never was. *There's no way anything happened! How to respond to this? Think!*

Trying her best to keep her normal tone, "I'm fine with 'us,' why wouldn't I be?" She air quoted the us.

Pete appeared to loosen up slightly. "Well after that text, I honestly wasn't sure where it left us, and more honestly, I was worried about that."

The enormity of the sigh Cris blew out was probably blatantly obvious to him. Assuming there was nothing before then, it was just a text, phew! *I can handle that!*

"I'm really sorry Bryan, I don't even remember the text last night."

It looked like he was a little disappointed. No way did something happen before this apparently disturbing text he would be upset about!

"You don't remember? Are you sure you're okay? Were you drinking?" Concern was written all over his face now.

Cris was really wondering what happened last night and was starting to get annoyed about it. Trying to keep her cool, she still ending up snapping at him a little.

"Bryan, look, I'm sorry! I don't remember, okay?! I took your advice of drowning myself in a bottle and maybe had a little bit of wine last night. I think I was just really exhausted after the day. I also took a run which probably didn't help my exhaustion." *Did he already know this though because he was there last night? Was he how I got home?*

"I'm sorry you were worried about whatever I said in the text."

She quickly took a big breath in. *Inhale strength and courage, exhale the weakness.* "So, what the hell was it I said anyways?"

Pete let out a long sigh. "I knew you went for a run..." *Uh Oh!*

The sound of heavy footsteps cut Pete off from finishing the rest of the story. It sounded like a ferocious bear hunting down whoever took her cubs. Steele and Bryan both looked in the direction of the oncoming noise. Cris knew exactly what it was, or should she say *who* it was. Sure enough, there was Chief Bolton thundering around the corner in their direction. His cheeks were rosy, and his breath was coming hard. *Like a bull charging after the red cape.* She gave a quick rub inside the pocket that was on her left thigh. *Here we go. Pull all the strength and courage you've been inhaling right now Steele, you're gonna need it!*

It looked like he was trying to compose himself before opening his mouth to unleash on her. She'd never seen him look so pissed before and she had never heard him truly yell at anyone before. Chief always acted professionally and calmly and got his point across sternly, not from a loud, embarrassing scolding. His team respected him for it and were more likely to listen to him and follow his orders. Cris was really praying, as she was rubbing inside her pocket, today would not be the day his composure would be beyond reach.

"Steele, I thought I saw you walk by! I'm quite sure I was clear when I left you yesterday saying you were to use bereavement time!" Again, the stern voice, but he was not yelling.

Cris knew by the look of his face and stature that even though he had managed to stay calm, this was not the time to tell him what he could do with his bereavement time offer like she normally would have. It was like Chief was taking this personal, because of *her* for some reason. *Tread lightly Steele!*

Not wanting to show weakness, but also not wanting to appear defiant and further set him off, she squared her shoulders as best should could with the shitty coffee in her right hand, trying to show strength, but her words did not hold that same potency. Cris gave a little sideways glance at Pete, who was pretending to be busy with paperwork now. She felt awkward discussing this with Bolton in front of Pete, not to mention their conversation which had suddenly got shut down. Oh well, nothing could be done about any of it now.

"Chief, please hear me out! I understand you want me to take a leave and use the time but think about it. What would I do? You know me, I'm a busy body. I can't sit still and can't stay home. You tied my hands of looking into this case myself, I understand and accept it, but what will I do then?" Cris paused, hoping her pleading, sincere face was helping break his insistence.

"Sir, look at my desk." She pointed to the stacks of paper in neat rows on her desk. "I have lots of paperwork there that needs to be finished up and filed away. When I'm on a case I have no time to get these caught up. This is a perfect time. It keeps me busy, productive and sane. Plus, no doubt it won't be long before another case will be thrown at me with the way this sick world works. Please! I can't sit home and do nothing, I will go crazy."

She winced as she said the word crazy, but quickly covered it up with a grin. "Which would prove my neighbors right, and we can't have that, can we?"

She ended with a little tilt of the head. That was it, all she had, and she knew it wasn't great. Was it enough?

Chief stood there stoically the whole time, just listening with his hands clasped at the small of his back. *Parade Rest* she had found herself thinking. She had no idea what to expect. He finally showed the first signs of actual life and let out an exasperated sigh as he swiftly moved his arms naturally down his sides by his seams, but she noticed. *Attention.* This was not the first time she suspected he had a military background.

A slight shake of his head and he was back in his Chief mode. "Ah, hell Steele!"

Was he going to concede? Cris realized she still had her left hand in her pocket. She quickly pulled it out, at the same time gently set her coffee cup on the corner of Bryan's desk and stood at her own attention, giving all of it to Bolton.

"I will allow you to stay and catch up on your files until another case comes through for you. I suspect you're right, it probably won't be long. In all honesty I can't make you take a bereavement leave. But, let me make myself absolutely fucking clear, I will be watching you closely. If I even get a hint things are getting to be overwhelming and you refuse to take a leave, I will make you leave pending a full psych review. I will not tolerate you risking your mental health. Are we clear on this?" Chief's voice was raised and firm, but not yelling.

"Crystal, Sir!" Cris wanted to salute him but thought better of it.

Although she felt victorious, it was obvious he was still not happy about it and certainly would not welcome her normal smart-ass remarks or gestures.

Chief Bolton looked over at Bryan, who must not have been very invested in his paperwork because he apparently felt Chief's stare since he returned the glance.

Looking back at Cris, Chief's eyes almost challenging her. "Well, since you want to be here today, I guess we might as well get your questioning for Luke's case done and over with. You may change your mind about wanting to stay after that."

Uh-Oh!

Chapter 10

Chief escorted her and Pete to his office. Upon entering his small office, Chief held his left hand out, indicating for Cris to sit in the chair in front of his desk, and Pete to sit in his own chair behind the desk. Bolton parked himself on the corner of his desk, well at least one cheek of himself. He had his hip resting on the corner of his desk, one hand on the desk balancing himself as he was turned towards Cris, the other holding a cardboard cup of the shitty coffee.

This wasn't her first time being in his office by any means, but this time felt different, awkward, and she was tense. She sat on the hard, uncomfortable chair and looked around with new, nervous eyes. Though Chief had lots of files and papers, everything was neatly stacked and in its place. She recognized an organized mind when she saw it. She would even go so far as to wager his was in the same order as her own stacks; by priority. Cris did not like being on this side of the desk with these two facing her like the Spanish Inquisition. *Might as well get this moving.*

"So, I gotta tell ya, the way the two of you are sitting here facing me, I feel like I am going to be interrogated or something. I know you said you had some questions, but this feels more serious than just some questions. It's a little weird being in your office this way Bolton. What's up?" She gave a little chuckle, was trying to act casual, nonchalant.

She realized she was rubbing her thumb against her fingers, another nervous habit. She was thankful to be on the other side of the desk so they didn't see that at least, they would pick up on it immediately. *Always watch the body language.*

Pete sat there and didn't respond right away, but instead looked towards Chief. She noticed Chief shift his hip slightly on his tiny corner plot. He took a little sip of his swill before speaking, Cris couldn't help but wonder if it was his own nervous habit.

"Pete is going to ask you a few questions to try to get more information for the investigation. I wanted to be here as another set of ears, to potentially see another angle, or have something you say trigger another way of thinking. We can't have too many ideas on this case. I also wanted to help explain why Bryan is asking some of the questions that he is if need be."

Cris felt some heat coming to her face. "Chief, I'm not a fucking moron. I understand the questions needing to be asked and why, this is also my job, remember?"

She noticed Pete do a little shift in the chair. *Good, let him be uncomfortable and intimidated, I'm not a friggin' baby to be coddled.*

Chief exhaled loudly as he gave a slight eye roll. "No, you're not a fucking moron, but what you are is on the inside of this one, not looking at it through the same eyes. You are also very stubborn and hard-headed sometimes; shit, all the time! I don't want any misunderstandings here."

Trying to compose herself, knowing this was no way to start the investigation, and not wanting her face to get any redder, tipping them off to her real feelings about it, Cris calmed her tone.

"So, if this is an official interrogation then, why are we in here instead of the interrogation room?"

"I would prefer to call this an interview, not an interrogation. I felt it would be more comfortable for you in here, no need for those sterile formalities and no need for anyone else to know it's going on. They have enough crap to talk about, no reason to give them any more. Things are a little different in this case Cris, you said so yourself, remember?"

Nothing like having your boss throw your words back in your face when you were being stubborn and hard-headed before. Damn him for always being right!

"Yes Sir, I know they are. Thank you for thinking of what's better for me instead of following normal protocol." She gave a little smirk. "Despite my stubborn, hard-headed ass, I do appreciate it."

She looked over at Pete then, who looked like a boy in the schoolroom knowing he was going to have to stand up and give an oral presentation and was dreading hearing his name be called. Cris decided to cut him some slight slack, just a little, especially since she still had no idea what happened last night.

"Alright Bryan, you ready? Let's get this shit show on the road."

That at least warranted a little grin out of him, it looked like the tension eased a little bit. Both his face and body loosened up. He gave a quiet throat clear and leaned his body forward, grabbing his pen from his ear and opening up his notebook which already had things written down.

"Alright Steele, let's start with the logical, basic questions. Can you think of anyone who might have wanted to hurt Luke, even from his past? Did he seem nervous or upset recently?"

"No, I have racked my brain going through all this. I've known him and been his best, and probably the only true friend since we were 10. There's nobody from his past who would want to hurt him. There was the usual childish schoolyard taunts, nothing more. There was nothing unusual about his behavior. He was loved by his students and fellow faculty members. He was such a good-hearted, genuine person. Who could possibly have anything against him?"

"That's what we're trying to figure out. So, it's safe to also assume there was not anyone he recently had a disagreement with that he told you about? No threats?"

"No, of course not, nothing."

Cris suddenly wished she had thought to bring a bottle of water. The wine from the night before had left her dehydrated and the questions and memories were not doing her any justice either. She was fidgeting her foot. Another nervous habit. Thankfully they couldn't see that either, the desk was a great shield. She would have to remember this with her own suspects and be sure to always use the interrogation room with the open table underneath.

Cris noticed Pete seemed to tense up a little. It was almost imperceptible, but she caught it. The slightest movement of his butt in the chair, an almost inaudible clearing of his throat, glancing at his notebook just a second too long. He was good, but still, she noticed. It takes an anxious person to see the anxiety in others. She waited for Pete to proceed with his next line of questioning. It was only a matter of seconds that passed, but she noticed. If Chief did, he gave no indication, just like her. Either Chief didn't notice, or he was as good with his poker face as she was. With less than five seconds passing, Pete spoke.

"Okay Cris, I want you to think about this one for a minute. This may even be something where you can't think of anything right now, but something in the night tickles your brain and you realize maybe there was something you missed or misinterpreted as stress from Luke, or an over active imagination on your part."

Cris had been in his spot plenty of times before. She knew it was something the witness would probably deny because they weren't ready or able to face the truth. She also knew she personally had no acceptance issues, there was nothing wrong that needed her denial, at least when it came to Luke.

"Yes, I understand Pete, go ahead." She saw a slight shifting of Chief's hip on the corner of the desk again.

A quick draw of the breath from Pete, again, nobody else would've noticed, but she did.

"Was there ever any sign, a hint, indication or accusation of Luke being a little too friendly with a student? Maybe a ticked off dad at some rumors going around?"

Anyone would've noticed Pete's voice a little lower this time, his eyes slightly more averted.

 At this round of questions, Cris came unleashed. She knew he was reaching for something that probably wasn't there, "doing his job", but it still lit her fuse. This case was different, he didn't have to go to that line of questioning.

"You have got to be fucking kidding me Bryan! You can't even ask me in a serious tone!"

She was getting ready to roll and inhaled a deep breath. Bryan seeing the opportunity to speak, tried to jump on it.

"Cris, please! I know these are not things you want to think about, but I have to ask them. I am only trying to help find the bastard who murdered your husband. I am trying to help *you,* please let me help!" Pete now had a sad, pleading in his eyes.

Cris was furious and having none of it. She looked between both Bryan and Bolton but focused her cutting glare on Bryan.

"Why the fuck are you guys trying to be so nice to me all the time? I'm not some helpless female."

A sickening thought struck her just then, her eyes narrowed. "You're both a little too nice. Chief, I don't know what your deal is, but I do know where you were at the time of the shooting. You were here, with witnesses, and if you weren't here, you would be home where your wife would have you by the balls, she's a good woman. But Bryan! Where were you yesterday morning, do you have any alibis?"

Pete gave her his own set of narrow eyes back. "I was alone, as you would well know!"

What the hell was that supposed to mean? Cris was at a whole new level of rage now! She lunged up, chair scraping across the floor, pointing her finger across the desk directed at his face.

"So why the fuck do *you* care so much? You can't be that nice or you wouldn't still be single! Did you have some motive to kill my husband?"

Pete's face got scarlet red as he started to open his mouth, probably to either defend himself or tell her off.

"Steele!" Chief's voice boomed, immediately cutting her off and taking full control of the room and the situation.

He turned quickly to Pete. "Bryan, go ahead, I think you asked everything you needed to at this point. I will finish up here."

Without saying a word, Pete grabbed his pen and notebook and quickly stormed out. It was clear he was fuming, but he had the self-control and smarts to keep his mouth shut. Cris was wishing she had utilized that restraint herself.

Chief turned back to her, glaring. He snapped a sharp finger at her chair. "Sit down!"

She knew enough to follow his order without so much as a breath of noise.

"Let me start by saying *that* shit right there, *that* is the reason why you cannot be involved with the case and why I was in the room today to alleviate those "misunderstandings." This couldn't possibly be any closer or more personal to you! Your judgment is clouded on this, understandably. Now, I don't want to hear any more accusations like that again unless you have some kind of evidence to back it up, besides Bryan just being too nice."

Chief's voice grew calmer as he spoke, but his curt tone was very clear this discussion was not going to be had again. He really was a great leader, he got his point across without making you feel like a total incompetent steaming pile of dung heap at the end. You were left with respect for him and wanting to please him. He ran a tight ship, but he commanded it well! Chief gave a little pause, his raised eyebrows and direct stare indicating he was looking for some kind of agreement from her.

Cris obliged him with rounded shoulders and averted her gaze to the old coffee stains on his desk as she replied.

"Yes, Sir, I understand. I'm sorry I lost it. You're right, I am too close. The questions of Luke being with a student felt like an accusation, even if only implied. I couldn't see straight after that one. Thank you for being here and stopping me."

She felt like a little girl disappointing her father and she had a feeling her cheeks may be slightly pink.

Chief probably realized she was feeling bad about her reactions. Cris always appeared hard, cold and unfeeling. Showing these emotions today was certainly uncharacteristic. Bolton lowered his voice and leaned forward slightly with his arms on his desk.

"Cris, I am not perfect by any means. I have done a lot of bad shit in my life. I try to be a good and fair person, I try my best to uphold my 'do unto others' belief and attitude, probably very similar to yourself if I had to venture a guess." Chief gestured his hand towards her.

She looked back at him with knowing eyes. Despite her outward coldness, she did live by those same beliefs. Again, you recognize your own types and quirks when you see them.

"So having said that, I'm glad I come off as a nice guy to you. It's not always easy in my position, but at the end of the day I want my team to know how much I appreciate and respect them, along with all their personality quirks." Bolton gave her a head nod on that one, followed by a slight sigh.

"I will admit, although I try to be fair, I probably do treat you a little differently than the rest. I try not to, but I can't seem to stop myself. I think it's only fair I tell you, especially since you want to know what 'my deal' is." Chief must have seen her furrowed brow and confused, concerned look.

"Let's just say I have some knowledge about your childhood and leave it at that. I have compassion for you, I can't help it. I feel the need to protect you, whether you need it or not. It's probably why I come off as "too nice" to you. Hopefully, this confession takes me off your suspect list."

Bolton gave her a low chuckle at the attempt of humor, but her own mouth probably hung wide open at his words. *He must have been given background information when I was hired, which apparently included my childhood, shit!* She didn't want anyone to know that! Cris knew he would keep it private, thankfully, but still, those were her demons to keep locked in the closet!

Cris tried to act nonchalant, but she was sure her face must be giving her away, her mouth drier than cotton now. "Chief, I'm not sure what it is you know, and I know this would go without saying, but I have to say it. Please do not let whatever knowledge you have go anywhere!"

She was going to say more, but Bolton held up his hand and stopped her.

"Cris, say no more. You know it will not be spoken. The only reason I mentioned it at all was so you had a little understanding of why I am 'too nice' to you. Conversation over. Now, I think Bryan is out there licking his wounds after the lashing you just gave him. Get your head out of your ass, swallow your pride and go talk to him, make up. You guys are friends. You don't want to lose your dog sitter, do you?"

Chief smiled at her and stood up. It was clear his lecture and admission of her past was over and there should be no need to discuss either of them again. Cris rose and gave a polite head nod as she turned, indicating she was in agreement and thankful.

She took a deep breath as she made a right out of Bolton's office and headed for the little areas of mock cubicles, more specifically, Pete's desk. Not only did she owe him an apology, but she still needed to find out what happened last night. *Damn it, this is gonna suck!*

Cris came around to the opening of Pete's desk area, having no idea what she was going to say, feeling like a total screw up. Looking in, she saw Pete was shuffling through some papers in a file, Luke's she assumed. *Let's get this done and over with.* She knocked as best as possible on the cheap wall. He looked up, his face completely unreadable.

"Shit, remind me not to play poker with you!" Cris kind of blurted it out. She had no idea what she was going to say to him, but it sure as hell wasn't a smart-ass comment like that. Pete looked back at her confused.

"Um, I'm sorry, why's that?" Still the unreadable face. How mad at her was he?

"Sorry Bryan, that was not at all what I meant to say. You just have this face that is completely unreadable. I have no idea what you're thinking right now."

Cris gave a small pause, thinking about her words to him for the first time today, she looked down at the dingy gray floor and conceded.

"I guess I've said a lot of things to you I shouldn't have this morning, I'm sorry."

Pete stood up and took her hand, pulling her further into his non-private office, then quickly let it go. His voice was low as he spoke, not wanting the nearby co-workers to hear.

"Cris, I know this is all really difficult for you and I knew those questions were going to be equally as difficult, and knowing you as well as I do, I knew you weren't going to take them laying down. All that aside though, the accusations you threw at me were really fucking hurtful!"

Cris noticed even through his anger and hurt he still kept his voice low, still protecting her. She puffed out a sigh.

"I'm really sorry Pete! And of course, I know why you're still single, nobody can handle you always being gone and dealing with death in one form or another. It's not an easy career for a serious relationship. I should never have said any of those things to you. I really am sorry!"

She was not accustomed to this showing of emotion, was not sure how to properly express it. She hoped he believed her.

Pete gave her a non-committal shrug. "I know this is not easy for you on many levels. I just hope you will take a minute and think before you speak as the investigation goes on. We are colleagues, but we are also friends. I don't have many true relationships, I really don't want the ones I do have ruined."

"I was out of line Pete. I'm truly sorry and I promise to try my best to think first next time. It's not easy for me, but I will work on it."

Cris gave him a smile at the admission of her personality fault, then she went to her own poker face. "While we are already on shaky ground, I guess I might as well ask if we can go back to our conversation that was interrupted about last night? You had said you knew I went for a run right before Chief came for the first round of handing my ass to me."

Pete gave a smile at the ass handing reference, a good sign. "You texted me when you got home saying you had gone for a run and were just getting home and noticed my truck was gone."

Okay take a breath, that's how he knew you went for a run.

"Long story short, you wanted to know what I had found out so far for the investigation. When I told you I couldn't share it with you, at least not yet, you got pretty pissed. You texted some nasty things then stopped responding to me."

Cris was both relieved and upset with herself. Nothing had happened, except her mouth again.

"Sorry Pete, I swear I'm trying to work on cutting my sharp tongue. I should have never said those things to you. I know you're just doing your job and I promise I won't push you like that again. Hell, I won't even ask you about the investigation, I know you will tell me if there's something important. I really think I was just exhausted last night, and, okay, maybe a little drunk."

Pete seemed slightly, temporarily, relieved. Cris knew how he must have felt, their relationship was at least stable at this point and hopefully she really wouldn't ask him about it again. She gave a slight pause, getting that courage again.

She winced a little as she lowered her voice to almost a whisper. "Did I happen to mention how I got home last night, or anything about a priest?"

Pete gave her a sideways glance at that one, poker face gone. "Shit no! You don't remember that either? Damn it Cris, you weren't drinking while you were running, were you? Did you run to a bar?"

He took a moment to shake his head, no doubt thinking about her lapse in memory and possibly judgment. "Priest? Did you partake in a little too much of the blood of Christ with a priest?"

All good questions, she thought to herself with a little trepidation.

Chapter 11

*C*urled up on a wooden bench on the side porch, 10-year old Cris was lost and submerged in another life of her book when she heard Old Lady Steele's car pull in next door. She had no reason to break her alternate life fantasy for her old neighbor, that was until she heard her talking to someone. That piqued her interest, she never had company. She raised her eyebrows as she looked up and over her sunglasses. There at the rear of the old powder blue Plymouth stood a scrawny looking boy, with tousled brown hair, helping get bags and luggage out of the trunk. From a distance, he looked awkward and scared, and also close to her age. She sat up straight, straining to get a better look. He must have noticed the movement because he lifted his head and looked over. She didn't really know what to do, it was obvious she was staring, she was busted. She just gave a low, awkward wave and sat back down on the bench quickly. She could feel her cheeks burning and was thankful he was too far away to see.

The rest of the day Cris kept looking over there, and the rare times she was indoors, she was sneaking peeks through the blinds. It must have been Old Lady Steele's grandson. He was probably only visiting for vacation or something, but it might give her someone to hang out with while he was here. After she made herself macaroni and cheese for dinner Cris decided to go outside and play in the field between the two houses, hoping maybe this elusive boy would come out. She filled a wagon with blocks and rolled them out. She started stacking and balancing blocks on each other building little houses and a city. After about 15 minutes she had a good little city going already, and she heard the creak of the neighbor's door opening. She looked up from her mini city to see Old Lady Steele holding the door open and motioning and talking to the inside of the house. A quick point of a finger towards Cris *followed by the tousled brown hair, peeking his head out. They both looked over at Cris then and she was again busted by her blatant staring. Awkward again, she gave the same quick low wave she had earlier in the day. He gave a similar wave back and came the rest of the way out the door. Another small exchange between him and Old Lady Steele then he was walking down the steps heading her way. He shuffled over slowly with his hands in his pockets and his head down.*

As he got closer she looked up at him and tried to smile. "Hi, I'm Cris."

He replied shyly, "I'm Luke."

"Are you here visiting for vacation?"

Luke looked like he didn't really know how or want to answer that. After a brief pause, he responded.

"No, I'm going to live here with my Grammie now." He had tears in his eyes but didn't let them spill.

Cris cocked her head. "Where are your parents?"

She didn't even think before she asked, it just came out.

"They're not here."

Luke gave a little sniff but didn't elaborate and she didn't want to ask him anymore. She didn't know how to deal with it if he started crying. Crying was an emotion she was not used to.

She gave a diminutive shrug. "Well, want to build with me? I have lots more blocks, see?"

She pointed to the wagon next to her, still half full of blocks. Luke smiled then, it was a crooked smile and she liked it, it seemed to fit him. Cris felt her face get hot and she quickly looked down at her little city and continued to build.

Luke sat down on the other side of the wagon and grabbed some blocks. "Mind if I build over here?"

"Not at all! I never have anyone to play with me, this will be fun!" She was trying not to sound too excited, but it was hard.

"My Grammie said there aren't many kids on this street?"

Although it felt comfortable talking to each other, neither of them were looking at each other while they were talking, they just kept looking at their buildings they were creating, it was easier to overcome the nervousness that way.

"There's some older kids, teenagers, up the street. They don't bother with me though."

A thought hit her then. "Hey, since you're living here, you'll be going to school with me, we can sit on the bus together!"

"Um, yeah, I guess I will." Luke appeared to think about that for a minute.

"It will be good to know someone before I start. I'm going into fifth grade." It was clear by the quiver in his voice he was not looking forward to a new school and having to make new friends.

"Me too! We will be in the same class, cool!" Cris had a big smile now and was actually looking at him.

Not much after the words left her mouth though, she frowned. "I should warn you though. You probably don't want to become friends with me, or at least not at school in front of the other kids. I won't be upset with you if you wanted to hang out together outside of school but pretend you don't know me in school. Or, if you don't want to be my friend at all, I would understand."

Luke stopped building and tipped his head. "Why not?"

"Because the other kids don't like me. They pick on me and I seem to have a habit to get mad and stand up for myself when they do. Sometimes it turns into an all-out brawl."

"That's not right! Why do they pick on you?"

"They actually start most of the time by picking on my dad, then when I defend him and my family they call me 'Crazy Cris' and say I'm just like my daddy. I guess me tackling them to the ground after that makes them feel justified in calling me crazy."

She was sad telling him this because she thought they could be friends, but it wouldn't be fair to him. "No point in you having to be picked on just because you're my friend."

"I don't like being friends with people who are like that. I am only friends with good people, or, at least I was. I don't plan to change my ways now."

He paused, clearly thinking about this whole thing. "Ya know, just by you telling me this tells me you are a good, honest person. I have a feeling we are going to become really good friends Miss Cris."

At the "Miss Cris" she could feel the blush.

"Um, please just call me Cris. Miss Cris sounds funny." She actually let out a laugh.

"Sorry, I didn't mean to offend you. It's just how we, I mean I, talk to people."

"Oh, no offense! Just save that for the older people. If we are going to be friends, you need to call me Cris, or whatever you want, just nothing so formal!"

"Okay! I think I'm really going to like you!" Luke quickly turned

his head trying to hide his blushed cheeks.

Cris didn't know why he was going to be living here now, but at the moment she was really happy about it!

The rest of the summer they were inseparable, like the proverbial peas and carrots. Since Luke's Grammie was not really prepared to raise another child, and the fact both he and Cris were wise and responsible beyond their years, she pretty much let them play together all day. Cris had basically been on her own the past two years since daddy finally got out of the U.S. Navy and they moved here. Neither he nor her mom were the same since then. So, Luke and Cris would be together having fun from sun up to sun down. Sometimes with a break for food or drink of water, but most of the time they packed their own food and explored and had fun, making the reality of their lives disappear, at least during daylight time. They would build cabins in the back yard, hop the trains that went by, play all along the railroad tracks, pick berries then eat them all before they got them home and play by the river trying to skip rocks where it wasn't so rough and explore the nearby caves. Even the treacherous walk to get to the river was an adventure in itself.

Before they knew it, summer was over, and the reality of school bared down on them. The first day they stood together at the bus stop, trying to joke and keep each other's spirits up. Cris knew what she was facing, and she didn't care, but she did care about Luke. She had warned him, but he would have to truly experience the other kids to understand. She still wanted to spare him from that, at least give him a chance to see if he could make friends. As they waited for the bus, she told him not to sit with her, to not affiliate himself with her just yet, give himself a fighting chance. The bus came, and Luke made her go on first. Of course, got to be a gentleman, she thought. She sat at the edge of a seat that had the seat open on the opposite side, so he could sit there, and they could still be close. Luke squat down next to her and pushed her over towards the window with his little hips so he could sit down.

Luke looked at her with his crooked smile as the bus took off.

"Maybe you really are crazy if you think I'm going to ignore you and pretend I don't know you."

She punched his arm in response but couldn't wipe off her grin from ear to ear.

"I don't care what they think of me Cris, you are my best friend no matter what!"

When they got to school, the morning was busy listening to the teacher tell them the daily schedule and what was expected of them while passing out some of the books. Things were going fine, up until recess. Luke immediately sidled up next to Cris. Before they could escape anywhere on the playground, a group surrounded them. One of the ring leaders, Raquel, started right in.

She sneered with a high pitch voice "Hey Crazy, welcome back."

Not missing a beat, Cris snapped back. "Screw you bitch."

Luke looked over at Cris, he had not heard her talk like that, she knew he must be surprised, and probably disappointed in her, but she was going to stand her ground and hope for the best in her relationship with Luke. She was surprised when she glanced at him quickly and his face looked like he was proud.

Raquel bit right back, with an outstretched pretend shaking of her hand. "Oh, I'm so scared Crazy! You'll never guess! I heard my dad talking this morning..."

Cris cut Raquel off before she could finish and moved right up to her face. "Oh, you heard him telling your momma he knew what a whore she was and he knows you're not really his? Well everyone already knew that, welcome to reality you female bastard!"

Raquel's face got scarlet red and high pitch gone, she blurted in her normal voice "No! That last night, just like all summer, your crazy dad's truck was at the bar again, and it was still there this morning. His home away from home, huh?!"

Cris laughed in her face. "Why is your dad always driving by the bar anyway? Looking for your momma, or trying to find his illegitimate daughter's real daddy? It's a new year bitch, you've had all summer to get some new material. Oh yeah, you're not bright enough!"

She was shaking her head from side to side in Raquel's face at that point, showing no fear. The rest of the kids were still standing around in a circle, just watching the show. Luke was still in the middle, at this point starting to grab at her hand to pull her back, trying to save her. Raquel saw him and pounced, voice high pitched again as she looked to the side of Cris' head at him.

"Oh, hey there new kid! Luke, right?" Raquel didn't wait for an answer but kept going so Luke couldn't talk, trying to establish dominance. "Look, I see you trying to help her out. You probably don't know enough yet, but let me tell you, she's crazy. Save yourself the trouble and let her go."

Raquel gave a slight pause, enough for Luke to jump in. "That's where you're wrong. I do know her, and I'm NOT letting her go!" Luke was not nearly as brusque as Cris was, but he was still strong and firm in his response, obviously not going to back down or condemn Cris.

Raquel again lost her high-pitched voice and got in Luke's face, she threw her head back and gave a deep laugh, obviously happy with new meat to pound. "I heard my dad tell my mom about you too! Living with Old Lady Steele now because your parents died in a head-on car accident and you were in the back seat, unhurt, and tried to revive them. I bet you're crazy just like her, no wonder you like her! How's life living with Grandma now?"

Raquel barely had the last words out before Cris slammed her to the ground and threw a punch that landed square on Raquel's nose and blood came spurting out.

Chapter 12

Pete trudged into the office a little before eight, for the first time in his career feeling nondescript, like an outcast who didn't belong. Steele and Bolton were already there. They were in their own separate corners of their respective offices, submerged in papers, or at least pretending to be. He still felt uneasy about everything that had happened, from the one-sided texting war Sunday night to yesterday's blow out and Cris' accusation of him being a murderer, but it was time to buck up and get over it. He had a job to do and today could be a potentially big day with the ceremony and funeral just a few hours away. Chances were good the killer would be there to revel in his work, basking in the pain and suffering he caused.

Pete set his keys down on his desk and plunked down in his chair, setting his coffee mug next to his computer as he hit the button to fire it up.

"Mornin' Bryan." Pete looked over and saw Cris looking at him from her desk.

"Oh, hey Steele. You're here early, I thought you might stay home this morning to get ready." He noticed the dark circles under her eyes even from this distance. "You should've tried to sleep in a little."

"That's wishful thinking. I didn't sleep well, I woke up from a dream and couldn't fall back asleep. Figured I might as well get a workout in then get to work where I might be able to be productive, especially since the rest of the day will be shot." Cris took a long pull from her water bottle.

It was clear they didn't really know what to say to each other, both reverting to small talk. Pete hoped things would get back to the way they used to be, and he was really hoping maybe they would become closer. He could be there for her when she needed someone to fix things around the house and anything else she needed. Not like he had a social life anyways.

"Do you need any help getting things set up at the church?" More small talk.

"No, I should be good. The church is actually setting things up, told me not to worry about doing anything. It's going to be small anyways, there can't be much to do."

Cris gave a shrug, then stood up and stretched. Pete could tell she was trying to act like it was no big deal, just another day, another business chore to cross off her list.

"Well, if that ends up being the case, it will be easier for us to spot anyone who doesn't belong. That could certainly work to our advantage."

Pete noticed the office getting busier now, louder. More phones beeping and chirping, voices loudly conversing like the receiving person is hard of hearing. Detective Campbell pranced by in her heels, blonde hair flowing behind her, adding to the noise as she apparently felt the rest of the office needed to hear her cell phone conversation. Her desk was on the other side of Pete's, adjacent to Cris'. Pete looked at Cris and rolled his eyes. She responded by coming over and sitting on the corner of his desk.

"I can't compete with all that noise. So, is there a game plan yet for today?"

"Of course. Bolton already has it all planned out."

Cris cut him off with a mutter. "Of course, he does."

She shook her head but had a little smile on her face. "Sorry, I didn't mean to say that out loud, proceed." She gave him a little head bow and roll of her hand as she told him to proceed.

Pete smiled back. "Smart-ass. He and I will both get there early to greet as many people as we can before it starts. At that point, Chief is going to go sit by you. His wife will already be sitting by you, so he will just slip in. He said you won't have any family there so they are going to be there for support."

He paused giving her a second to expand on that, he knew nothing of her past and she never talked about it, but she just sat staring at him waiting for him to continue. Pete took the hint and carried on.

"...at the same time also getting a view from the front for suspects, while the rest of us are scanning from the back."

Cris nodded. "Who else will be back there with you?"

"Chief set up a few plain clothes officers to be mixed in, he didn't tell me who; and Campbell will also be there." Pete motioned his head to the direction of Campbell's desk.

All business, Cris had no smart-assed remarks. "That should be plenty, like I said, it's going to be very small."

She stood up and stretched again, her shirt riding up a little showing some of her abs. She quickly pulled it back down. "Alright, it's getting loud in here, I think my productivity is over for now. I'm going to run home and get dressed, I'll meet you guys at the church in a few."

Cris turned brusquely, grabbed her keys and water bottle from her desk and walked away. She gave a short wave as she passed by Chief's office. Pete watched her ass sway all the way down the hall until she turned the corner.

Pete stood up, shaking his thoughts off. It was time to focus and get to work. He grabbed his keys and coffee mug and made a point of not looking at Cris' office space as he left his own. He peeked around the wall to Campbell's pink and purple lined lair. She had her face submerged in a compact mirror, touching up her makeup.

"Hey, Campbell."

Kim Campbell looked at his reflection in her mirror but didn't stop her application when he started talking, instead, she moved to her lips, sticking them out and applying some bright red lipstick, almost seductive looking. He released a sigh and gave a slight eye roll, hoping she didn't actually notice because he didn't want to be rude to her, but at the same time, he couldn't help himself. He was pretty sure she didn't notice, that was giving her too much credit in his book.

"Look, I'm going to head over to the church now, walk around the grounds and scope things out until people start to arrive. I'll see you there."

Campbell swiveled around in her chair, apparently finished with her makeup session. She gave him her thousand watt smile with her bright red lips and perfectly straight, white teeth.

"Okay Bryan, sounds good! I've just got a few things to wrap up and I'll be there."

"No rush. Take your time, we still have awhile."

Pete walked away, hoping he didn't sound as sincere about her taking her time as he actually was. He was going to walk past Chief's office, but he noticed Chief saw him, so he figured he might as well update him.

"Hey Chief, I'm going to head out. I got a few things to check on and I want to be at the church early to walk around the grounds and see if anyone is lingering, watching."

Pete was trying to sound upbeat, but he wasn't feeling it. He needed to get away from people, he wanted to be alone, which was pretty sad considering how solitary his life already was. Pete knew this case was going to tear him apart, it was personal for him too.

Chief looked at him with furrowed brows. There would be no fooling him. "Alright, I'll meet you there in a little while. Everything okay, Bryan?"

"Yes Sir, just focused on the case. This could be a big day, the break we so desperately need. I want to be as proactive and prepared as I can be." Pete turned on his heels to leave.

"I'll see you there, Chief." Pete waved as he started to walk down the hall.

When Pete got there, he noticed the church was already bustling with people, but they mostly appeared to be the church members. He couldn't believe what he saw when he walked in. The altar was surrounded by huge, beautiful flower arrangements and multiple collages, and they were still placing more things around. He couldn't believe Cris would do all this, she was not a "showy" type of person. She wanted something small. Since he still had plenty of time to walk the grounds outside, he decided to walk up and look at the elaborate displays. Looking at the cards on the flowers and the pictures, he quickly realized it wasn't Cris, the assortments were from Luke's students and his fellow teachers. The collages were all kinds of pictures, some of him by himself and some with his students at different classes and sporting events. He had to look away from the pictures of Luke. His happiness and love of life were always so evident, these pictures were a sad reminder. Again, he thought how this was too personal for him, he was too close.

Pete turned to walk outside. He suddenly realized the small service Cris was expecting was probably not going to be small at all based on how the altar already looked. That was not in their favor for the investigation. It would be too easy for someone to blend in with the crowd. He knew they were going to have to be checking out every single person, and it was going to be a daunting task. He had to get his head out of his ass. *No time for emotions. Think of it as nothing more than a high-profile case.* He knew it was easier said than done, but he had to try something to stop his feelings from being all over the place on this one.

He walked out back. The grounds were beautiful. He had never been here before, and quite honestly, he was shocked the service was in a Catholic church. Once Pete thought about it though, he knew he shouldn't be shocked by anything since he didn't truly know anything very personal about Cris. He also knew he had to stop thinking about her.

Clearing his head, he looked up at the large trees, the squirrels chasing each other through the branches, jumping from tree to tree, shaking the Spanish Moss as they did. The shadow of a hawk passed through the bright sun.

"Better hide squirrels or you're going to be lunch." The screech from the hawk confirmed his words.

He continued the walk around the backside of the church, back by the pond. There were benches over-looking the small pond at different spots all the way around it. Pete decided to go to the backside of the pond where he could see everything and take a seat on the bench. He sat there for a while, just watching. Looking for any movement in the bushes, anything. There was nothing or nobody unusual, except the gator sunning himself on the grass at the water's edge, but he didn't appear to be interested in talking.

After a few minutes, Pete saw Bolton appear and got up, jogging back towards the front to join him. "Hey, Chief!"

"Hey, Bryan. Were you able to walk the perimeter?"

They began walking towards the entrance of the church. "Yes, I've been here for a while. I haven't seen anyone or anything that doesn't belong yet. There is also quite a display at the altar, I expect it's going to be a huge turnout."

"Shit. That's what I was afraid of."

They both took their places at the entrance doors, one at each side. Unless you knew them, you would just assume they were ushers for the church. They nodded as team members came through. Everyone knew where they were assigned to be, no need to speak and potentially blow cover if the killer was watching.

It was almost time for the service to start, time for them to go in and continue the observations inside. Bolton went in and sat in between his wife and Cris, while Pete stood off to the side in the back. He would be nonchalantly wandering around a little bit, making sure he could see all angles.

Standing over on the side he could clearly see Chief and Cris. Pete noticed Cris with her shoulders straight back and eyes focused on the altar, she looked stoic and strong. *Of course, she won't show any emotion!* Then he noticed Bolton, who also had his arm around her. *What the fuck is that? Look at her, she's good, she doesn't need that. What is Chief's deal with her? He* realized he was starting to get annoyed, then knew he needed to focus on the job at hand. *Chief said he was going to be there to support her, that's what he's doing, with his wife on his other side, and besides, what is it to you?* Pete gave a slight head shake as he slowly walked towards the back of the room.

Looking at the church, he realized there was not an empty space in the pews. He also noticed besides their own team, there was nobody there by themselves. It was all students who were with their families or faculty sitting with other staff members, and there was not a dry eye from any of them. They were all beside themselves with grief, it was genuine. Luke was clearly very much loved and respected.

Surely, the killer could not be here with any of these mourners. Pete rubbed his right hand over his buzzed head habitually. *Could one of these "mourners" actually be the killer?*

Once the service was over and the long line of condolences to Cris was finally through, Mrs. Bolton kept Cris busy talking with Father Tony, while the rest of the crew all convened in the cry room where it was private.

Chief spoke first, removing his glasses while wiping the sweat from his brow. "Alright, guys what have we got? Anyone see anybody suspicious, that didn't belong?"

Nobody spoke, but they all shook their heads no.

Pete spoke up. "Sir, there was nobody who stood out, no unfamiliar faces. Besides the few of us, everybody was here with someone. There was nobody here alone. You know as well as I do, the chances of the killer being here with someone is almost nil."

Chief mopped his brow again before replacing his glasses. "Well fuck!"

They all looked around the church they were standing in when he said that, but it was clear, everybody's sentiments were the same.

Chapter 13

Cris was sitting Indian-style on the living room floor watching the Saturday morning cartoons as mom was cleaning the house. This was their Saturday morning routine, sometimes her mom would let Cris help her with the dusting. She worked in the cafeteria at the school all week, then spent the evenings playing with Cris. Saturday mornings were the time to get the housework done and over with by noon, then they had the rest of the weekend to do whatever they wanted, which usually consisted of the nearby playground, playing board games, drawing pictures and sending them with letters to her dad and sometimes his shipmates, building tents in the living room and watching movies. If they were real lucky they might even get a call from dad!

Mom was just finishing mopping the kitchen floor. It always symbolized the end of the cleaning. Apparently, she had heard the mailman come as she was almost done.

"Hey, honey! I heard the mailman. I'm going to go grab the mail quick. I just finished mopping the floor so don't come out yet please."

The mail was a big deal in the Murray household! There was always the anticipation of letters from dad!

"Okay, Mom!"

Her eyes were glued to the screen anyway. It was close to noon, the show was almost over, she had to watch it to the end.

She heard her mom come back in. "Cris! Come on honey, we got a letter from dad!"

They both loved it when they got his letters, but mom was always so happy when she got them, it really made her day. She had already opened the envelope by the time Cris shut the big old console television off and came bounding into the kitchen, sliding, still in her footsie pajamas. Dad had usually included a letter for both of them, plus a letter just for her and a letter just for mom. Mom had obviously started reading hers because she was looking at a piece of paper and crying. She looked up at her mom, worried.

"What's wrong mom? Is dad okay?" Cris never saw her mom cry, she was sure she must not be able to; up until now!

Her mom wiped her eyes and looked down at Cris with a huge smile. "Yes, baby! I have some wonderful news! Daddy will be coming home soon, for good!"

Cris couldn't believe it! "Really?" She squealed. "Read it to me, mom!"

Mom read her letter to Cris, although she was smart enough to know she was probably changing and leaving out some of his words, but it didn't matter, she told her the important stuff! He wasn't going to reenlist. After this deployment, he was done! They were going to be able to buy a house of their own, were going to move to an area where dad had some friends, no more renting or moving around to different duty stations! She just couldn't believe it! Although she was a little sad to be moving and scared to change schools, it wasn't anything she wasn't used to. It didn't matter as long as dad was going to be home!

The next few months flew by as she and her mom were busy getting everything packed and sorting the things they wouldn't take. She was already wise for her eight-years and like an "old soul." She was a big helper in packing things up and didn't argue or complain when she was told to place items in the donation pile. Things would be ready for when dad got home, she would be sure of it!

The day of the ship's arrival came quickly. She was at the port with her mom, like they had done a gazillion times before. It never got old, seeing them in their dress whites (or blues, depending on the season) all lined up along the rail! Ever since Cris could remember, she always had a lump in her throat at their arrival. Pride and shear excitement! Today was mixed emotions. She was so happy her dad would now be home with them, but it was also sad to know this was the last time they would be at the port awaiting his arrival. She already knew the meaning of bittersweet all to well, this was no exception.

The ship finally docked! The parents who had new babies born while they were deployed were the first ones off. Cris waited impatiently, trying to see over everyone's heads. Finally! She saw her daddy coming! The same red hair and blue eyes she had, was sprinting in her direction. He found them in the crowd and threw his sea bag down to scoop them both up. She was so happy he would be with them forever now, she wanted to cry. She kept swallowing the lump in her throat down. They didn't cry, they were always strong. At least that's what she always saw, so it was all she knew.

Daddy said "see you soon" to lots of his shipmates before we could actually leave the port. Even at her young age, Cris knew this must be hard for him. He spent most of his 12-year military career with many of these guys, they were also his family. Bittersweet, she understood all too well.

Over the next couple of days, he finished things up on base before they could officially move, which was perfect because it also allowed for her to finish the last of her school year. It was great having him home though! She noticed he was a little different than before, when he was home between deployments. Cris chalked it up to not being in the military anymore and starting a new civilian life. He would get used to the schedule she and mom had, and everything would be much better soon, she just knew it!

It was the end of June when they moved into their new house. It wasn't huge, but it was their own! There weren't any kids right in their neighborhood to play with, but she didn't care. She had her parents to hang out with and dad had some friends nearby. She overheard mom saying how important it was, to have his friends around to help him out. She didn't know what he needed help with since he could do anything, but if mom said it was a good thing, that was all that mattered to her!

Dad kept saying he had to find a job and she heard him complaining how he was having a hard time getting one. Employers didn't want Veterans with their military mindsets and issues, was what she would hear him say. She didn't understand that, she thought they were the best, but it was the employer's loss as far as she was concerned. He was quieter than he used to be, though he still played with her, it wasn't with the same zeal as she remembered. He also seemed to drink a lot more than he used to. Some nights he would just drink beer, but most nights Sailor Jerry on the rocks was his beloved companion. Of course, Cris thought it was just the coolest thing since he was a sailor, but mom didn't seem to see the same humor in it.

Before she knew it, the fourth of July was upon them. Cris was so excited, they always celebrated the Fourth of July! Any day that acknowledged America or the military in any way was always celebrated as appropriate in their house. This year, it was not as exciting, right from the get go. The same buzz was not in the air that there used to be. Sure, they had a cookout, and of course, they all wore some form of patriotic clothing, and a few of dad's friends even came over, but it was not the same enthusiasm. She noticed Sailor Jerry seemed to be the fellow traveler of choice for most of them today, but she was enjoying playing with the other kids, so beyond noticing the drinks, Cris paid little mind.

Normally, mom and Cris would go watch the local fireworks, and dad if he wasn't deployed. This year, that was different too. Mom said dad didn't want to hear the fireworks this year and they were going to stay home and hope it was quiet. Cris didn't really understand, but if that is what was really needed, then she was okay with it. Since they were staying home, and she was tired from playing most of the day, when mom told her it was time for bed a little before dark, Cris didn't complain.

It wasn't long before she heard some fireworks going off in the distance. They weren't right near their house, but certainly close enough to hear. She wondered where they were, and if she looked out her window could she could see them? She quietly got up and tiptoed to her window. As she heard what sounded like the grand finale of the show nearby, she heard a similar, but fearful, grand finale going on in her own house.

She prayed she would not make a sound as she turned the knob on her door. That being a success, she tiptoed down the hallway. The fragments she saw were absolute chaos. Her mom was running to the phone in the kitchen, looking at a small piece of paper in her hand as she dialed. Dad was in the living room shouting, at who or what, Cris could not tell.

"There are fucking women and children there! They are innocents!" Dad turned suddenly to face another wall, flailing his arms and obviously seeing some other world. "Damn it! Run! Go, get out of there!"

She could not understand why her dad was acting this way. Everything at that moment was pandemonium. The fireworks were booming in the distance; dad was screaming at the walls which had Sailor Jerry running down them with broken glass and cubes of ice on the at the bottom and on the floor, and mom was frantically talking to someone on the other end of the phone. Cris' heart was slamming in her chest, but she couldn't walk away. She knew she needed to help, but she was scared and had no idea which one to go to.

Mom hung up the phone, her eyes like saucers. She turned and saw Cris peering around the wall, trying to hide at the end of the hall.

Mom glanced in the living room at dad, who was still yelling at some unseen apparitions, and decided to quickly run over to her.

"Baby, go in your room! I know this looks crazy, but everything is going to be okay, I promise! I have help coming for daddy. Please, just listen to mommy right now and go!"

Mom's eyes were pleading and no way could Cris put up a fuss right now. It was clear mom had enough on her plate.

Cris quickly ran to her room but kept her ear close to the door. She thought she heard the rumble of exhaust slowing down, and promptly looked out her bedroom window to see a pickup pulling in their driveway. From her window, she could not see who got out, but she knew it must be "the help" mom said was coming. She dared to feel a little less dismayed and prayed this would fix whatever was wrong. Her ear back to her door, she heard mom's hushed voice and some other man's voice talking back calmly to her. Right after, she heard the same voice talking more loudly, but firmly, to her dad. She heard her dad talk back to him now, not like he sounded before when he was screaming at the walls. The rest was quiet and too muted for her to make out, but she heard the front door close followed by silence in the house. The familiar sound of the truck exhaust coming to life, she ran back over to the window. As the truck slowly rumbled and backed out of the driveway and drove past her window, she noticed dad was in the passenger seat, his head resting on his hand against the window. Her focus out her own window, Cris never heard mom's quiet feet padding into her bedroom.

The next two years proved to be much of the same. Dad continued to have difficulty separating what he had to see and do over the past 12 years, with his life now as a civilian. It was not a simple "flip of the switch" to adjust. He still was not able to get a job and he now spent most nights at the bar, and most of his days sleeping it off. The bartender would end up calling his "friend" to take him home. She knew by the sound of the truck, it was the same one that came that fourth of July night. Mom ended up working two jobs trying to make ends meet, while Cris spent most of her time alone.

Her mom knew how much more responsible she was compared to her biological age, so she knew she could leave her alone when she was not in school. It became the new norm in the Murray household.

Because of all of this, school was not her friend. Bullying had become an issue, "Crazy Cris" became her name; except Cris refused to be bullied without a fight, so she stood up for herself and her family. Most of the time, this resulted in her being labeled as the bully, instead of the other way around. She didn't care. She held her ground, believed in standing up for what was right, no matter what the results. She was a sailor's daughter and she could cuss and fight like one when times called for it. She had learned a lot in her short 10 years, but most of all, she had already learned what was truly important.

She was thankful when the fourth grade was finally over, and summer break had arrived. At least she didn't have to deal with the crap for a few months. She would never forget how it ended up being the best summer of her life, when Old Lady Steele pulled into her driveway that day with Luke, and Cris got to meet him, only to see the hollowness in his scared green eyes.

Chapter 14

At the imagery of Luke's hollow looking eyes, Cris startled and woke abruptly. Feeling slightly adrift, she had to shake off the remnants of the vivid dream, it seemed so damn real! Still smelling some lingering Sailor Jerry in the slumbered distance, the reality of where she was quickly set in as Stormy laid her head on Cris' chest. Another night on the couch. She still couldn't bear sleeping in their bed. After giving Stormy her due, she glanced over at the glowing time on the cable box. 4:30. She looked down at the dog who was laying quite pathetically on her chest now.

"Might as well get moving, Storm old girl. They'll be no going back to sleep now anyway."

She fleetingly thought of her dream, thought of Luke, now in the ground next to his parents. His life concluded way too early. Then she thought of her dad. The smartest and strongest of men, having to make split-second decisions under pressure most people could never comprehend, and yet, even he could not withstand the shit storms of life. And the fragile, empty shell which was left of her mother. Cris didn't even tell her about Luke's untimely demise, afraid it might finish breaking her cracked shell and toss her over the edge. Feeling fully frustrated and pissed off at the unfairness of life now, it was time to hit the gym equipment in their workout room and burn off that fuel of rage running through her veins.

After 45 minutes of core training and weight resistance, she was amply sweaty and sore, but the anger still oozed, contaminated in her blood. Cris decided to finish kicking her ass with a run on the beach. The hooting of the owls were again her companions for the first stretch of the run. As she got closer to the ocean, the smell of salt water tantalized her nostrils and rejuvenated her soul. Running right along the shore, the water lapped at her pounding feet as the waves crashed down, at times kissing her knees when the waves were higher. Her legs and lungs were both starting to burn, like the sun now coming up in the sky. She knew it was time to head home. Her self-torture successfully completed for today, her attitude was now adjusted.

A little more at peace on the run back, she noticed the surrounding beauty more to its entirety. It was high tide, so she was surprised when she saw a few dolphins jumping and playing about 75 yards off shore, knowing they usually preferred low tide and calmer waters. *They were meant for me to see*, Cris thought as she ran along, trying to watch them and where she was running. There were several washed up jelly fish and horseshoe crab shells to dodge, so she had to be mindful of it all. The pelicans were dive-bombing in from above trying to snatch their breakfast, while a few other locals were also getting their morning runs in. Upon leaving the sand and beach, and heading homeward bound, the owls seemed to have abandoned her, but the gentle breeze moving the fronds of the palm trees and the Spanish moss dancing to the music of the breeze, was a calming, welcome, companion.

After showering and spending a few minutes playing and having quality time with Stormy, she figured she better get her lunch and things together. Stormy content and lunch packed, she quickly looked at the time.

Still having a few minutes to spare, Cris knew she really needed to put all the food into the freezer that was left on her porch after the service yesterday. She arrived home late to an overwhelming support from the school community; an abundance of casseroles, lasagnas, and other variety of foods with sympathy cards attached. She temporarily stuffed them in the fridge, but she knew it would take forever to eat all this food by herself, so she would have to freeze it. Upon freezer task completion, satisfied she had been as productive as she could be, she gave Stormy her treat and headed out the door to see what fun today had in store for her.

The day hadn't started to heat up too bad yet. Cris put the windows of her GT down on the drive to work instead of using the AC and slipped on her sunglasses. Driving up the bridge crossing over the Intracoastal Waterway, at the peak, she enjoyed the view of the boats docked and the ones already out in the water, sailboats in the distance and the bright sun glinting off the water. The tall billowing cord grass looking a beautiful shade of green in contrast to the water. She inhaled the familiar smell of fish, salt, and pluff mud and both grimaced and smiled. The smell wasn't particularly pleasant, but it was a welcome smell, it had come to represent home and all its surrounding beauty.

The commute wasn't long and lost in thought Cris found herself at headquarters before she realized it. It was like the red sea parting as she walked by the break room, a.k.a. gossip within the shitty coffee area. She saw Moretti standing there talking to Reed. She paused a quick moment, surely not wanting to seem rude by not saying good morning. Moretti was facing the door, but wouldn't even look at her, pretending to be busy in his conversation with Reed. Just to piss him off, she smiled big while she gave a little wave and yelled over.

"Mornin' pencil dick! Morning Reed!"

As Reed turned to say good morning back, she saw the grin he was unsuccessfully trying to hide. Moretti, on the other hand just flipped her the bird with a seething red face and matching ears. Again, feeling successful in her tasks, Cris decided to move along.

She set her keys and water bottle down in their specific, precise, designated spots on her desk and noticed Bryan was also sitting at his. Really trying to keep her promise of not asking him about the case, and still trying to smooth things over a little, she reminded herself she was not going to ask if he found anything at the services yesterday, or otherwise.

"Good morning, Pete!"

Pete looked over from his computer screen at her. "Hey, good morning Cris!"

Pete quickly, stealth-like, closed the file of papers that had been open beside his computer. Cris noticed. *Well, you know he's working on the case, true to his word.*

She didn't want to acknowledge she noticed and make him feel uncomfortable or make him feel like she was watching and wanting to ask about the case. She had no idea what to say to him now, everything felt like it would look like she was digging for information. *What have you got going on today?* Obviously, it will look like she's prying. She hated the fact it felt like there was a wall between them now. It felt like they were pretending and weren't capable of anything beyond small talk. She expelled a big sigh as she walked over to Pete's desk. *Screw it.*

"I'm sorry, but this friggin' sucks Bryan!"

Pete looked back at her with a confused and, or, scared look, she couldn't quite tell which.

"We used to joke and talk and now I feel like I can't have any kind of conversation with you. I feel like anything I say will make it look like I'm on an excavating expedition for information. We are reduced to small talk and I hate it!" She was thankful to see he looked genuinely relieved.

"I know, Cris. I have felt the same way. I can tell all we are both doing is small talk, and it is so damn uncomfortable."

"Look Pete, I promised you I would not ask you about the investigation again, and I meant it. I know you will tell me when there is news worthy of telling. In the meantime, can we agree to try to be as normal as we can be towards each other?"

Pete let out a snicker. "Well, normal needs to be a word used loosely with us. I don't think our crazy asses fit the definition."

That was more like it! "Well, no shit! Why do you think I said as normal as we can be?"

Cris had a smile on her face now. "Maybe one of these nights you can stop over for a cook out, or the tons of food left on my porch yesterday. I'm sure Stormy would love to see you too, it's been awhile."

Pete smiled wide, perfect white teeth showing as he softly spoke now. "I would really love to, Cris."

"Good, me too. It's time to get back to the chaotic routine of life." She looked back at her desk then. "Speaking of which, I need to get this stack finished."

"Yeah, I have a few interviews I have to follow up on myself."

Pete looked at her a little pained. It was obvious he felt uncomfortable discussing his day now, but at the same time, he really wanted things to be the way they used to be between them.

She smiled at him again. "Well then get your ass off that chair and get to work, don't let me stop you, cowboy."

"I won't. I'll probably see you around later." Pete paused for a quick second. "And, hey, try to behave yourself a little today okay? Go easy on the some of the guys around here, they don't all have their big girl panties on like you do."

Cris couldn't resist! "Oh! You mean like pencil dick, I mean, Moretti?"

"Yeah, I mean like pencil dick. You hit him right where it counts, which everyone I know finds hilarious. Moretti, on the other hand, is a little butt hurt."

Cris smiled wide. "Good, he deserves it. I'm not the only bitch, karma runs alongside me. Good luck today Bryan."

With that, Cris turned back to her desk, as she heard a muffled "Thanks, see ya, Cris!"

Feeling a little better about her relationship with Pete, Cris was ready to tackle the last of her paperwork. She was just sitting down at her desk when she saw Bolton was walking her way. He was obviously making a bee-line to her humble abode.

Well stone the damn crows, this can't be good!

Chapter 15

Chief Jeff Bolton hung up the phone and ran his fingers through his salt and pepper hair. He felt the thick coffee burning its way back up his esophagus. Opening the top drawer of his desk, he grabbed his container of antacids and popped two, quickly chewing them down.

The Jasper Town PD was asking for help from his department, knowing they were fortunate enough to be harboring a few of the counties best homicide detectives. While it wasn't unheard of, it certainly wasn't customary to send their team to the other end of the county. Even so, Bolton had already confirmed with them he would send two detectives up for as long as they needed. Now he had to break it to those two detectives. That might go over like a fart in church. If he was lucky, they would take their new orders with a smile. He wasn't counting on it though.

Deciding to start with Cris, Jeff walked out and headed towards her desk area first. He passed Bryan en route. They exchanged nods of greeting as they passed, and both kept moving, each on their own missions. As he approached Cris' little office space, he noticed she was just getting to her desk and sitting down, and that she saw him coming.

"Hey, Chief, what's up?"

Jeff gave a little snort and shook his head, just a little. *Leave it to Cris to try to get a jump on the conversation. No beating around the bush for her.*

"Hey, Cris. How are things going?" Chief nudged his chin forward towards her files she had been working on.

She habitually glanced over at the stack. "Not bad, I've got most of them done. Probably one more day should get them all wrapped up."

"Ah, that's good. I would also be willing to bet you have been working through them in order of priority, meaning the ones left are not very pressing?" Bolton knew how her mind worked, the same way as his in most cases.

"Yes, Sir. That would be an accurate statement. Maybe you should take up betting." Cris gave him a smirk.

Chief chuckled back at her. "Thanks for the tip Cris, maybe I'll take it into consideration. If I win big, I'll keep you in mind."

"Like hell you would! You would get your winnings and go retire in the Caribbean somewhere, never to be heard from again."

"It's a great thought, but it's not my style or personality, as much as I might wish it was."

"Yeah, I know it's not. Typical retirement is not going to work for you. You need to be around circumstances where you can help people. As tough as you may try to act, I see through you. You are a kind, caring and protective person by nature. But, hey, don't worry, I won't spread that shit around on you. Your secret is safe with me." Cris waved her hand downward at him as if to say "no problem".

"Well, try to keep that nice warm image of me in mind then." Bolton paused and took a breath. "I have a case for you, the rest of those files can wait."

"Great, I could use some action in my life right now."

For once Bolton couldn't tell if she was being sarcastic or serious. "Hold down the excitement. This case is at the other end of Sun County. It's going to require you guys to stay up there."

Cris raised her pointer finger up, quickly cutting him off as she made air quotes. "Wait! Who's "we" and how long will "we" have to be gone? I have Stormy to think about too, nobody is home to be with her anymore."

"Campbell will be joining you on this one." Cris instinctively responded to him with an exasperated eye roll.

Bolton immediately held his hand up, stopping her. "I've made my decision. Bryan is strictly working on his assignment. I'm hoping he will also be able to take care of Stormy while you're gone. As far as how long you will be gone, depends on how long it takes you to catch the perp. I already told them you were both coming and you would both stay until it was solved. Chief Williams is expecting you by tonight."

Direct and to the point. He was trying to make it clear this was her next case, no choice about it. He knew it would do her good to get away from the area for a few days. He could have told Jasper PD no, but he was secretly thankful for the opportunity to get Cris away from here and get her mind working on a hard case. Jeff knew this was just what she needed.

"Let me check with Bryan about taking care of Stormy. If he can't I don't know what I will do with her."

"I'm sure he will. He loves her and I know he would be happy to help you out. But, by all means, try him now. I'm going to go let Campbell know. I'll brief you both with what I was told about the case. In my office, 30 minutes."

Chief turned away as she was picking up her phone. Satisfied with how it went with Cris, Jeff was ready to let Kim Campbell know her next assignment.

Campbell's sparkly office area was just two spaces down on the right, just after Bryan's. Chief found her sitting at her desk with her well-manicured fingernails typing on her keyboard and a case file laying open next to it. Since they didn't have actual doors, Jeff gave a knock on her wall.

"Morning, Campbell." Chief greeted her as she turned around, her blonde hair following her sudden movement.

Kim flashed her perfect smile at him. "Morning, Chief! How's it going?"

"Well, I have a new assignment for you."

"Oh good. This one just come in?"

"Yes, but it's not here. It's up in Jasper." Chief saw the look of confusion on her face.

"Isn't it like two hours away?"

"Yes, it is. You will be partnering with Steele on this one, and you will both be staying up there until this case is wrapped up."

Campbell shrugged her shoulders. "Okay. I'm always up for a little travel, see some new sights."

"Happy to hear it. I want you and Steele in my office in 25 minutes for a briefing."

"Alright. That gives me time to finish this up." Campbell flicked her hair behind her as she spun back around and returned to her work.

Jeff saw Cris was on the phone as he walked past. He knew she must have gotten a hold of Bryan because she was talking about Stormy.

Bolton wasn't back in his office very long before Cris knocked on his open door.

"Hey, Steele, come on in. Is Bryan able to help you out with the dog?"

Cris walked in and plopped in the same chair she had just sat in two days before for the "interview."

"Yes, thankfully he said he could take her as long as I needed him to."

"That's good. You know, I was just thinking, you and Campbell should hang out and try to destress a little one night while you're up there."

Cris gave a little laugh. "I think her idea of destressing and mine are two different things. Don't get me wrong, I don't have a problem with Campbell, I just don't have anything in common with her."

Jeff smiled patiently at Cris. "You never know. You guys have been partners plenty of times, but never overnight somewhere. Maybe you will find a few commonalities, or maybe you won't, but my point is, try to lighten up a little when the opportunity presents itself."

"Thanks, Chief. Maybe I'll take it into consideration." She used his own words spoken just a few minutes ago, back at him.

Jeff grinned at her and shook his head. "You certainly keep us on our toes around here. You know that Steele?"

She looked back at him with a dead serious face. "I've been told something along those lines a time or two. Maybe more along the lines of offending people than keeping them on their toes though." Cris shrugged. "But that's usually reserved special for the ones who deserve it."

Bolton was laughing just as Campbell walked in.

"Well, crap guys. Did I miss comedy hour?" Campbell pretended to be upset by it.

Chief straightened in his chair. "Not specifically. We were just discussing Steele's personality."

Campbell smirked. "Ah, I see! Say no more!"

Bolton stood as he grabbed his notepad containing his case notes. "Alright ladies, I don't have a lot of details on this case, but here are the basics. The Jasper PD had two teenage girls, unrelated, reported missing within a day of each other. They found the body of the first missing girl this morning. They fear they will find the second one the same way. Even worse, there is a greater fear of this being a serial killer, and rightly so. They are getting nowhere on their own and need this person caught before any more girls come up missing or dead. That's why they called us. Sorry, it's all I got. Chief Williams will give you more specifics when you get there."

Cris was the first to speak. "Sounds like we have our work cut out for us."

Chief looked between them both but focused mostly on Cris. "Sounds like it. You will both be working on this, but Steele I want you to be the lead. Take your county issued Explorer and call me if you run into any problems. Go home and pack for a few days and you guys can figure out if you want to meet back here or pick up Campbell at her house. I want you on the road by noon though."

Both women nodded in agreement.

"We'll go put this bitch to bed, Chief!" Campbell shouted back as they stood to head out. Cris rolled her eyes.

Steele and Campbell walked out the door together. Campbell placed her arm over Steele's shoulder and as she pulled her close, he heard her tell Cris "A road trip, this could be fun! Maybe I can teach you some tips on cosmetics."

Jeff could tell by her high-pitched voice and barely contained laugh she was busting on Cris.

Judging by Steele's response of "Fuck off, Campbell," followed by throwing Kim's arm off her shoulder, Cris was making it clear she did not share the enthusiasm.

Bolton shook his head and smiled. The poor Jasper PD had no idea what they were in for.

Chapter 16

Cris came home to Stormy jubilantly greeting her at the door. It always melted her heart, but even more so now. She couldn't even bring herself to yell at her for jumping up on her. She basked in the welcome she was receiving from Stormy and spent quite a bit of time just snuggling with her. She knew she was really going to miss her girl, she was already starting to just at the thought of leaving.

Getting Stormy to come sit on the couch with her, Cris continued the affection party there. "Hey, Storm, Mommy has to leave for work for a few days. Pete is going to take good care of you though, okay? I promise I'll be home as soon as I can."

She was hugging, petting and kissing her as she was talking to her, and was rewarded with Stormy's big brown eyes giving their full attention to what she was saying.

She knew people would probably think she was unbalanced for having full-fledged, one-sided conversations with her dog. She didn't care. Stormy had been with her through lots of tough times and she was always there for her no matter how Cris was feeling. She knew the love was unconditional and she would always have someone happy to see her when she got home. Someone whose happiness and existence revolved around her. Stormy was her companion and best friend.

Cris knew she had to get moving and get ready, whether she wanted to or not. Trying to decide what to bring, not knowing exactly how long she would be gone, did not make it an easy task. Staring at her clothes in the closet, with Stormy sitting right at her heels, Cris promised herself she was not going to turn around to look at Luke's clothes hanging behind her. Making up her mind to grab three days worth, she walked out of her closet with her arms full of work and workout clothes. Working out was her form of stress relief. No way was she going to go unprepared. She threw her clothes on the couch while she went to the coat closet and grabbed a backpack to put them all in. Stormy loyally following her every step of the way. Placing her few toiletries in the front compartment of her backpack, she was as packed as she was going to get.

Packing complete, along with all Stormy's things gathered together with a note for Pete, she couldn't resist spending a few more minutes playing with Stormy. She was throwing Stormy's red Kong ball around the house for her to chase. It bounced into the kitchen and rolled behind the trash can. Not wanting Stormy to knock the can over, she went to get the ball. That was good because it also reminded her she needed to get all the trash out before leaving. She then looked at her kitchen table, and all the papers and notes neatly stacked on it she had left there from her own investigative work so far. She had been very busy with her moonlighting after work the past couple of days. Cris grabbed it all up and put it on her desk in the office, adding it to the other charts and items she had already gathered and organized in there. Not wanting to get caught and have anyone to see what she had done, or that she was even working on the case, she shut the door behind herself and quickly looked at the time.

She had a few more minutes and she intended to use every last one. She was procrastinating, and she knew it. Cris realized not only did she not want to leave Stormy, but she didn't want to leave her house empty overnight. She felt like she was abandoning Luke. She knew it was ludicrous, but she still couldn't stop the thoughts that harbored in her head. Sometimes the darkness was hard to overcome.

Cris walked around the kitchen and living room making sure everything was straight and in order, where it belonged. Busy, anxious, procrastinating work. But also necessary for her OCD and her mind to be decluttered and clear. The organization and having everything in their precise place calmed her.

Not being able to resist reorganizing the silverware drawer after opening it, she started pulling the knives out. She stepped backwards to open the drawer a little further, so she could reach a few that had slipped to the back. As she stepped back, she hadn't realized Stormy's Kong ball was now there. Her foot landed right on top of the ball and suddenly she was trying to balance on it like a low budget circus performer. Quickly, but not swiftly, flailing her arms out to try to keep her balance, the knife in her right hand sliced through her left forearm.

"Mother Fucker!" She yelled as she instinctively dropped the knife and she slammed down on the hard tile floor.

Stormy yelped and high tailed it to the couch to suck her blankets.

Cris looked down at her arm. "Son of a bitch!"

She wasn't cursing at the pain, but at the bloody mess now spattered all over the floor and counters.

"Ugh, I don't have time for this shit!"

Getting up, she grabbed a paper towel and held it over the gash. Even at quick glance, she knew it needed stitches. Applying pressure to her inner arm and trying not to step in the bloody mess and spread it further with her footsteps, she rushed to the closet in the bathroom which housed the supplies. She quickly grabbed the Peroxide, Neosporin, gauze, scissors, and tape with her right hand, trying to keep the paper towel in place on the left forearm. At least with all the sticky blood, the saturated towel was pretty much staying in place. *Thank God for all miracles big and small, right?* Twisting around, Cris placed the items on the bathroom sink, then, she situated her arm in the basin as best she could. Holding the Peroxide bottle with her left hand to twist the top off with her right, was not a pleasant experience. She grit her teeth and got it done.

Pouring the liquid over the gash, she watched as it fizzed. Letting it continue to do its bubbling job, she prepared the gauze and tape as best she could with her teeth and right hand. Without drying up the Peroxide, she layered on the Neosporin and began wrapping the gauze as tightly as she could, then taped her forearm. As satisfied as she could be with her one-handed work, she finished by cleaning up the blood from the bathroom areas. Knowing she would need a bandage change quite often, she placed the necessary supplies in the backpack with her toiletries.

Cris was sweating at this point. Not sure if it was from the adrenaline or the rushing to get cleaned up, she wiped her brow with her bicep and checked her watch.

"Shit!" It was time to clean up the bloody mess in the kitchen and quick!

Normally, she would have scrubbed something like this all down by hand with bleach, but not having the time, she had to settle for her bleach spray. Doing a quick sweeping spray to the floor and cupboards, she grabbed the mop and wiped the floor, then finished the cupboards speedily with a rag. Placing the mop and cleaning rag back into the mudroom to dry, she was as patched up and cleaned up as she could be with these time restraints.

Chief wanted them on the road by noon, and she still had to go to Campbell's house to pick her up first. Knowing her time was beyond up at this point, she grabbed her backpack and Stormy's treat. As Stormy jumped on the couch awaiting her treat, Cris started choking up. She kneeled at the couch in front of Stormy and let her backpack fall to the floor.

Tears started burning at her eyes threatening to fall. "Oh, for the love of fuck, pull yourself together, Steele! What the hell is your problem? You're only going to be gone a few days. Stop being a pansy ass bitch!"

She gave Stormy one final pet and kiss, then her treat. She lifted the backpack onto her back and headed for the door. She looked back at Stormy as she swallowed the lump in her throat.

"Be a good girl!" Then she turned the lock on the door knob before she closed it behind her.

Walking out to her county-issued SUV, Cris gave a sigh, knowing the adrenaline rush had passed, and the darkness, not to mention the pain in her arm, had begun to settle back in.

Campbell also lived on the island, as most of them did, it was only a 10-minute drive to her house. Cris left the windows up and cranked on the AC this time because she was in the government issued vehicle and didn't want everyone to hear as she blasted the music the whole way there, trying to drown out the darkness before it started to consume her.

After getting cleared through the security gate, she pulled into the parking space of Campbell's upscale townhouse. Before she could beep, or otherwise announce her arrival, Campbell came out, sporting a completely different attire from this morning. This one comprised of a perfectly tailored gray skirt suit with vertical white pinstripes, and dressy gray flats. All of her curves and muscles were accentuated perfectly as she carried multiple bags on her shoulders and rolled a small suitcase.

As Cris opened the back for her, she couldn't resist making a comment. "Damn! Are you planning on staying for a month or what?"

When Campbell looked at her to answer, she saw her bandaged arm. Her face held a combined look of concern and suspicion. Reading her face like a book, Cris sharply stopped her from commenting.

"Don't even fucking ask."

Campbell shrugged her shoulders, obviously listening and deciding to ignore it, and went back to the sarcastic question at hand. "It's just the necessities."

Campbell tossed her long blonde hair back and started pointing to the individual bags. "This bag is my toiletries and make-up, this one has my work clothes, this one is my after-work clothes and PJ's, and this one is a variety of shoes based on what clothes I might be wearing."

Campbell paused briefly as she looked around the cargo area. "Where are your bags, in the back seat?"

Cris rolled her eyes and said, mostly under her breath, "You have got to be fucking kidding me!"

She pointed to her meager backpack sitting in the side corner of the cargo area. "It's right there. Just the necessities."

She slammed the door down and shook her head. "C'mon, let's roll."

Chapter 17

Pete slammed his foot on the gas after putting his rig in gear. The tires spun and squealed as the ass end of the truck kicked around before the rubber finally made good contact and gripped the asphalt, sending one final sideways spin as is snapped back straight. Hitting the buttons on the steering wheel a little too hard, he cranked up the radio.

Today was his last hope at getting any real leads on Luke's case. Meeting with Luke's colleagues, students, and parents of students, proved to be a wasted use of time. He even met with every single player and family of Luke's soccer team. It was one glowing review of Luke after another, nobody could come up with any person, event, or circumstance remotely negative or suspicious. He had even interviewed parents and students separately, in case something needed to be said in private and confidentially. Pete was sure they all told the truth. They all sat calmly and maintained eye contact, none of them showed any of the telltale signs of lying, or nervousness. Nothing but raw grief and remorse. There was nobody left on his list to question.

It was like the bullet came sailing from down from the atmosphere. Except. They had the bullet and the clearly marked matted down area where the killer took its prey. Even that was useless in its own way. No clear footprint to look for or compare. The bullet was a standard 45 cal. commonly used for hunting in the area, and of course, no finger prints on it. It would have been shot from an ordinary gun which probably 90% of people in the area own. And just about everyone owned a gun, hell most people even had their concealed carry permits. The only evidence they had was so common, it made it all the more difficult. How could he track something that was "a dime a dozen" and could be found almost anywhere?

Today just solidified the supposition he was already preparing for. What would the response to that be? Will he get accused of not trying hard enough? Giving up too easily and missing something or someone?

Just after making a right-hand turn, Pete slammed his fist on the dashboard. "Fuck!"

Upon entering Cris' neighborhood Pete turned the music down. It was a small, quiet community. Even in his rage and frustration, he still wanted to be respectful to her neighbors. Reaching the end of the street, he pulled into her driveway. Before even getting out, he noticed the front porch. Cris had left the green light bulb on. At first, he was thinking she must not have realized it and he would shut it off for her, but before he was even closing the door of his truck, he knew it was a mistake. She would want that green light going every night, and since nobody would be there to turn it on, she chose to leave it going the whole time, as opposed to the alternative of not at all. He could almost hear her saying "Green Light A Vet" as she switched it on. Approaching her door, Pete looked up at the light. He already decided no way in hell was he messing with that!

He hadn't even gotten his key in the lock, and he already heard the customary thwack of Stormy's tail rapidly whipping the door on the other side. For the first time today, he gave a genuine smile. Pete loved dogs, and Stormy certainly held a special spot in his heart. Opening the door, he was greeted with a wet nose in his hands, which quickly turned to his face as he knelt to greet her, barely getting the door closed. Chuckling now, he already felt so much anger and frustration melting away. With each kiss it got lesser and lesser.

"Hey girl, I'm happy to see you too!"

He was rubbing her soft ears and caressing her head, while simultaneously trying to keep her from knocking him over. Calming her a little bit, Pete got her to sit. As he was still petting her, he lifted his head and looked around, then wished he hadn't. He saw Cris and Luke everywhere. Uneasiness starting setting in again.

"Oh, hell no!"

He stood up and talked to Stormy like she could understand every word. "C'mon, girl! Let's get your stuff together. We've got another play date and it's been awhile! Are you going to leave some room for me in the bed tonight?"

Stormy bounded right beside him, tail wagging, like it was second nature. "Let's go see if Mommy left us a note in the kitchen like she usually does. I can't imagine her veering from her routine."

Paws prancing alongside him, they meandered into the kitchen. Just as expected, there was a note on the counter. The usual. Cris had already gathered Stormy's favorite things together and had them waiting in a pile for him. Additionally, she told him to take a dish from the freezer to have for lunch or dinner over the next few days.

Still looking at the piece of paper, Pete talked to the note, or the thin air, or whatever. "Thanks, Cris, but I would rather wait until you get home and come over and share one with you."

He looked from the note down to Stormy. "You would like that too, right girl?"

Stormy responded with more thumping of her tail on the floor, then not able to contain herself anymore, she jumped up putting her front paws on his chest, tail swooshing through the air. Pete grabbed her paws and slid down the cabinets with her and started talking in a higher pitched, silly, voice to her.

"See, I knew it! It's a date then! When mommy comes home, we'll all have dinner together."

As he was talking to her, he noticed a few little red spots on the baseboard next to him. In his line of work, he knew blood stains when he saw them. "Well, that's weird! First of all, there's blood there, and second of all, Cris didn't clean it."

Realizing it was clear he was no longer talking to her, Stormy stopped her love attack and laid down. Pete got on his hands and knees and saw there were a few more spots on the other side of where he was sitting.

He felt his heart beat faster. He knew forensics hadn't been in here because this was not the crime scene. Did something happen here before they went on the picnic? *Of course not, Cris would've said something.* His mind started racing, maybe this was the break he needed! Cris was covered in his blood when Pete saw her at the scene. She could've been bleeding, and he wouldn't have even noticed, nor would anyone else. Did she find out Luke was screwing around with a student and confronted him? Was there an altercation and she convinced him to go on this picnic to talk things over, only to take revenge? Stormy must have sensed his agitation because she suddenly came over and nudged his hand.

Pete looked down at her and coming back to reality, he quickly shook his head. "What's wrong with me Storm? I just lost my mind for a minute there. No way could either of them have done the things I was thinking."

Stormy started banging her tail again, obviously agreeing with him. He then realized it could've been Stormy. He quickly checked her over, even though he knew it couldn't really be her. Stormy's fur was mostly white, there were a few brown patches, but he would've already seen if there was blood. As expected, he saw no indications of current or previous bleeding. Maybe it was her tail! It wouldn't be the first time the end of her tail had bled from hitting it so hard against the wall and other objects because of her excitement.

It could've happened days ago, and Cris missed this spot when she cleaned it up. He felt along her tail as Stormy tilted her head and pricked her ears, looking at him quizzically. Nothing.

Pete knew he had to call Cris. He really didn't want to. He didn't want her thinking of home at all, much less worrying about Stormy, but this really had him apprehensive. He couldn't just ignore it. Looking down at Stormy he began almost unconsciously rubbing her ears, hoping to somehow get some transference of courage from her, he grabbed his phone from his pocket and clicked on Cris' name.

It only rang twice before her voice filled his ears. "Bryan, what's up?"

Pete swallowed hard, as his heart seemed to do a triple beat. *It's only because you're nervous about the blood, big guy.*

It sounded like Cris was talking through her speakers. He knew she was driving up to Jasper, and he also knew she had Campbell with her.

"Steele! Hey, sorry to bother you!" Nerves shot, Pete was ready to ramble on, but Cris cut him off.

"No bother, is everything okay?" Always matter of fact and gotta have the lead. Thankfully, he didn't mind.

He heard Campbell cut in, and he grit his teeth instead of biting his tongue. "Hi Pete, it's Kim! How's it going?"

He wanted so bad to ignore her, but Pete didn't have the heart, or the upbringing, to be rude. "Hi, Campbell. Hey Cris, can you take me off speaker?"

Noticing Campbell had used their first names, he intentionally used her last name, but Cris' first. It wasn't rude, but he felt like it got his point across. Petty as it may be, sometimes it's the small victories that get us through.

"Yeah, just give me a second." He could hear the concern in Cris' voice. "Okay, what's wrong?"

"I'm not really sure how to approach this to tell you the truth, so I'm just going to say it. I was sitting on the kitchen floor with Stormy and I saw blood spatters on your baseboard. I checked her over, I can't see anything on her."

He took a quick deep breath. "Do you know where this came from?"

He was praying he hadn't come across some secret and she was going to be upset. Cris let out a laugh. Pete hadn't realized he was holding his breath until he released it out upon hearing her laughter. Damn, he loved the sound of that!

"Shit, Pete, you got me! Alright, I had an intruder come in and let's just say I took care of him and leave it at that. Sorry man, I thought I cleaned the area up. Could you be a dear though and dispose of those spatters for me? The bleach is under the kitchen sink right there."

Pete had to smile, she was such a pisser. "Yeah, I'll get right on it for you. I'll leave the bill on the counter. Obviously, you still have your sense of humor, so I'm assuming you're okay at least?"

"Oh yeah. I got a little scrape on my arm in the altercation, but it's all good."

It was clear Cris knew what the blood was from, but she had no intentions of telling him the truth. Satisfied with the fact Cris and Stormy were both alright, he decided to let it go, at least for now.

"Well, as long as you're good then. I'm sorry to have bothered you while you're driving. Have a safe trip and show them mainland country folks how it's done!"

"That is a deal! Thanks for checking in Pete and taking care of my girl! See ya soon!" Then, Cris promptly terminated the call.

"See ya soon Cris." Pete said almost wistfully to the already disconnected phone.

He decided to clean up the blood spatters for her quick, especially since she told him where the bleach was. He convinced himself he was not being an accomplice to or covering up anything. He wanted to clean it to help her out, and also to be a smart-ass back. He would be sure to leave a bill on the counter with a "free of charge for first time service" message in the amount due. If nothing else, it would get a smile out of her, and that in itself would make it all worth it.

Bleach clean up task completed, Pete started to gather the belongings Stormy had strung about. Her food was still sitting by her dishes, as were most of her toys and blankets. Right where Cris left them. There were a few though Stormy had obviously pulled away, either to play with or get comfort from.

Pete knew all of her favorite toys. As he was gathering it all together, he realized her red ball was missing. He started walking around the house looking for the elusive ball. Stormy was hot on his heels but seemed to have no intention of giving him a clue as to its whereabouts.

Walking down the hall, Pete couldn't help but notice the office door was shut. Most people would not think twice about a closed door, but he did. Cris was a creature of habit where her belongings and ways were concerned. He continued his search, but the closed door stuck in the back of his mind. He had been to her house several times, all doors were always opened, he was very curious about this oddity. He knew her well enough to know her OCD would not allow for a door of a room to be closed when all the rest were open.

He didn't see the ball with a quick scan of the workout room, bathrooms, or bedroom. During that brief inspection though, he couldn't help but notice Cris had unplugged all her electronics that were not necessary to be plugged in while she was away. Even in her time of grief, she was still a creature of habit.

Walking back by the closed office door on his way to look more thoroughly in the living room, kitchen and dining room, Pete contemplated opening the office door. He was trying to justify it by saying Stormy's ball could have been shut in there by mistake. He thought better of it.

"Not my business, no need to further upset her. Just my luck I would turn a piece of paper 1/8 of an inch as I walked by. It would not go unnoticed by her, I would be busted."

Stormy cocked her head at him then snorted. He took that as an agreement from her. He shook his head. Maybe he was thinking too much into it. Steele is extremely OCD, she would not have accidentally left that door closed. But then, she just lost her husband in a horrible, tragic way. Who could blame her if there was a crack in her OCD shield!

Continuing on, he looked down at Stormy. "If we don't find it one of these other rooms, then we will have to go in there to look for it. I don't want to leave without your ball."

Stormy padded ahead, going towards the dining room. "Okay, girl. Let's start in there. Not many hiding places to search through."

A quick glance of the dining room did not reveal the ball. The dining room was an open floor plan into the kitchen. Pete quickly glanced at the kitchen too, seeing no red ball. He got down on his hands and knees to do a more thorough search. He was immediately distracted by Stormy half tackling him, thinking he's coming to her level for play time. Gently holding her aside, he scanned under the table and chairs. At first, he didn't see anything, but when he moved his head to the side slightly, he saw a slice of red in the corner behind the table. Fully moving over, he was able to see, it was, in fact, the elusive red ball.

"Well, there you are! You have been quite the challenge." As he reached in and grabbed the ball, he softly whispered under his breath. "Guess there's no need to open that office door."

Chapter 18

T he two-hour drive up to Jasper was beginning to feel more like 10. Cris missed Stormy a little more with each passing mile, and she still couldn't shake the notion she was abandoning Luke at home. *Shake it off Steele, you cannot let your dark, crazy, hang out. Tuck that shit back in!*

Campbell, riding shotgun, had been touching up her makeup, texting people, or checking her social media constantly. She would make some comments about some of the texts or posts, something funny, or stupid, someone said. Cris did not know these people or the rest of the story. She couldn't share in Campbell's enthusiasm, nor could she bring herself to give a shit.

Kim was nice, Cris really didn't mind her, they were just polar opposites. Kim was from some ridiculously rich area north of Chicago. She was used to the finer things in life and having everything handed to her.

Since Cris hadn't been responding to Campbell, she figured she should at least explain why. "Look, Campbell, I'm sorry, but I don't know these people or their history, or even much of yours for that matter. I really don't have anything to say about their comments, I truly can't relate."

"It's okay. I was talking out loud anyways. Some of these people are so ridiculous in their complaints and life's problems, it makes me laugh, and honestly, thankful I'm not there anymore."

"You grew up in some ritzy area north of Chicago, right?"

"Yeah, we were about 30 minutes north of the city. I'm kinda the family black sheep now."

Cris didn't respond, she had no response really, but gave Campbell time to continue on should she feel like it, which she evidently did.

"My brother is an attorney in Chicago, just like my dad. Shit, he basically had the job, and company, waiting for him. My mom hoped and planned I would marry some rich man and be a stay at home mom like her. Now, keep in mind, that really means hanging out at the country club or local coffee houses, playing tennis, having social hours and drinking wine all day. Not much actual "stay at home" or "mom" time involved there. It was more of an image that needed to be kept up."

Cris gave a little chortle. "Okay, so that explains the prima donna part."

"Well, I always did have a rebellious side. I really went to school for criminal psychology, in the beginning, to piss them off. To be a "professional" but on a different level, getting into the minds of monsters." Campbell gave a brief pause, but then kept on going.

"I really do love my job and feel like it was what I was meant to do, my calling if you will. I strive to be great at it, not only for myself and my colleagues, and to get the dirt bags off the streets, but also to piss my parents off even more. Oh, the shame!" Campbell cackled.

"So, how are your parents with you now? Do they still support you even though you didn't follow the path they had hoped?"

"Financially, yes. I mean, how could they not? They couldn't uphold their haughty image if they didn't. They paid for all of my schooling and even bought my townhouse near the ocean. But, personally and professionally, they are highly disappointed. They don't want to hear anything about my job. They refuse to let me speak if it entails anything about work or my co-workers. I don't care. I love my job and the fact it rubs them like sand in their underwear, all the better."

"That's funny. Well, I guess that explains why you don't act like a total rich douche and why even though you're a "girly girl" you aren't grossed out or bothered by this profession. So, why didn't you stay near the Chicago area where the big money is?"

"I didn't want to be that close to where they were, or to their influence. Really though, I've always had a love affair with the ocean. When we would go to one on vacation, I could sit there for hours, just watching and listening to the waves crash. When I applied for, and landed, the job on Shine Island, shit, it was my dream come true!" Campbell started looking out the window, Cris assumed she was probably thinking about her past and her present.

This gave Cris a new view of her partner. Thankfully, Campbell was actually good at her job. Even though she was born with a silver spoon up her ass, Cris had to love her rebellious side and the fact she wasn't a snob, nor did she want to be. It still didn't change the fact they were polar opposites, but it did create a different level of respect. Campbell wasn't entirely the rich, blonde bimbo she outwardly appeared to be.

Cris was thinking about their complete opposite childhoods. Campbell had no idea what it was like to move to different houses or get bullied on the playground at the public school, or just to have to fight for every single friggin' thing in life. Similarly, Cris couldn't imagine having slumber parties in a grand house, or hell, even having friends close enough to have them with. Pretending to have makeovers and play dress up with your friends, getting manicures and pedicures. The biggest problem was who you were going to go to the dance with or that your latte wasn't to perfection. Nope, Cris couldn't imagine. She also couldn't imagine wanting that life.

Even though Campbell chose this path, even if questionably for the wrong reasons, and she was good at it, still, it didn't change her roots. Campbell still had to have the finer things in life, the mani's and pedi's and makeup on as soon as her feet hit the floor. Something Cris would never understand, and likewise, she would never expect Campbell to understand her roots and resulting personality and simplicities.

Lost in thought about their lifestyle differences and how her own had made her strong, yet humble, Cris' cell phone snapped her back to reality with its melodic tune. Glancing quickly, she saw Pete's name displaying across the screen. Her heart leapt a moment, worried something was wrong with Stormy, she quickly clicked the button on the steering wheel to answer. As Pete spoke, she couldn't help but notice Campbell squirmed slightly in her seat at the sound of his voice. She also noticed Campbell tossing her hair back when she said hello to Pete herself, like he could actually see her. The disappointment on her face when Pete asked her to take him off speaker was unmistakable and Cris found it slightly gratifying, even though she knew it was wrong. She was very focused on her conversation with Pete, but she still observed that now Campbell was staring out the window, no longer texting or playing on her phone. Cris knew she was trying to listen to every word and figure out their conversation. She figured she might as well give her and Pete both a good tale about what happened to her forearm.

They were just getting ready to pull into the parking lot of "The Jasper Inn" when Cris disconnected the call. If Campbell was trying to keep her eavesdropping a secret, she blew her cover.

"Just to let you know, your "little scrape" you encountered during your "so-called altercation," looks like it's about ready to bleed through. You might want to make a bandage change the first thing on your list when you get to your room."

"Yeah, I planned on it, thanks."

She would swear she felt some hostility coming from Campbell. *What the hell is that about? Seriously, whatever, I really don't care and I don't have time for that shit.* Cris put the SUV in park, unbuckled, grabbed her keys and phone as she got out.

Opening the rear hatch, she waited for Campbell to unload her battalion of baggage, so she could grab her single backpack. Cris gave a little smile and shake of her head while Kim was trying to finagle all of her essentials.

Apparently, Kim saw it. "What?"

"I just think it's funny to see the difference in our 'necessities'."

Cris was gingerly pulling the straps of the backpack over her arm on its way to her shoulders. She really did need a new bandage and was careful not to rub this one and have the blood start dripping. She slammed the door down and listened while the beeps indicated the doors were now locked.

"Hey, it takes work to look this good." Campbell was trying to keep a straight face as she said it.

Cris tried to bite her tongue, but she always did struggle with that. She remembered her mom telling her how her mouth was really going to get her in trouble one day. That was after yet another call from the principal. Of course, dad was always proud she stood her ground.

Try as she may, there was no biting down this time, her quick tongue was going to be heard. "Oh yeah, with your perfectly white, straight teeth from, I'm sure, only the best dentist and orthodontist in the whole Chicago area, and your expensive facial products that are probably better than Botox injections. It takes a lot of work? Nice try, but you can't bullshit me with that."

She held out her right hand. "Give me a damn bag, I'll help you carry one."

"You're a piece of work Steele, you know that?" Campbell was smiling.

"Yeah, I've been told that a few times. I've also been called worse. I don't care."

"Well, here. I'll gladly give you a bag since you had to park clear at the outer edge of the parking lot."

Campbell handed her a designer bag. Just which designer, Cris did not know. If her memory served her correctly though, this was the toiletry bag.

"Stop complaining, you should be thanking me for helping you burn a few extra calories with the longer walk. Geesh, I try to help a bitch out and this is the gratitude I get." Cris was shaking her head with over abundant zeal, the sarcasm obvious.

As they got closer to the building Cris saw how cheap it looked. Plain beige stucco walls and basically nonexistent landscaping. The sign out front looked like it was the original from the 70's. Obviously, not much of the budget was spent on curb appeal.

Evidently, Campbell noticed it too. "What is this, the freaking Bates Motel?"

"Now Campbell, come on. The department is paying for this. You know we're not going to get The Ritz! This will be somewhere between Bates and Ritz. Chief assured me it was clean. As long as we're not bringing bedbugs back home with us, it's all good right?" Cris managed to keep a serious face.

Campbell blatantly shivered. "Screw that! I see anything crawling, I'm out of here! I'll pay for my own damn place! I'll take blood and dead bodies all day long, but bed bugs and creepy crawlies, no way!"

She was trying to sound like she was pretending to be over reacting, but Cris knew better, Campbell was dead serious.

"Hey, don't worry! You can't really see the bedbugs crawling. They will scatter like roaches with the lights, you'll never know they're there until you wake up in the morning with red marks, scratching like a meth addict." Cris' serious face cracked a little.

She snapped her fingers like a light bulb just went off. "Ah, man, bonus! Imagine how mortified your parents would be then!"

"Fuck off Steele, not funny!"

"Aw, lighten up princess. Pull that silver spoon out of your ass and use it to swat at any bugs you come across." Cris started to chuckle. "I'm just busting on you! They are not going to put us up in some place that bad."

Campbell just snorted in reply as they reached the door. Cris smiled inwardly. *Hmm, I guess she doesn't want to talk anymore.* On the glass entry door, a sign read: Thank you for your patience during our renovation!

The inside was certainly not The Ritz, but there was at least some attention given to making it a pleasant appearance. There were a few live plants placed sporadically throughout the lounge, and though you could tell the furniture was well used, it was still in pretty good condition. It smelled fresh, the wooden floors looked clean and things appeared to be dusted. *Good enough for me.*

As they walked up to the check-in counter, Campbell set her bags down. Cris could see her eyeing a bottle of hand sanitizer sitting on a higher counter, next to the check-in area.

"Oh, I could use some of this right now." Campbell slid over to the value sized sanitizer.

Cris noticed how much higher the counter was and found it odd, it seemed like a design flaw. But, she had to say it was probably a good place for the sanitizer, out of the reach of kids. She wasn't really paying attention but waiting for the attendant to come to the counter for the check-in process.

In her peripheral vision she saw Campbell pump the hand sanitizer, then she turned as a mild chaos quickly ensued. When Campbell pushed the pump down a big glob squirted out in her hand so hard it splattered all over her face and into both eyes.

"Ah, shit!" Her eyes were clearly blurry by the way she was holding her hands forward so she didn't bump into anything.

She had managed to open her purse and was feeling around inside it. "I need a fucking tissue, son of a bitch, my eyes!"

Cris was trying so hard not to laugh, she knew it had to sting, but hot damn, if it didn't look like a comedy routine! Cris saw a box of tissues sitting there on the counter, right near the demonic hand sanitizer, and grabbed a few.

"Here, start with these." She thrust them into Campbell's hand. Campbell grabbed them blindly as she frantically started rubbing at her eyes.

By this time, Cris noticed the check-in attendant had come up and was silently watching the show, as was she. After about 30 seconds of rubbing, Campbell looked up and was blinking incessantly. She had mascara running down her face and her eye shadow was either smeared or completely worn off. Cris couldn't hold back anymore and she let out a huge burst of air as laughter immediately ensued.

"I'm sorry Campbell, I don't mean to laugh, really. But holy shit was that funny! Are you okay?"

Cris had to wipe her own eyes a little from tears of laughter. She noticed the attendant had turned his back and was pretending to do something. Cris had no doubt he had tears of laughter running down his face too.

Campbell was beginning to calm down, and even had the makings of a smirk. "I can't believe that just happened! I mean, seriously, leave it to me! Holy hell, my eyes are spicy!"

Cris laughed even harder, and noticed the attendant actually walked away into a back room. "Spicy eyes? What the hell? That's hilarious!"

Campbell was smiling. "Cris, your laughing is infectious. But seriously, it's how they feel, they burn, like something spicy would."

"No, I guess it makes sense. I've just never heard, or thought, of eyes being spicy!"

Campbell was trying to appear offended but wasn't able to hide her smile. "Gee, I'm happy I can be your entertainment this afternoon."

"Me too. That laugh felt good."

Cris wiped her eyes again, let out a breath and turned, deciding to ring the bell to check-in. She figured she would save him the embarrassment of admitting he saw the whole scene. She didn't think Campbell ever saw him behind the counter with her blurry and spicy eyes. When the attendant came out they exchanged a look of raised eyes and an incognito head nod, which made it clear his secret was safe with her and he was grateful. She saw him glance at her bloody bandage as she brought her left hand up the hold the paper while she signed with her right, but he returned her favor by not saying a word. She gave him a smile as she handed him the signed paper.

Thankfully, the rest of the process was uneventful. Steele and Campbell each went to their adjoining rooms. Cris knew Campbell would take a little bit getting unpacked, then would have to wash her face and reapply her makeup from the damage done in the lobby.

That would give her plenty of time to clean up her gaping arm and re-bandage it.

Makeshift doctoring successfully completed, she called Chief Williams to let him know they were in town and had checked into their hotel. He briefed her on the case, there was not much more information than Chief Bolton had already given her. They exchanged numbers, and both agreed it would be best to get a good night's sleep and start fresh in the morning. She had all the meager details the Jasper PD did, not much else could be done tonight, tomorrow would be the day to dig in and look outside the narrow boxes they had already looked in.

She decided to call it a night. Campbell seemed happy with that decision when she called to let her know, Cris thought perhaps her eyes were still a little spicy. Tomorrow they would finally get down to some action. Now, Cris just hoped she could shut her mind off to get some sleep.

Chapter 19

*L*uke *and Cris slid as best they could on their feet, down the narrow dirt path of the steep embankment, small shards, rocks and pebbles joining them in their sliding descent. Reaching the tiny ravine before a slight incline began, they paused at the narrow, mucky water in the middle.*

Cris looked back at Luke, dead serious. "Jump all the way over, don't let your feet touch the shit stream."

Luke's eyes widened and he stood frozen. Cris wasn't sure if it was because of her language or because he was afraid of touching, or falling into, said "shit stream." She didn't take any time to reflect on it, just jumped over to the other side.

"C'mon! Your turn! Don't think about it, just do it. It's not that wide!"

Luke took a deep breath and jumped. Successfully planting his feet on the dirt at the other side, he released his breath and glanced back at it.

"Is that really what that is?" He pointed to the brown sludge with iridescent interspersed and slowly swirling throughout it.

Cris shrugged nonchalantly. "I don't know. I just know that's what I've heard it called. That's what it looks like, so I assume so. I've never had the desire to actually think about it."

She had already started the trek forward. "Watch out for the poison sumac trees up here. If you touch them, you'll itch like crazy! And the smooth berries you'll see along the way, don't eat those, they're dog berries. If you want, we can go raspberry picking later!"

Cris looked back to make sure he was keeping up and hearing her. Luke looked a little frazzled.

"Um, yeah sure we can go pick some raspberries later. I'm not sure if I got everything you said though, so I think I'll walk by your side as much as the trail allows." He picked up the pace to get next to Cris.

"Okay, good idea. It's wide for a little while up here. Once we hit the top of the cliff, you'll see the path that goes down and around is really narrow. Until then though you can be right next to me. Am I talking too much?"

"I'm just not used to it, that's all. You're fine."

"I'm not used to having someone with me, I'm excited to share my adventure with someone! My dad does call me motor mouth sometimes. I'm actually quiet most of the time, I will sit by myself and read or do quiet things. But, when there's something I'm excited about, I'm kinda like a squirrel on speed." Cris decided to shut her trap for a little bit, the next few minutes of the walk were nothing special to talk about anyways.

It was quiet, nobody else ever came through here that Cris knew of or had ever seen. There were a few puffy white clouds in the sky, but the sun was shining and there was a slight breeze. Luke was looking around at the trees and surrounding area as they meandered along. Before long, they came to the top of the cliff. Cris walked close to the edge of it so they could peer down. She noticed Luke was standing back farther than she was, so she grabbed his hand and squeezed. His cheeks got pink, but he didn't resist. They leaned their heads forward looking down and he squeezed her hand even harder.

"We don't go down this way do we?" Luke asked quietly over the noise of the water echoing up.

Cris laughed slightly. "No! The narrow path I was telling you about, it's right over here to the left."

She pulled him in that direction but didn't let go of his hand. She realized he didn't bother to try to dislodge it either. They came upon the narrow, winding, path. It was covered with thin black shavings from the rocks being worn by the water at some point in time. She had to release his hand to get close to his ear, so he could hear her over the water below.

"Just stay close and follow me. This path goes around the cliff to some rocks at the bottom, then the water. These pieces are a little slippery, but not too bad."

"Okay."

They were about halfway down the slope and rounding another spiral turn when Luke's foot slipped. Cris turned around to look when she heard the ruckus of the rock shards cascading like a landslide. Too late. Luke had completed his slide and his feet went into the back of Cris' calves, taking her with him. The two of them were stuck together, sliding down like they were sledding down a snowy hill. Only, there wasn't any snow, or a sled, only their butts and legs on the shards of diminutive rocks. She could feel her calves getting cut and scraped as they slid to the bottom.

As soon as they came to a stop, Luke jumped up and grabbed her hand and arm. "I'm so sorry! Are you okay? I'm so sorry!"

Cris started laughing. "Man, I've never gone down that way before, what a ride!"

She could see Luke's relief as his facial expression eased. Luke gently pulled on her to help her up.

Immediately he saw her scraped up legs. "Oh no! You're bleeding! I'm so sorry!"

Cris looked down. "Oh, it's nothing, don't even worry about it! It will clean right up when I get home. I guess you're lucky you were wearing jeans. That ended up being a good choice!"

For once, Luke couldn't contain his excitement and his words quickly rambled together. "I can't believe that happened! I was kind of sliding down instead of picking my feet up, and my foot just kept sliding too fast, then before I could try to catch myself both feet were sliding, and I was on the ground!"

"Just think of the stories we'll have to tell later. The time you tried to take me out at the river." Cris was laughing, but Luke looked like he wanted to throw up.

"I'm kidding! C'mon, let's go down to the water and skip rocks for a little bit."

Cris picked up a rock and skipped it across the river. It went a few feet before it hit a rapid and sank. Luke had joined in, or at least was trying. The rapids were pretty fierce here and he really had to raise his voice.

"So, you usually come here by yourself?"

"Yeah. It's something to do, and the walk getting here is its own adventure, as you now know. There's some small caves down here too. I'll show you." Cris grabbed Luke's hand again and turned to the right, trampling over the huge wet rocks, trying not to slip.

They walked down about 50 feet to an opening of a small cave. The caves didn't go back very far, but for a kid, it was enthralling. They explored a few more that were fairly close, in each one imagining getting stuck in one due to a storm or bad weather, or because they were lost and had to wait there for help to arrive. Just like when she was hiding while playing hide and go seek, Cris always felt the urge to pee as her imagination took off in these dark caves. She couldn't help but wonder if Luke did too or if it was just her, yet another character flaw. They let their creativity go wild while they explored, then decided to sit on the boulders at the shore and just watch the rapids splashing over the rocks. This being one of the many times Cris would be silent.

After a few hours, both of their stomachs started grumbling, reminding them about the raspberries. They mutually decided to head back and were thankful the trip back was uneventful. The ascent back up the black shards of rock did not lead to any more blood and no feet touched the shit stream as they jumped back over. Judging by the crooked smile on his face, Luke even seemed to enjoy having to use a rope to help pull himself up at the last steep hill before being back on level ground.

"That was fun, thank you for taking me there and showing me everything!"

"Sure! Let's go to my house and grab a bowl to put the raspberries in."

Cris led the way back through the small grassy area and back to the street to cross over. When they reached the driveway, Cris noticed her dad's truck was home. She turned to Luke with enthusiasm again.

"Please come meet my dad, he is awesome! He's not crazy like everyone says he is. Sometimes things just bring back bad memories and he feels like he is there again. Once he realizes he's not there, that he's here with us, he's fine."

Luke didn't respond but continued to follow her up the steps.

They walked inside, entering the kitchen. Cris quickly wet a paper towel and wiped the dried-up blood from her legs. She didn't want her dad to see the blood, she never knew what might trigger him and she didn't want to take a chance of setting him off when her mom was not home to help, or with Luke there. She threw the towels away, placing them under some other garbage so he wouldn't see them. Just as she reached the cupboard and grabbed a bowl, she heard her dad come into the kitchen.

"Hey honey, I thought I heard someone come in. It's not getting dark yet, I'm surprised to see you inside."

"We are going to go raspberry picking, I was only coming in to get a bowl. This is Luke, the one who moved in next door last week." Cris pointed to Luke who was standing behind her, just inside the door.

"Oh, hi, Luke! My daughter finally has someone to hang around with. It's very nice to meet you! Cris has certainly talked a lot about you."

"Nice to meet you, Sir." Luke looked like he wanted to crawl under a rock.

"Sir? You've been taught respect. Kids around here don't talk like that, and it's a damn shame. So, Luke, where are you from?"

"Shine Island, Sir." Luke's cheeks were blushing, but he maintained eye contact.

"Ah, Shine Island! Yes, I know that place well. I was stationed there for a while, back when I first joined the Navy." He looked down at Cris. "Your mother loved it there. It was one duty station she didn't want to leave when I got the change of orders." He looked away almost wistfully.

Cris got excited and started firing a barrage of questions at him. "Really? You guys were there? Mom loved it? Why haven't we ever gone there? Can we go visit it now you're home for good?"

Her dad started rubbing the top of her head. "Easy pumpkin! I don't think your mom would want to go back there now. It's hard to explain. She has really good memories of it there, how it was, how we were." He spoke softer. "Things are different now, and if we went back there now, those old memories would be ruined by the new ones." His blue eyes were searching her own matching blue eyes.

She sighed. "I get it."

"I figured you would. You are too smart for your britches." He tousled her hair now.

Cris laughed as she started to swat his hand away, embarrassed in front of Luke. "Britches! What a funny word."

"Well, you guys better go get picking those berries. It was very nice to meet you, Luke." He shook Luke's hand and chuckled. "Maybe you can make a lady out of my daughter."

Luke's face got really red. "Um, I'll do my best, Sir. It was nice to meet you too."

Cris looked back as they walked towards the door to leave. She noticed her dad going for the cupboard that held his companion, Sailor Jerry.

Chapter 20

Cris bolted awake, her dad and Luke heavy on her heart and mind. She looked around the dark room, feeling for Stormy, disoriented after the dream. Spying the time on the alarm clock next to her lumpy bed, she remembered where she was, and once again, reality hit her like the bitch it is.

Cris rolled over, pulling the blankets over her head, praying to get a little more sleep. She was trying to forget the dream and how much she wished her dad was here to help her through her loneliness and loss of Luke. Of course, she wished he was here, in the capacity he was before his discharge and PTSD. Thoughts were fully drifting to her dad then, going where she didn't want them to go. *Nope, not going there, time to shut that shit down.*

She tried to manipulate her thoughts to this new case but found it difficult with such minimal information. She started making a mental checklist of questions to ask and avenues to check when they got to the station this morning. Rolling back over looking at the clock, she quickly realized there would be no going back to sleep now. The hamsters in her brain were up and running, spinning their wheel at full speed.

"Ugh, screw it!"

Throwing back the covers, knowing her body and mind needed to exercise to try and alleviate some of the stress, she grabbed her running clothes. Since this fine establishment didn't have a gym yet, a notice indicated there would be one upon completion of the renovations, which was of no help to her now, Cris knew it was going to have to be a run outside. Not knowing the area, something told her it would be wise to put on the shorts that housed the concealed carry holder at the small of the back.

After the seeping bandage was sufficiently changed, Cris was dressed, hair snapped up in a high pony, and room card in her pocket in less than five minutes. She quickly made the bed, cradled her government issued Smith & Wesson in its built-in holster at her back, grabbed her cell phone and head phones and placed the do not disturb sign in the slot on the door as she closed it.

Taking the short jaunt down the hall she could smell the aroma of the Continental breakfast being prepared. By the time she reached the lobby, her stomach was clamorously reminding her she hadn't fed it the night before. Nodding to the attendant at the desk and giving a quick "Morning" as she passed, Cris inwardly promised her stomach whatever form of food was available upon returning.

Before going out the lobby door Cris promptly put one earbud in her right ear and fired up her workout playlist before fully completing the exiting process. Giving a warm up jog through the parking lot while the music began to get the adrenaline pumping, she abruptly realized she had to make a spur of the moment decision on which direction to navigate her little pedestrian journey. Kicking herself for being preoccupied on the phone with Pete when arriving, she couldn't remember what the immediate, surrounding area looked like. There was no way to tell from this view.

She decided to take a right at the end of the parking lot. The plan would be to stay straight on the same road, or make no more than one turn, so she would be sure to find her way back to the hotel and not get disoriented.

The hotel was located in a residential area, certainly off the beaten path of the busier commercial streets. The first little stretch of the run was clearly working-class family homes. Cute little places and mostly well kept, American flags hanging at the front of more homes than not and decent cars in most of the driveways. Small, native trees sporadically lined the sidewalks, providing some shade and natural beauty. It was not like an upper-class community that would have identical trees precisely spaced apart, with wire or mulch around the bottom. Personally, Cris preferred the naturalness in life.

It was probably no more than a mile from the hotel and its modest little area, before the surroundings started to change. It began with the homes becoming more run down and not cared for, not much beyond those was the addition of old rusty cars in the yard, grass growing up alongside them. Even the smell changed. She realized there was more of a dirty smell in the air. Cris didn't know if it was different, multiple smells combining from the houses and mixing together outside or what, but it was clearly there.

There was a slight curve in the road and as she rounded the corner, she was immediately assaulted with the scene of old abandoned buildings. Haunches immediately up, she was thankful for the decision of bringing along her companion, Smith & Wesson. It was quiet this early in the morning. This part of town had probably just gone to bed not long ago, where the previous area was most likely hitting the snooze buttons on their alarms, trying to steal a few more minutes before getting ready for work.

Even though the call with Pete had her distracted coming to the hotel, Cris knew she had made a turn down one of the many side roads not far from the hotel. She had not come in from this way, she would have remembered this area.

Looking around as she ran just a little farther, she was thankful her mind had switched from her dream and old life, to the present case. She couldn't help but think this area could easily be housing the killer or where he is holding his latest abduction, assuming it was related as they suspected it was. It could even be the kill or dump site of the poor girl they already found.

Cris turned and started heading back to the hotel the same way she came, hyper vigilant as she passed through. Seeing things with new eyes now, thinking about the one dead girl and the other one still missing. Also thinking about the fact she had her cold steel companion with her, it was not an intention to be in a situation where it would need to be pulled out. *You critters just stay asleep, or at least inside your habitats where you belong.*

This run had served its purpose. Cris was focused on the case now. Anxious to get back and showered so they could grab a quick breakfast and go to the station to get busy, Cris pumped her legs into high gear. Her sneakers pounding the pavement as the beat of the accelerating music poured into her ear, matching her strides, sweat poured down now and she gave a smile while her expanded lungs gasped for air.

Just before making the left back into the parking lot, she slowed to a jog, then a fast walk before reaching the door. No time for a cool down, it would have to do. Cris was fully engulfed with the smells of breakfast as soon as the glass doors slid open. It smelled heavenly. She knew she must be starving to be looking forward to what would no doubt be a disappointment of a Continental breakfast. Rubbing her belly as she passed, she walked briskly to her room. Not only was she starving and wanting to get moving to the station, she also knew she smelled of sweat and didn't want to subject the staff or other passerby's to it any more than she had to.

Removing the Do Not Disturb sign from the key slot with her left hand so she could enter her room, she saw the bloody bandage in her peripheral vision. Opening the door and replacing the sign in the slot, she swore under her breath as the door slammed shut.

"I don't have time for this shit, or enough supplies at this rate. I guess the run got the blood pumping a little too much. Damn it!"

Cris grabbed fresh doctoring supplies along with her clothes and headed for the shower. She let the shower water run to get warm while peeling off her dripping wet clothes and unwrapping her bandage. Even after that length of time, the shower water was barely tepid. Since the hotel only seemed to have cold water, she was thankful for the run and sweat. Wincing as the water hit her forearm, she tried to ignore it and focus elsewhere. Whatever fogginess the run hadn't cleared, the frigid water certainly took care of. It quite possibly could have been her quickest shower ever. Cris could feel her mind certainly had sharpness and clarity now.

Shivering, she was trying to hurry to dry off so she could get dressed to warm back up. Getting out and reaching for her clothes, she was mentally kicking herself for only bringing short sleeved shirts, there would be no hiding her arm. Of course, she couldn't have known when she packed, but still.

The run or the water hadn't helped the gash in her arm at all. It took her extra time to keep patting it dry and applying more pressure. Thankful it at least looked clean, there was not much concern for infection. Pouring more Peroxide, then slathering on the Neosporin before starting the wrapping process, Cris was hoping to keep it that way. She added a few extra layers to the bandage, knowing it might be awhile before getting to change it again. She certainly didn't need to have any spots of blood peeking through.

Just as she was applying the adhesive tape, her cell phone blasted its generic little ditty. "Who the hell?"

Figuring it was probably Campbell seeing if she was awake yet, she ran from the dingy bathroom out to the battered dresser where her phone was singing and dancing, tape flapping in the breeze from her arm as she went.

Snatching up the cell phone and looking at the screen, Cris realized it wasn't Campbell, but Chief Williams' number. Groaning and trying to finish adhering her tape, she hit the button to answer.

"Steele."

"Morning Steele, it's Chief Williams. I hope you were up."

"Yes, Sir. I was just getting ready."

"Good, I'm going to need you guys. We just got confirmation on a body found this morning. It's the other missing girl. I'll text you the address and meet you at the scene."

Son of a bitch!

Chapter 21

No sooner had Cris disconnected with Chief Williams, she immediately pushed the contact icon for Campbell. This time she put the phone on speaker, so she could set it down and finish taping her bandage in place. Kim's voice promptly cut off the ring on the other end.

"Hey, Cris, what's up?" At least she didn't sound like she had just been woken up.

"Hey, Campbell. I just got a call from Chief Williams. They found the body of the second abducted girl. He wants us to meet him at the scene."

"Ah, shit! So, it is beginning to look like their fear might be right. This just may be the work of a serial killer."

Cris sighed. "It appears to be a very good possibility. We need to get more specific details and crack this one soon so we don't have to find out the hard way!"

"I was just finishing up getting ready. How much more time do you need?"

"I'm ready now. I need to throw a few things in my pockets and I'm good to go."

"Okay. Give me about 10 more minutes."

"I'll meet you in the lounge for a quick breakfast in 15."

"Alright, see you there." Campbell disconnected the call.

Cris was down at the sad excuse of a continental breakfast within five minutes. It was fairly quiet, but she was surprised to see there were a few other people and one young family there already. She grabbed a cup of coffee and set it on a table to save it, a little further away from the general population. No point in ruining their breakfast with having to hear about the bodies of dead teenaged girls.

Going back up to the breakfast bar, she grabbed a few items that would be quick to eat and take on the road if needed. Campbell came alongside Cris, grabbing her own plate and utensils. Without picking her head up or breaking her concentration of gathering her breakfast, Cris acknowledged Campbell.

"I've already got a table saved for us over there in the outer corner. My coffee cup is on it."

"Okay, I see it, thanks."

Cris silently finished assembling her breakfast and headed for their table. After sitting down, she ritually arranged her food at her spot on the table to her specifications. Oatmeal right in front of her; a plate of eggs, bacon, sausage and muffin to the top left, coffee cup at the top right, and an orange, apple and banana that would probably serve as her midday snack or lunch directly in between the plate and coffee cup.

Momentarily, Campbell came over and sat down to the left of her. Cris noticed Campbell was immediately eyeing her specific arrangement of her personal buffet with raised eyebrows. She didn't care. She knew if someone didn't possess the same organizational skills, they wouldn't understand. The same concept went for the caloric intake needs. She currently did not have the patience or the give a sweet damn to try to explain any of it. Realizing time was of the essence, she started shoveling the food into her mouth, deciding to put the focus on the case where it belonged.

Giving a quick swallow, Cris started spewing the minimal details she knew. "So, the second girl they got the call on this morning was found by a runner passing through. It would appear our offender doesn't try to hide the bodies from being discovered. They were not in plain sight, but also it does not appear they are even attempted to be hidden in any way."

"And they're sure it was the second girl who was reported missing yesterday morning?"

"According to Chief Williams, yes."

"I know they are just getting the call, but do we know if the COD seems to be the same for both girls?"

"We don't know for sure, but apparently the first officer on the scene reported strangulation marks around the neck."

Campbell loudly exhaled. "Shit."

Cris took a big swig of the coffee, pushing the oatmeal down. "Exactly!"

Inhaling the food on her plate now, Cris realized she was rubbing inside her left pocket again. Apparently, Campbell must have noticed it too by the look on her face and furrowed brows.

"Do you have something in your pocket?"

"Huh?" Cris feigned puzzlement.

"So many times, I see you rubbing or fumbling in your pocket, it seems to be a habit you're doing a lot lately. I can't ignore it anymore, I gotta know. What the hell is that about?"

Cris sat quietly for a few seconds, not sure how to answer. It wasn't a big deal, but she felt weird sharing anything personal with anyone other than Luke. She knew she had to get over that, especially since she didn't have Luke to talk to anymore, but it was easier said than done. Could she form some kind bond with Campbell? Just because they had nothing in common from their childhood, or not even much now, it wasn't like Cris didn't like her, or that Campbell acted like a snob. She was cool and smart. She noticed Campbell staring at her, obviously expecting a response.

"If it's some top secret guarded thing then screw it, forget I asked." Campbell seemed hurt.

Cris knew she needed to answer her, there was nothing important to hide or have Campbell get upset about, it was merely her own insecurities. She let out a long breath.

"Honestly, I don't even consciously realize I'm doing it most of the time. When I do, I notice I'm doing it in times when I need strength." She sighed.

"I carry a...." Just then a little girl dropped a ceramic plate and immediately starting crying. Cris tensed internally a little at the unexpected shattering.

Campbell leaned forward. "What was that?" Indicating the conversation they were having, not the broken plate.

Cris shook her head trying to ignore the knot suddenly in her stomach from the sound of the plate shattering. "Nothing, forget it, it's not important."

She glanced at her watch. "C'mon, we gotta get moving."

She grabbed her trash and stood up. After throwing it away she quickly grabbed the apple, orange, and banana from the table and pushed her chair in, making it clear the conversation was over.

She took the keys out of her pocket as they rushed through the sliding glass doors and clicked the doors of the SUV unlocked as they got closer. They both climbed in and got buckled. Cris tossed the fruit in the back seat and began eagerly punching the address Chief Williams had given her into the GPS.

Within minutes they arrived at their destination of the latest crime scene. Cris seeing all the yellow crime scene tape draped, quarantining off the area, and uniforms and techs crawling around, immediately brought her back to her last crime scene. Luke's. *Focus! We're not going there today. We are going to get justice for these girls so you can get home to Stormy and continue to resolve Luke's.* Justice, answers and closure. She was sure the families wanted this, it was what she wanted for Luke.

Giving a mental shake as she shut off the vehicle, Cris looked over to Campbell. "I know it goes without saying, but I'm going to say it anyway. We need to canvas the crowd and the immediate visible surrounding area. Chances are good the son of a bitch is still here, in the crowd savoring his work."

"Yeah. After the initial look at the body and crime scene and questioning the techs, I'll start looking for and talking to any potential witnesses in the crowd, including the runner who found her."

They had exited her SUV and crossed around the front of it. "Perfect. We know most likely the killer is here, watching, and probably not too far away."

Cris was already observing the area and surroundings as she got out and walked towards the crime scene tape. She noticed a person sitting on the sidewalk, out of place, not far from where she parked.

"Go on ahead Campbell, I'll be right there."

Cris briskly walked over to the man hunched on the sidewalk, partially leaning up against a building. She could tell he was homeless. As she approached him she saw he was sporting a hat that was once a vibrant American flag, but now was dingy and in desperate need of a wash. He appeared to be apprehensive as she got closer, but he made no attempt to run or move. She reached the man and crouched down so she was level with him.

"Good morning, Sir."

The dirty man looked over at her with fear and trepidation but was polite none the less.

"Good morning, Ma'am. I've gotta tell ya, if you're here to ask me about whatever is going on over there, I don't know anything about it, I'm sorry." His eyes looked genuine.

Cris smiled at him. "Well, I was going to ask if you happened to see or hear anything unusual this morning, but since you already said you didn't, I can move along to my next question."

He looked at her quizzically now. Cris realized he did not seem very old, and cleaned up, he would probably be a nice-looking chap.

"Yes, Ma'am. What can I help you with?"

"Well, I couldn't help but notice your hat. I hope you don't mind me asking, are you a Veteran?"

She thought she could see a blush under the scruffy beard and dirty face. "Yes, Ma'am, I am."

Cris reached her hand out, indicating she wished to shake his. He timidly held his out in return, grabbing hers.

"Thank you for your service, Sir!"

The poor man looked like he didn't know what to say or do, but as he released her hand, he finally spoke. "You're welcome, Ma'am. Just doing my duty."

"Don't be so modest, no you weren't. We are not in the time of the draft. You volunteered to give your life for your country, I'm grateful to you! Hey, would you please wait here a minute?"

"Um, sure."

Cris ran back over to her Ford, clicking the FOB to unlock it as she approached. Reaching onto the floor of the back seat, she quickly grabbed a filled plastic bag. Slamming the door and turning to go back over to the man, she noticed Campbell was staring at her. *Fuck it, I don't have to explain myself to her.*

Cris returned to the Vet and talked to him briefly about his previous military life. At the conclusion of their short conversation, she asked him to stand up. She could tell he was confused by her request, but she knew with him being a military man, he would not deny or question her. Once he rose to his full height, she threw her arms around his neck and gave him a tight squeeze, a genuine hug.

"God Bless you!"

Upon hearing those words, he squeezed her back. "Thank you!"

Cris felt a drop hit her shoulder and pretended not to notice his fallen tear as she pulled away. She forced the plastic bag she had set on the ground into his hand.

"I wish I could do more, but this should help you for a day or two anyway. I'll keep you in my prayers that you will get the better life you deserve and have more than earned."

 As Cris began to walk away, she could see the thankfulness in his eyes. She gave him a quick wave before she turned and headed back across the street to the crime scene. Campbell had not moved the whole time but stood there just watching the show.

"I thought I was going to interview the gawkers?" Campbell tried to appear genuinely confused.

"You are. The guy I just gave the bag to is good though. No need to question him."

"What the hell did you give him in the bag? Clean clothes I hope." Campbell was trying to be funny, but Cris didn't see the humor.

"No Campbell. As a matter of fact, the bag is full of food and water. A necessity for him. He's fucking earned it!" She knew Campbell didn't understand, that she had been trying to crack a joke, but as usual, Cris couldn't bite her tongue completely.

"C'mon, let's go to the scene, then you can go start your questioning of the rest of them." Cris stormed off towards the yellow crime scene tape without looking back.

Chapter 22

Steele and Campbell arrived at the Jasper PD well before noon. It was a small brown brick building with a nicely manicured lawn and colorful flowers interspersed with some greens along the front.

Campbell pushed her designer sunglasses on top of her head as she leaned forward slightly and looked out the windshield. "Well, doesn't this just look like a quaint little place."

"Yeah, a regular Mayberry, or should we be listening for banjos?" The two girls burst out laughing.

Cris rarely gave much more than a snort or a chuckle when she found something humorous. To see and hear her laugh like this was priceless to Campbell. *Maybe she is letting her guard down, just a little.*

Campbell looked over at her. "It seems good to hear you laugh, Cris."

Cris stopped as she turned the key back in the ignition. Clearly, that comment made her think about something.

"You know, I've gotta tell ya, Chief told me before we left to try to lighten up while I'm up here when the opportunity presents itself. I, of course, told him the odds of that. But, I feel like maybe I am lightening up a little at opportune moments. Maybe getting off Shine Island and away from the shit right in my face was good. Or maybe I'm just fucking nuts! Either way, don't tell Chief, okay? Keep this between us."

"Yeah, sure Cris. I won't let Bolton know he may have been right."

They both got out and shut their doors. As Campbell shut hers and got ready to walk towards the back, she noticed something white on the back-driver's side floor out of the corner of her eye. She looked in her back-passenger window to see what it was and immediately realized they were the white shopping bags filled with food and water. Thinking back to just a few hours ago, she remembered Cris had opened the back-driver's door to grab the bag. *She has a whole little supply of them. How the hell did I not notice them back there before now?*

Campbell didn't say anything to her about them, and instead kept going like she never even saw them. Not that it was a big deal, it wasn't like Cris was trying to hide them. Campbell just had a feeling it might make Steele uncomfortable if she mentioned it, too personal. No need to ruin the moment they just had.

Campbell pushed her hair back over her shoulder. "Well, I don't hear any banjos, I'll take that as a good sign."

"I'll take what I can get right now."

"Damn, Steele, now you're talking my language!"

"I meant with luck, or breaks, not men."

Campbell pretended to be hurt and held her hand over her heart. "Ugh! I am insulted!"

Cris looked at her and grinned. "Why? Because you'll take what you can get for men, or because I'm not talking your language?"

Campbell didn't miss a beat. "Take it how you will." She turned and gave Cris an over exaggerated wink.

Both of them walked into the police station smiling. Campbell realized it was probably not the most appropriate thing to be doing, so she quickly wiped the smile off her face. The little comic relief was a nice diversion, but now it was time to get back into work mode. *Damn, is Cris rubbing off on me?*

Walking up to the volunteer at the desk, Cris held out her badge. "Good morning, Ma'am. Detectives Steele and Campbell to see Chief Williams."

Campbell was fumbling in her purse for her badge, but it wasn't necessary. Before the volunteer could even ask for hers or call back to Chief Williams, he was coming through the door.

Chief smiled at all of them. "Thank you, Deb. C'mon back detectives."

"Thank you, Chief." Cris looked back at the volunteer as they walked past. "Thank you, Ma'am."

Following closely behind Steele, Campbell gave the volunteer a smile and a nod as she went by. The department seemed as small on the inside as it looked on the outside. It appeared this department had even less of an office space than they did. At least they had some makeshift walls. Jasper PD just had desks huddled near each other throughout a medium sized room.

Chief Williams weaved through the desks and slowed as he approached one all by itself in the corner. It was the most private area of them all. "I want to officially introduce you guys to our detective on this case, Beau Wymer."

Beau stood to shake their hands. Chief gestured to Steele and Campbell respectively. "Beau, this is Detective Cris Steele and Detective Kim Campbell."

Campbell was trying to be inconspicuous about checking Beau out as he stood. *Damn, he looks rock hard.* She felt his hand grab hers at the mention of her name. *Nice strong, firm grasp, wonder what else they can do?* Kim heard his deep voice speak and floated out of her fantasy.

"Steele, Campbell, nice to meet you and please call me Beau. Thank you for driving all the way up here to help us out with this one, and I wanted to apologize that we missed each other at the crime scene this morning."

"It's okay, our timing just happened to be a little off this morning. We're happy to come up and try to help out." Cris lowered her voice, tilted her head and put her hand up alongside her mouth. "I personally think Chief Bolton just wanted to get rid of us." Cris smiled at Beau and Chief Williams.

Campbell gave Cris a playful nudge on the arm with her shoulder. "Maybe he wanted to get rid of you, but me, I'm a constant delight."

Beau smiled then looked at Cris' arm. "Dang Steele, that's quite the bandage on your arm."

Campbell was standing beside her shaking her head no while moving her hands from side to side near her face as if to say "stop."

Cris shrugged her shoulders. "You should see the other guy."

Beau and Chief Williams both had huge smiles. Williams shook his head. "Chief Bolton warned me about you two. He said you were the best at what you do, but your personalities needed to come with a warning label. He didn't give me any more details than that. Now I think I understand what he was saying. I'll leave y'all alone to get caught up on the case."

Chief turned to look at Beau before walking away. "Good luck!"

"Thanks, Chief. They may give me a run for my money, but I think I can handle these girls." Beau was sporting a wide grin.

Chief snorted as he walked off.

Beau pulled up two chairs that weren't being used from other desks. "Please, make yourselves as comfortable as possible on these rock-hard chairs. Let me start by saying welcome, and let me add, I'm *really* glad you guys have a sense of humor!"

"Thank you. It looks like we may all need to pull out our sense of humor in this case to try to keep ourselves sane."

Cris, always getting right down to business. Campbell had to admit though, she was impressed Cris actually did as much small talk and joking as she had.

They all sat down, and Campbell couldn't help but notice Beau did not have a ring on his finger and also no pictures on his desk. *Hmm.* "So, we know the cause of death with the first victim, Lilliana, was strangulation. And preliminary from the looks of victim number two this morning..."

Steele cut in, "Annabelle"

Campbell continued on, "...looks like it will be the same. What else have we got?"

Beau cleared his throat. "Lilliana and Annabelle, both 16 years-old, had brown hair, hazel eyes, approximately 5'4, Caucasian, and a slim build. But that's where the similarities end. Annabelle went to Jasper public school, and Lilliana attended a local private school. They did not know each other and there were no crossing of extra-curricular activities we could find."

"So, it appears he is abducting them strictly based on their physical characteristics. Do we have any other reports back yet?" Cris made a few notes in her notepad as she spoke.

"No, but I was planning a trip to see Wyatt, the M.E., this morning to check in. I would love for you both to join me."

Campbell stood up. "Sounds like a plan."

"He is in a separate building not far from here. We don't have the space to house everyone under one roof."

They were all standing now, and he looked at both girls. "We normally walk over. Do you mind walking? It's really not far. We can drive if you prefer, but the walk over is much more peaceful."

Steele and Campbell were both nodding their heads. Campbell noticed Cris tucked her notepad and pen in her pocket as she replied. "No, we don't mind at all."

"Alright then, let's get rolling."

The three amigos headed out the back door. Beau leading the way, with Steele and Campbell hot on his heels, almost beside him.

Beau and Steele were talking more about the case. Campbell knew she should be listening and chiming into the conversation, but instead she was looking around and enjoying the view. *I can catch up on the conversation later, Beau was right, this is a nice peaceful walk.* There was a pond in the back with several ducks and birds, surrounded by small trees with their limbs gently swaying with the breeze. Just around the side of the pond was a small building, made out of the same brown brick. It seemed that was the building they were aiming for.

"Well, here we are. I told you it was a short walk. I hope you didn't mind it."

Campbell piped in. "No, it was nice to get the fresh air and it really is very peaceful back here, just like you said. I'm glad we got to do this."

"Pleased to hear you liked it. That's saying something if our old country town can impress you island girls."

Cris sounded like she was blowing raspberries. "Pfft! Oh please, neither one of us are native island girls, we were both just fortunate enough to end up there."

"Well, Sun County is all the better for it."

Cris stood widely with her hands on her hips. "Okay, Beau, that's all the sunshine and rainbows I can take in a day."

All three of them laughed. "Well, that's good because that was about all I had left in me. Dang, you ladies *are* gonna give me a run for my money."

Beau tried to stop laughing as he knocked on the door before entering. "Hey, Wyatt. How's it going?"

Wyatt walked from the steel table over towards them. "Hey, Beau, perfect timing. I was just finishing up with our latest."

The trio entered just inside the door. "Wyatt, I want to introduce you to Detectives Cris Steele and Kim Campbell. They came up from Shine Island to help us out on this one."

"Pleasure to meet you ladies. I apologize for not shaking your hands, but as you can see, my gloves and hands aren't the cleanest, I was just getting ready to start my clean up. Shine Island, huh? I hope it was a nice trip."

Campbell gave him her full-fledged white toothed smile. "It wasn't bad, thank you." Campbell didn't look at Steele, whom, she was sure, was rolling her eyes.

Beau looked hard at Wyatt. "Thanks for expediting this one for us. There's no need for us to come in any further, no point in taking the time get all gussied up in gowns, masks, and gloves. Did you find anything additional from yesterday or useful from today?"

"A little bit. My preliminary on the blood work done here in the lab shows traces of chloroform in both of their systems. Of course, I can't say anything officially until the formal toxicology results come in from the county, but I would be willing to stake my career that he used chloroform to subdue them."

Campbell watched as Cris moved her vision from the young girl laying on the cold table behind the glass and directed her attention now to Wyatt.

"You said trace amounts? It takes a large amount of inhaled chloroform to actually make a victim unconscious. Based on your preliminary findings, does it appear to be a large enough amount?"

Wyatt raised his eyebrows to Cris. "My preliminary findings do not suggest the amount was great enough, and I do expect the official toxicology reports to reflect my own findings."

"Meaning he would have only stunned or subjugated them a little, for lack of a better word."

"Yes, that is most likely accurate."

"Which also means he must live close by, or at least have his holding place close by. Too risky to drive very far with someone who could come around after a few minutes and make some serious noise."

"Also, a most likely assessment in my opinion."

Beau and Campbell were standing there watching them, their heads moving in unison looking like they're watching a ping pong tournament.

"Okay, so beyond the chloroform, anything else discovered upon examination?"

"Well the official COD was Ligature Strangulation in both cases."

"What about signs of sexual abuse or defense evidence under the finger nails?"

"No sexual abuse, or skin or debris under the nails for either one."

Cris furrowed her brows. "Hmm, Strangulation is highly typical to coincide with sexual abuse, interesting. Also, maybe there is no debris under the nails because he used the chloroform before the strangulation, instead of at the abduction. Or perhaps both times." She seemed to be talking more to herself but was still loud enough for everyone to hear.

Wyatt looked over to Beau with wide eyes. He was clearly not prepared for Steele to be as knowledgeable as she was.

Beau smirked back at him. "Detective Steele is now the lead on this case. Detective Campbell and I are assisting."

Campbell was listening to it all and watching Steele. She couldn't help but smile. It was like Cris' wheels were rotating at high speed and she was trying to keep up with all the thoughts. This was how she normally was, and Campbell was happy to see she didn't get lost with Luke's death.

Cris looked up, like she was finally through with her rampant thoughts. "Thank you, Wyatt, you have been very helpful. We have a few more avenues to search now. If I think of any other questions, I will have Beau give you a call."

"You're welcome, Ma'am. It was a pleasure meeting you both." Wyatt looked between Campbell and Steele.

Campbell looked back at him, "Likewise."

Steele was already heading to the door.

Beau turned back to face Wyatt. "Thanks again for getting that done so quickly, I owe you one!"

Both men gave a short wave before the trio departed out the door. No sooner had they stepped foot outside, Beau's phone rang.

"Hey Chief, what's up?"

Campbell saw Beau's face get pale.

"Chief has something he wants us all to hear, he's requested to be on speaker phone." He hit the speaker button. "Go ahead Chief, we're all here."

"I need you back here now. We just got the call from missing persons, there is another girl missing, her name is Delilah. The morons got the call from her parents hours ago but didn't tell us because they didn't connect this girl to the recent murders until now. Delilah has the same attributes as the first two victims, and she never came home last night. I don't have many other details. I don't think I need to explain the importance of finding this pecker head before victim number three ends up like the first two."

Three voices chimed in as one, it couldn't have been choreographed more perfectly. "Yes, Sir!"

Chapter 23

Cris' grumbling stomach reminded her they had worked through lunch. The apple and banana she had taken from the hotel this morning and eaten as soon as they got to the SUV hadn't done much. Campbell had eaten the remaining orange and didn't appear any more satisfied. They were just now leaving, and it was 7:00 at night. A few bottles of water and fruit had been stretched as far as they were going to be.

Cris started the ignition and threw her head back on the head rest, blowing out a big breath of air. "What a fucking day! We have zero evidence to go on and now have another girl missing. If he sticks to his timing, then we have less than two days to nail him, or Delilah will be the next body found. And, damn it, I'm starving!"

Campbell smiled. "Let's look at what we do have. We have a general area for the location based on last known location of the girls and where their bodies were found. By tomorrow, we will be ready to have a more accurate profile and be able to warn the public to keep vigilant and if they know girls who fit those parameters to keep them inside, or with an adult at all times. We know he is targeting this type, so we can search that aspect, find out if there is something that happened to an individual by someone fitting those characteristics. And, lastly, we do have a little pub right down the road that is on our way back to the hotel, I saw it this morning. I'm starving too."

Cris backed out of the parking spot and put the SUV in gear. "It's too much broad information to sift through and figure out in one day, any longer and Delilah is Dead-Lilah."

She could feel the shadows chasing her, the darkness creeping, ready to pounce and completely devour her. She grit her teeth and pushed her foot on the gas a little too hard, spinning the tires as they barreled out of the parking lot.

"Let's get some food in us, then I bet we will be able to think more clearly." Campbell fished her cosmetics out of her purse, pulled down the visor, looked in the mirror and began reapplying her makeup.

Cris didn't respond. Her eyes were focused on the road, but her mind was anywhere but there. They had to get more information and solve this case before another girl was gone before her time and anymore were abducted. She also needed to get home to solve Luke's case and see Stormy.

She heard Campbell's voice more prominently than before. "It's right there!"

Cris snapped out of her thoughts to see Campbell's hand pointed to the right side of the road towards the pub. "Ah, shit! Hang on."

Cris slammed the brakes and rocked into the dirt parking lot, dust swirling around like a cyclone in the dessert. "Sorry about that, but, hey, we're here!"

They walked into the entrance through the heavy wooden door. *It looks like a decent little place, clean and homey. Probably a family business.* Seeing the sign to seat themselves they decided on a high top close to the bar. A young-looking girl in short cutoff jeans and a fitted white tank top promptly bounced over to bring them menus and "get them started." Cris ordered a beer while Campbell finally decided on a cosmopolitan.

"Well, isn't she just the chippy little thing!" Campbell flung her blonde hair back over her shoulder, as the waitress walked to the bar.

Cris was focused on the menu and didn't bother to look up from it. "A huh. It's kinda her job though."

Lil Miss Chippy was back in a flash with the drinks and a huge smile. "Y'all need a few more minutes?"

Cris looked over at Campbell while answering. "I'm ready, are you good?"

"You go first, and I will be." Campbell appeared to be scanning the menu with a little more urgency now.

"I'll take the bacon cheeseburger, medium rare, with the fries and also a side of coleslaw, please."

"Mmm, sounds great! I'm so hungry. I'll try the Jasper burger, well done, with onion rings, please."

Cris noticed Miss Chippy didn't write any of their orders down, but simply smiled saying "Thank you!" as she grabbed their menus and walked away.

Campbell was looking around the pub, commenting about the décor and atmosphere. Cris wasn't listening, she felt her eyes blurring, almost trance like, as she gazed at the sweat dripping down her beer bottle. She could feel the darkness of everything trying to pull her under, drown her. She barely heard Campbell say something about her silence and being quiet. Cris readjusted her eyes as she looked from the beer to Campbell.

"Huh? Oh, just thinking about the case." *No need to specify which one.* "Got a lot on my mind."

She shook her head. "The food and beer will make me feel better." *Act normal, talk about the case a little. Can't let Campbell, or anyone else, see the broken glass, the cracks, shards, and darkness actually inside me, consuming me. I am not going to show "Crazy Cris."*

She noticed Campbell was staring at her. Hard. "Ya know, you don't fool me."

Cris looked back at Campbell very seriously. "I wasn't aware I was trying to."

"You are private and quiet, except your sharp tongue inside that sarcastic mouth. I know under all that, you are actually a very caring person. You are always the first to try to help someone who needs it, even though you try to make it look like you're not."

"Oh, is that your professional opinion, Dr. Campbell?" Cris put the beer to her mouth, trying not to show the smile fighting at her lips.

"Just take that homeless guy, for example..."

Cris interrupted "Vet, he was a homeless Vet, there's a big difference to me."

"...Whatever. My point is, shit, you have bags in the back of your car just waiting to be handed out. Why don't you let your walls crack just a little and let some of your internal warmth seep out? Why don't you tell me *why* the Vet's are so important to you?"

Cris gave the only response she knew how. "Go fuck yourself, Campbell."

"Hey, it's been awhile since I've gotten any, I just might."

Cris rolled her eyes and responded by taking a long pull of her beer.

Saved by the music, Campbell's phone started ringing. She looked at the screen with squinted eyes and furrowed brows as she pressed the button to answer the call. "Kim Campbell."

In mere seconds, she hung up. "Ugh! Telemarketers. How the hell do they keep getting your number after you've placed it on the do not call list?"

Cris must have had a stupid look on her face because Campbell questioned her. "What's that look for?"

She started chuckling. "I don't know why I haven't thought of it before I heard you answer the phone, but damn! Your name sounds like a working girl's name. "Kim Campbell at your service, what'll it be tonight big guy?""

Steele and Campbell were both laughing as the food was brought over to their table. Miss Chippy asked if there was anything else they needed and they both simultaneously held up their drinks. They barely had the last drop drained out of their current drinks as she set the second round on the table.

"I wanna text Pete and check in on Stormy quick."

Campbell gave a snort. "Bryan, now there's someone I would love to get my hands on! What's the deal with you two anyway?"

"What do you mean? There's no "deal," he's just a really nice guy."

"I know he's a nice guy, but he seems extra nice to you. I heard him briefly on the phone with you. There was more than concern in his voice."

"Pete's our, er, my, dog sitter and we have all hung out a few times, we're friends."

"Yeah, you ever wonder if he's too nice? I mean, why is he still single then?"

Cris' voice went up an octave. "Because nobody can handle his job with him being gone and consumed by his cases. There's a reason he's the best, because he works his ass off." She was defending him, but wasn't she just wondering the same thing herself only a few days ago?

"Yeah, okay and you don't have to get so defensive about him. Well, I wouldn't mind being "friends" with him. That's one piece of ass I'd love to tear into and find out for myself if he's the best! Man, if you're not going after that, you are freaking crazy!" Campbell raised her glass.

Cris didn't comment, instead shoved the burger in her mouth and took a huge juicy bite. As she was chewing, she was texting Pete. That became her routine to not have to talk anymore. Bite, chew, text, wash down with the beer, repeat. *I can justify it by knowing I'm being productive. Filling my grumbling, angry belly, finding out about my girl, and okay, not having to have a real conversation.* Proud of her multi-tasking skills and happy to hear Stormy was completely fine, she felt herself grinning at the texts after the food was gone.

Campbell must have noticed Cris' grin appear too. "Must be some good texting judging by the smirk on your face and the fact you're still texting. That's some 'quick text to check in.'"

"It is, he's trying to give me crap saying Stormy doesn't even miss me because she's so happy to be with him."

"Uh huh."

"And he's sending me pictures trying to prove his point. I, of course, don't agree."

"I bet he's sending pictures, of more than just Stormy."

Cris looked over at Campbell, not even sure how she wanted to respond, if at all. Seeing Miss Chippy walking their way, she waved at her. "Check please!"

Cris didn't say anything else as she unconsciously and habitually stacked all her dishes in order by size, then placed her napkin and silverware on top. All in a neat and orderly pile. She saw Campbell watching her out of the top of her eyes, but she didn't care.

Thankfully, the hotel was less than a mile away. Upon arriving at their rooms, Cris had decided how she wanted to respond to Campbell's comment about the pictures.

"Try to get some sleep Campbell, it's going to be a busy day tomorrow. Oh, and I'll think of you as I look at those pictures Pete sent me. Hope your night is as good as mine will be." She left Campbell standing there staring at her as she went in and closed her door, locking the deadbolt behind her.

Grinning to herself, she walked to the bathroom and re-bandaged her arm. She was getting pretty good at it and was able to use less of the bandage as it was finally starting to scab over. It only took a few minutes this time. After she got all dressed and ready for bed, she took the rosary out of her left pocket and entwined it around her right hand as she crawled into bed.

She knew it wasn't going to actually be a good night, her mind was becoming consumed. *I walk a tightrope, on the edge of darkness every minute of every day. Nobody knows it, they all think I'm content with my sarcastic comments and positive with always being thankful and seeing the beauty in everything. Unless I chose to give them a glimpse of my walk, never will I fully expose my true dance with darkness. I feel it pulling, at any minute I will go dark. Have to fight it so nobody sees. My shield cannot be let down when anyone else is around.*

When the darkness is always there, a part of you, and you struggle every day to keep it away, struggle just to get out of bed. Then out of nowhere, it creeps in, you don't even see it coming, you kinda feel it and keep trying to push it down, but by then, it's already too late. It grabs you and takes you under with it. Fully submerged in the darkness and the numbness, you just wanna hurt yourself and stay there curled up in that darkness forever.... The darkness comes too often now.

Cris felt the tears running down her cheeks as she rubbed the beads of the rosary, before suddenly drifting off to sleep.

Chapter 24

It was a nice, peaceful Sunday morning. 10-year-old Cris had just finished a gourmet breakfast with dad, even if it was a little late to still be called breakfast. He was an amazing cook and always put on a big spread. Today's feature included made to order omelets, bacon, sausage, pancakes, cinnamon French toast and freshly cut fruit in bowls. Cris enjoyed chocolate milk, while her dad had coffee, possibly with his companion Sailor Jerry, she didn't really want to know. The best part was they chopped and prepared everything together, which usually included some singing, dancing and tickling on the side, and always included lots of laughs.

They were standing next to each other at the kitchen counter putting the remaining food into plastic containers. "Your mom might want some left overs when she gets home."

Cris gazed up at him and smiled, he loved her mom so much. Her mom was waitressing at the diner, as was the usual now. Dad must have seen her looking up at him because he quickly looked down at her with crossed eyes, head tilted and tongue sticking out. She held her stomach as she burst into laughter.

Food put away, it was time for the dishes. Her dad was washing the dishes and Cris was rinsing and stacking them to dry. She was watching out the window with trepidation as the sky got darker. She quickly glanced at the clock, which was really out of habit since she knew her mom wouldn't be home for a few more hours. As the clouds got lower and loomed darker, Cris' stomach churned. All that delicious breakfast now burned its way upward. She didn't want her dad to see her fear and began silently praying as she did her best to keep rinsing and stacking as usual. Please don't let there be thunder, please! I'll do anything you want! Just please no thunder! *Her pleading prayer became more like a repetitive chant.*

For whatever reason, it wasn't in the plans to have that prayer answered apparently because not too many chants in, did a strike of lighting come into view close by, immediately followed by a thundering boom that sounded like a bomb going off.

Experience had taught her to expect a reaction and thankfully her reflexes acted swiftly. She was already doing a tuck and swoop as the plate in her dad's hand went sailing across the room and shattered against the wall, just like her heart and stomach were now. She knew how things would go from here. Yelling, flailing arms and objects. She also was smart enough to follow her mom's orders to get out of the house if she was not home, to let him destroy the house and Cris was to get out of the line of fire. Refusing to let the tears fall that were threatening to spill, she kept swallowing at the burning lump in her throat as she hustled quietly out the door.

As Cris ran over to Luke's house, thankful to have somewhere safe to go now, she thought about their morning with remorse. Just like that, with one eruption of thunder, their wonderful morning was now another distant memory. She knew he wouldn't try to follow her or look for her, he was in another time and place right now, not here, in his home, with his daughter. Again, she bit back the tears and kept trying to swallow the lump in vain.

She knocked on their door. Grammie opened the door and smiled. "Well, look at who's here!"

She moved aside so Cris could come in as she turned her head to the side and yelled. "Luke, your little friend is here."

Cris couldn't help but smile as she saw Luke come around the corner. Trying her best to separate from the reality for her sudden visit, she thought about how a few months ago she didn't even know "Old Lady Steele," and now thanks to her fast bond with Luke, she was also calling her Grammie.

Luke's green eyes gleamed back at her. "Hey, Cris, this is a pleasant surprise!"

Cris turned and looked out as the rain began to hammer down, the noise drowning out their voices as it pounded on the roof, she swallowed hard. "Yeah, my dad needed some time to himself, so I thought I would come hang for a little, if that's okay?"

Luke gave her his crooked smile. "Of course! What do you want to do? Oh! Wanna play a board game?"

Cris thought a board game was a great idea. She could try to get distracted by the game and she wouldn't be expected to talk much, she could pretend she was concentrating and strategizing.

"A board game sounds perfect on this rainy day! How about Monopoly?"

"Ha! I love that game, I'll go grab it!"

Cris wanted to be able to look over at her house so she could watch for movements or anything indicating she needed to get back over there. She went into the parlor and sat at the table in the chair facing the window. There were only a few other claps of thunder since the first boom and even the rain was already slowing. It seemed it was just a fast-moving storm blowing through. Great, just enough to set dad off. You know, you could've answered my prayer by still sending the rain storm but skipping the thunder!

"Oh, there you are. I was wondering where you went." Luke had walked in with the game in hand. Cris, lost in her thoughts, hadn't heard him coming.

"I thought this would be a good place to play, lots of room here."

"Sounds good to me."

Luke sat down across from her and they began pulling out all the pieces and sorting the money. Cris told Luke he could be the banker. She knew she would be too distracted to even attempt to handle the money and she was really trying too hard to cover her inner thoughts and sickness.

She was challenging herself to act normal throughout the game, throwing in some trash talk here and there. "Ha ha! Boardwalk! The game is as good as mine now!"

Luke shot back, although with not nearly the same force. "You're going to have to get more than Boardwalk to beat me."

They were about three-quarters through the game when she saw her dad come out the door onto the porch. She noticed he locked the door and was thankful they had that spare key hidden alongside the house. He was obviously out of whatever place he was in before, but was still not thinking clearly considering he didn't wonder where his daughter was or if she had a key to get back in. As he got in his truck and started to back out of the driveway, she knew he was most likely traveling with his companion, Sailor Jerry, and/or was going to hang out with his companion now.

She was having a hard time staying in her seat and finishing the game. She wanted so bad to run home now and get the house cleaned up before her mom came home. She knew it would most likely still be a few hours as Sundays tended to be very busy at the restaurant, but she also knew it could take her hours to get the mess cleaned up.

"Cris, hey, it's your turn!" Luke broke through her thoughts.

"Oh, sorry. I guess I zoned out a little."

"It's okay, but I hope you're not preparing your excuse for why you lost."

"The game's not over yet!"

Of course, she knew it was over before it even started, and now, it was really over, but she had to pretend like she still cared. She carefully started to lose on purpose just to finish the game.

Luke was too smart. "Why does it look like you aren't trying anymore?"

"I decided to show you some mercy, I don't want you to cry because you got beat by a girl."

"Well, that would be a first."

"Plus, I really do need to get home now. I want to get the house cleaned before my mom gets home from work. With her two jobs, she shouldn't have to come home and clean and pick up." Cris knew she said more than she had wanted to, but there was no taking it back now.

She stood up and started picking up the game. "Thanks for the game Luke, it was fun."

Luke grabbed her hand as she was reaching for the money in the center of the board. She felt her cheeks get warm as she looked at him. He was now standing as well, and they were almost eye to eye.

"Stop Cris, I've got the game. You go ahead and take care of what you need to at home. I'll be here if you want to come back over later."

The lump came back to her throat full force and she felt her eyes well up with tears again. Before they could betray her anymore, Cris quickly said "Thank you, Luke," as she removed her hand from his and ran out the door.

On the short jaunt back to the house, Cris was splenetic. You stupid bitch, pull yourself together! Dry up your damn eyes and pull up your big girl underwear! *She grabbed the key from under the rock on the side of the house and ran to unlock the door.*

Opening the door, the first thing she noticed was Sailor Jerry sitting on the counter, then she noticed the aftermath of the storm. Her big girl underwear were pulled all the way up, so far they were practically riding up her ass, but it didn't matter. At the sight of the house, the tears uncontrollably fell. She didn't make a sound, not so much as a whimper, but she couldn't hold back the tears that spilled over this time. Trying to get that anger back to use as fuel, she stomped into the living room, put in a CD, and cranked it up. The tears quickly got replaced by anger as she thought of her dad, one of the best people she knew, and how scared and lost he was most of the time now. Her mom who now had to work two jobs to barely make ends meet, the empty shell she had become from working her butt off and trying to get dad through life as it was now. It wasn't fair, both of her parents were amazing people who deserved better.

She didn't remember getting the house done, her mom coming home, or collapsing into bed. She awoke to hearing the phone ring in the kitchen. Cris, blurry eyed, looked at the time, 2:14. The events of the day quickly came flashing back to her and she suddenly got scared about the message on the other end of the phone. As quietly as possible, she ran over to her closed door and pressed her ear against it as hard as she could.

"Thank you, Joe for calling him so I didn't have to come pick Patrick up and have to wake up Cris."

Her mom paused, obviously Joe was talking. She thought she could hear the sound of mom's feet pacing, at least as far as the phone cord would allow.

"Okay, so you're sure he's coming for Patrick then. That man is a saint I tell ya! I really don't know how we would get through this without him, and even you Joe. Thank you for always watching out for Patrick!"

Again, she paused, listening.

"I know, but I really hope someday I can find a way to repay you both! Thanks again Joe, and as usual, I'll walk down and get his truck after Cris goes to school tomorrow."

After another pause, her mom gave a loud sniff and the sound of her voice was a little different when she talked again. "Thank you, Joe, God bless!"

She heard her mom hang up the receiver, and, again, as quietly as she could, quickly padded back into bed. Only about ten minutes had passed when she heard the familiar sound of the pickup truck that dad's friend drove. Cris had never actually met this guy, but he was always the one to drive her dad home and on the few occasions mom had called him for help, he had come and picked her dad up.

Cris got up and looked out her window. Sure enough, it was the same truck. Her mom was waiting in the front yard and waved as the truck came to a stop. She grabbed her dad by the arm as he got out and continued holding it as they both walked into the house together. Seeing the truck pull away and hearing the click of the front door, she quickly jumped into bed and rolled over tightly in the covers. She knew they wouldn't come in to check on her, they never had before, but she wasn't going to take any chances. She closed her eyes tight and didn't remember drifting back off to sleep.

At recess the next day, Cris and Luke were sitting alone in the grass, picking dandelions and talking about what they were going to do after school. She saw Raquel and her band of bitches walking towards them. She looked at Luke and rolled her eyes. She was tired and wasn't in the mood to deal with them today. She also didn't need her mom getting a phone call about another altercation, she had enough on her plate already. Pretending not to have seen them coming, she continued her conversation with Luke. "We could have a rematch at Monopoly tonight, I won't go so easy on you this time."

At this point, the group was standing just behind where Cris and Luke were sitting, with their backs towards them. Raquel spoke very loudly to the group.

"Yeah, my dad said he saw the truck still parked at the bar again this morning. Must have been another crazy night at the "Crazy Murray House." Not that that's anything new." The whole group laughed as if by an expectation from an audio prompter.

She could feel her face burning and Luke must have seen it too. He looked into Cris' eyes, trying to refocus her as he spoke softly to her.

"Don't let them get to you, they're not worth it. You're better than they are, you're kind and caring, unlike those mean and nasty creatures." He was deep breathing, trying to get Cris to follow, and calm her.

The group was still laughing loudly behind them. Raquel's toxic voice cut in again. "And now she's got the new kid cloaked in her craziness. I'm not sure if he had a fighting chance anyway, but once he met her, it was all over, he got trapped in crazy town."

That was it, Cris wasn't going to keep listening to her, she always defended herself and her family, and now Luke, she wasn't about to stop now.

Raquel turned around and looked at Cris as she stood. "Aw, hey, speak of the devil, there's Crazy Cris. Just. Like. Her. Daddy!"

Cris looked at Raquel, peeled her lips and smiled, then started laughing wickedly. "Silly bitch, you just don't know who you're screwing with, and I can assure you, you certainly have no idea what crazy really is!"

The words were barely finished out of her mouth and her shoulders were driving into Raquel's abdominal area, knocking the wind out of her as she was pushing her backward and took her to the ground. Luke quickly jumped in and grabbed Cris' arms, pulling her away.

"Okay Cris, you made your point, you got her back. Let's not have any blood today, huh?!"

Cris could hear Raquel yelling and trying not to show how upset she actually was. "See, she is crazy just like her dad, Crazy Cris!"

Cris turned around with a huge sweet smile as she lifted one middle finger at Raquel, then the other middle finger at the whole group, waving it from side to side to make sure she flipped them all off equally.

Luke put his arm around Cris' shoulders and laughed as he turned her away from them. "Ah, Cris, what am I going to do with you?"

At the weight of Luke's arm around her shoulders, Cris felt her cheeks get warm again. She knew she was too young to feel like she loved a boy, but she couldn't deny the feeling fluttering in her stomach right then, and given the chance, she would have sworn right then and there she loved this boy!

Chapter 25

Cris woke up feeling the longing for her best friend, the only person who truly understood her completely and accepted and loved her fully. Rolling over and looking at the clock on the nightstand, she went to rub her eyes and quickly realized the rosary was still wrapped around her hand. "Ugh, stupid bitch!"

She sat up, turned on the light next to the bed, and began untangling the metal, seeing the little circular bead marks embedded in her hand. She flexed her fingers and shook her hand to get more circulation flowing to her finger tips.

Cris knew she still had a solid hour before sleeping beauty Campbell got up and moving. Still feeling the darkness trying to overpower her, she knew it was time to go for a run and try to leave those demons chained in some dark corner where they belonged. *Too much important shit to focus on, I've got to shake this off. Let's go, move your ass and snap out of it!*

Looking down at her bandage, she realized it still looked good, she decided she could wait until after her run and shower to put on a fresh one. Throwing the covers back, Cris set her feet on the cold floor then quickly pulled them back up as she was sure she just saw a giant roach run past. She grabbed her sneakers next to the bed, suddenly thankful for her oddity of being grossed out by walking on hotel floors. She only took her shoes off after she was sitting on the bed, ready to climb in, and put them on right after waking, or next to the shower if it was shower time. She shook out both of the sneakers to make sure the nasty thing hadn't gone in one. Satisfied the shoes were all clear, she put them on and began gathering her workout clothes. She also made sure to grab her Smith & Wesson again, remembering her uneasiness of the area yesterday.

Cris got changed into her workout clothes, secured her weapon in the holster at the small of her back, snapped her red hair in a high pony then tucked the room card in her pants pocket as she shut the door and placed an earbud in her right ear. She had her playlist already fired up before she even made it out the lobby door.

Lightly jogging through the parking lot, Cris paused when she got to the sidewalk at the end. She had taken a right at the end of the parking lot yesterday, which took her down into the run-down area and abandoned buildings. She looked to the left. She couldn't see much because the road went up at an incline just enough that her five-foot-two body couldn't see past it. There was a set of railroad tracks at the top, the crossing going through at the top of the hill. *Screw it, let's see what the proverbial other side of the tracks has in store.* Subconsciously reaching her hand around, feeling the steel at the small of her back, she took off up the incline to the left.

Cris was surprised to see much nicer homes as she reached the crest of the hill. There was an obvious socioeconomic class difference on this side of the tracks. It was like night and day from one side to the other. She thought about the small layout she had witnessed just by staying straight on the road while running. Right around the area of the hotel appeared to be the working-class area, slightly further down though as you got closer to the river, was where it was clear poverty. She tried to picture how it must have all started in history. People first built by the river, near the factories that went up right there, then spread closer to the tracks when they came in. Probably once the tracks were built the rest of the town expanded laterally with it. As growth came, near the river became poverty, closer to the tracks became the working class and on the other side, further from it all, were the successful business people. She had no idea if that was even remotely accurate, but she did find the housing differences interesting and she was thankful for the temporary distraction from her own life.

Cris pulled her arm up and looked at her watch, she couldn't believe she had already run a mile and a half while lost in her thoughts. The sun was starting to come up now and there were a few people coming out to walk their dogs. Most of them were in some kind of robe with a cup of coffee in one hand and the dog's leash in the other, and the few she saw, all held small dogs. *Guess Stormy wouldn't fit into this neighborhood.* The thought of Stormy made her smile and push a little harder. *The sooner we solve this case, the sooner I can get home to Stormy and Luke.*

Pulling herself back to this case made her look around the neighborhood again, wondering if one of the girls came from a place like this. She thought of those poor girls, still so young. Then, Cris thought of their parents and the devastation they must be feeling, and Delilah's parents worried every time the phone rings that it's a call saying the body has been found.

She remembered Luke always saying he didn't understand how she could do this every day. To look for, and get in the heads of these monsters, and live with the visions of the destruction they left behind. He didn't realize it was no worse than the visions already in her head. She was driven to try to figure out why people do the things they do. What made them become this type of person? And, if she was able to save lives by getting these psychos off the streets, then that in itself over rode all the bad shit she had to see every day.

Cris realized she was already back to the railroad crossing at the top of the hill. She began to slow as she ran down the incline and was at a light jog when she reached the hotel parking lot. Disconnecting the earbuds and shutting down the music, she decided to call Campbell to make sure she was up.

Campbell picked up on the second ring. "Good morning, Cris."

Cris was still short of breath. "Hey, Kim. Just making sure you were up."

"Yeah, I'm up. I still need to shower though. Why do you sound out of breath, what's wrong?"

"Nothing's wrong. I'm just getting back from a run. I need to shower quickly too. Meet you in the lounge for breakfast in 20?"

"Well, shit I don't think I can get ready that quick! We could always hit a drive thru on the way to the office."

"Not me, I'm not wasting money when I can get it right here for free. I'll see you in the lounge."

Cris disconnected the call and took the room card out of her pocket as she briskly walked the remainder of the distance to her room. After inserting the key card into the slot, she replaced the do not disturb sign, closed the door and locked the deadbolt.

She grabbed her backpack on the way through the small room to the bathroom and hung it from the hook on the back of the bathroom door. She turned the shower water all the way on hot before she did anything else. Undressing, setting her weapon down on the sink counter and removing the bandage from her arm, she tried to mentally prepare herself for the Arctic shower that was probably in store.

Just as she turned to get into the shower, she saw the giant roach scatter from the side of the bathtub and across the floor. "Son of a bitch!"

Cris grabbed her sneaker right next to the bathtub. "Come here fucker, you're mine! I'm not sleeping with you another night!"

She was slamming her shoe at it like a mad woman as they circled around the tiny room. It took flight and landed at the base of the toilet. She bent down and connected with a hard splat and smiled as she lifted her shoe and saw the remnants. "There, you piece of shit!"

She stood up and quickly realized she just performed this whole scene completely naked and burst out laughing. *Holy shit! It's a good thing nobody was recording that! I can't even imagine how that must have looked. Did you see that Luke? Are you laughing at me up there?* She lifted her face up towards the ceiling.

Thinking about the naked roach killing adventure, Cris wasn't thinking about the freezing temperature of the shower as she stepped in at full force under the streaming water. "Holy Mary, Mother of God! Ah, fuck me!"

She took the fastest shower she could, she felt like she should start an Olympic sport for speed washing. *Or maybe one for naked roach killing?* She chuckled to herself as she shut the water off and lunged for the towel. *You're such a moron.*

Standing on the towel she had laid on the floor she quickly got dressed in place and put her sneakers on. In less than five minutes, she was completely dressed and her arm freshly bandaged. Rolling her dirty clothes and placing them in the front pouch of her backpack, she glanced at the time. She still had seven minutes before she had to meet Campbell for breakfast.

Cris placed her weapon at the small of her back and pulled her t-shirt down over it. Taking her rosary off the nightstand, she placed it in her left pocket. Lastly, her car keys and the case which held her ID and key card went into her other pocket. All that was left was to make the bed. All her tasks completed, she still had five minutes. *Hell with it, I'm going down to get started.*

Cris snagged the same table they had yesterday morning, then went over to get her swill and slop. She was halfway through her plate when Campbell finally came marching in. Kim was sporting a black pantsuit today with a silky beige camisole under the thin jacket and matching beige heels.

"Ugh, I'm going to have to finish my makeup on the drive. I didn't even have time to blow dry my hair, I had to resort to *this*." Campbell pointed to the tightly wrapped bun on her head.

"Oh, the indignity of it all. Go get your plate, Campbell. We've got a lot of work to do today and a very short fuse could be lit anytime on Delilah. I don't think she cares about your hair or your makeup right now. Now that I think about it, take your plate to go."

"What's the matter? The pictures Bryan sent you last night didn't give you sweet dreams?"

"My dreams were friggin' spectacular. But, I bet Delilah's weren't, so it's time to put my own dreams aside and work on getting her back home alive."

"Damn, Cris. Always so serious."

"Yup, I've also been told that a time or two. You say that like it's a bad thing. Come on princess, get that plate, times a wastin'. I'll meet you outside."

Cris stood up, pushed her chair in, threw away her plate and cup and started walking towards the door. She was smiling to herself. She wasn't trying to be a bitch, she knew this was the only way to get Campbell motivated and moving. She looked over just before walking out the door. Campbell had her plate ready and was just putting the top on her coffee cup.

She waited just outside the door. As Campbell came out, Cris took the coffee cup out of her hand.

"Here, let me take this before you spill something."

"Gee, thanks."

"You know, I was only busting on you to get you motivated in there."

"Shove it, Steele."

"Oh, are we talking your language again?"

Both girls started laughing as they finished their jaunt to the SUV. Hopefully, it was a sign it was going to be a good day.

Chapter 26

Pete was sitting at his desk bouncing his feet and alternating between tapping his pen against the cold metal and riffing through his papers and notes. He wasn't prone to nervousness or anxiety, but this case had changed that, this time was personal and he had more at stake. He looked through the notes again, searching for anything he may have missed or anything that would trigger another line of thought or investigation. He kept coming up empty every time. *Shit!*

He took a drink of his cold coffee and almost gagged as the sludge went down. Conceding, he sighed as he rubbed his hand over the stubble that had crept onto his chin. Pete knew he couldn't procrastinate any longer. It was time to talk to Chief and give him his conclusion on Luke's death. Maybe by some miracle, Bolton would come up with something he'd overlooked.

Might as well warm up the motor oil in my cup before going in. I wish I had some other liquid courage to add to it. Pete knew this was still procrastination but getting up and moving was also progress. He stood up and stretched and automatically looked over at Cris' empty desk space. *Ah, hell!*

He grabbed his coffee cup and turned towards the break room. Walking by Chief's office, he noticed the door was open and Chief was sitting there. *Might as well commit myself, so I can't come up with any more excuses.* Pete walked over to the open door and knocked, Bolton must have seen him coming, he was already looking at him.

"Hey, Chief!"

"Hey, Bryan, how's it going?"

Pete responded with a shrug. "I think I've got all my evidence, interviews and information together. I'm as ready as I'm going be to sit down and put our heads together on this. When is a good time for you?"

"I can make time right now, come on in."

"I was just going to warm up this shit in my cup quick, can I bring you back any?"

Bolton adjusted his glasses. "No, I guess not, my indigestion is bad enough this morning."

"Yeah, I guess I'm just a glutton for punishment today. I'll be right back."

Pete walked the short distance to the break room, deep in his thoughts about what he was going to present to Chief, how he would even start the conversation. Rounding the corner, he saw Moretti standing at the counter near the coffee. The sight of Moretti made him think of Cris and he inwardly grinned.

"Moretti, do you ever leave this room and get any real work done?"

"I work circles around you. Fuck off, Bryan."

"No, I'm talking about actual police work, not standing around gossiping with whatever poor sap crosses your path. And, thanks for the offer, Moretti, but word around the precinct is your "Johnson" is a lot smaller than what you're proclaiming. I don't think I'm interested in what you're offering."

"You're an asshole."

"Hey, I'm just telling you what I heard."

Moretti attempted to say something in response, but Pete turned his back and ignored him as he poured the thick coffee in his cup. He looked over at Reed who was at the end of the counter throwing his cup away.

"Hey, Reed. How's life treating ya?"

Reed gently smacked Pete on the shoulder. "Not too bad buddy. How bout you?"

"Ah, can't complain. Nobody listens anyway." Pete finished making his coffee and turned to leave.

"See ya, Reed. Oh! Hey, Moretti, don't worry, I hear they make pills for your problem."

Pete walked out of the room but could still hear Moretti squawking as he walked down the hall. He smiled to himself. *That was for you, Cris.*

"What the hell are you smirking about?" Chief obviously saw him coming.

"Oh, nothing, just giving Moretti shit."

Bolton laughed. "That's always a good way to start the day, take him down a notch or two."

"Well, I can't compete with Steele's wit, but hopefully I would have made her proud."

Bringing himself back to reality as he shut the door behind himself, Pete thought of the reason he was in Chief's office. "I guess there's nowhere to go but down from there."

Chief took in a long pull of air and puffed it out. "All right, what have you got?"

Pete shook his head. "Nothing good, Sir. Honestly, I'm hoping you can find something to contradict my conclusion because I've got nothing."

"I'll try my best, but don't hold your breath."

Pete took a gulp of the thick swill in his hand and fought to keep it down. *Stop procrastinating, just lay it out.*

"Well, as you already knew from the scene, the 45 cal. that was removed is a common hunting ammo, shot from a standard gun. Shit, most of the residents around here probably have these in their homes. Luke has..." Pete shook his head. "...had, brown hair and was wearing a tan shirt. There are no surveillance cameras in the area, there were no foot prints, tire tracks, nothing. All we have is the matted down leaves on the other side of the trail where the shot came from."

He paused but Chief gave no indication of doing anything but giving his undivided attention, so he continued. "That area is known for wild boars and it is not uncommon to have hunters with pistols in there after them all year round."

Chief sat there listening, but not responding.

"All of the interviews came up just as empty. Nothing but good things to say about Luke, nobody could think of a single person who would want to hurt him or heard anything threatening. Hell, when I tried the questioning of parents about seeing, hearing, or having a gut feeling about anything potentially inappropriate with their child or any other student, I half wondered if they were going to shoot me they were so appalled and pissed off by the question."

Chief still just sat there stoically, listening. Pete took it as a sign to continue.

"Looking into his childhood for potential enemies, threats or records, it was even worse. Luke was originally from Shine Island until the age of 10 when his parents were killed in a head on collision. Luke was also in the car, but unhurt. After that, he moved up to Virginia to live with his grandmother. There were no siblings. Luke ended up with a small amount of money from the insurance company after the accident. His parents didn't have much money and no life insurance. It appears he spent the money he did have on supporting himself and helping his grandmother while he was there. So, nobody to be vengeful over an inheritance. That's where he met Cris and it seems she was his only friend. They finished college and then moved back here together. There's nothing eventful in his past either."

Bolton finally spoke. "Yes, I'm aware of his history."

Something about that statement gnawed at Pete, he couldn't put his finger on it. But, he quickly brushed it off and assumed Bolton had done some of his own research already.

"Luke had a small life insurance policy through the school. Cris was the sole beneficiary. Considering the direction he was shot and laying on her, I think it's safe to rule her out as a suspect for some pretty measly insurance money."

That was all the evidence he had, or lack thereof. Glutton for punishment, he took another drink. It just made his mouth feel even more like cotton and he was really wishing for a water right now. *Or better yet, something strong enough to drown this whole nightmare away.*

Maybe Bolton took his momentary silence as a cue to give his thoughts because he finally had a response of more than one sentence.

"I didn't spend as much time as you looking into this case, but I will say, I have read the forensics and M.E.'s reports and I had a feeling there wouldn't be anything useful in the interviews. I've been trying to prepare for this possibility and have been thinking of any other angles, interviews, or research to look at. I don't have any other brilliant ideas other than what you've already done. Is there anything else?"

Pete's shoulders slumped slightly. "No, Sir. We still have a killer to look for, but I don't believe it was intentional, Sir. I don't think this person meant to shoot Luke, I think it was a hunting accident, an unbelievably unlucky shot by an amateur. My conclusion is we are looking for an Involuntary Manslaughter, not a murderer." Pete shuffled in the chair. "I'm sorry, Sir, I know you were counting on me to solve this, but this is an epic fail in my career, I have no fucking idea how we are going to find him."

Bolton pulled open the top drawer of his desk and pulled out a few antacid tablets. After chewing them up quick, he took a deep breath.

"Look, Pete, let me tell it to you this way. When I think of Cris, I think of a shot of whiskey, or perhaps even a whole bottle." Pete could see this analogy in his own head, he was wondering what Chief's view was.

Bolton continued on. "She is neat, strong and full of purpose. The kicker is, like whiskey, too many underestimate her punch."

Pete smirked, this was slightly different than his own thoughts, but it was spot on.

Chief crossed his arms on his desk as he leaned forward and looked Pete hard in the eyes.

"Take this as a warning, Bryan. Steele will not receive this news well. Be ready for that punch."

Chapter 27

It was just before 7 am when Steele and Campbell sauntered into the station. They had set up a temporary war room yesterday at the back of the station in the small conference room and that's where they were heading now to get started. As they were walking through the office towards the back, Cris was pleasantly surprised to see Beau already at his desk.

Beau looked over at them. "Good morning ladies!"

Beau paused briefly then smirked. "Hope I don't offend y'all by saying that."

Campbell jumped in. "I don't mind being called a lady, Steele on the other hand, I don't know."

Cris rolled her eyes. "Morning Beau. Let me guess, you heard the clickity clack of her heels coming from the parking lot?"

She lowered her voice and put her hand alongside her mouth as she leaned closer to him. "Oh, and just as a head's up, don't mention her bun!"

Beau looked at them both and grinned. "Ok, so don't mention your bandage and your bun." He pointed to each girl respectively as he spoke.

He turned to lead the way towards the war room, keeping his back to them as continued to speak. "Too bad about the bun, because I was getting ready to say it's a good look for you. It makes you look like a serious, strict school teacher, like I'm waiting for the ruler to come out and crack my knuckles."

Cris could see Campbell's cheeks turn pink, even through her makeup.

"Hmm, well even though I think I may have an outfit at home befitting that role, er, profession, I don't think I could be quite that mean, unless circumstances really permitted, of course."

"Campbell, nobody wants to hear about your outfits or anything else that's in your closet, drawers or under your bed. I think you twisted that bun a little too friggin' tight."

Beau glanced back quickly as he continued walking. "Okay, so I can already see how this day is going to go. Obviously, you both got your fill of piss and vinegar this morning."

Cris was done playing nice and was all back to business now. "Yup, but now it's time to get to work."

Cris saw Campbell roll her eyes, she didn't give a shit. She was sent here to solve the case, not to fool fart around all day. She didn't want another girl dying on her watch, and she was anxious to get back home to Stormy and solving Luke's case.

The three of them entered the makeshift war room. They had only gotten the boards up yesterday, all the details now needed to be added. Cris immediately went over to the whiteboard and wrote "characteristics" in all caps across the top and underlined it. Below it, she began making 3 columns, one for each girl and under that wrote the list of the characteristics all three girls shared. Lillianna (private school), Annabelle (Jasper public school) and Delilah (different private school); all 16 years-old, brown hair, hazel eyes, approximately 5'4, Caucasian, slim build.

Cris didn't even pay attention to Beau and Campbell standing to the side watching her write. She was in a zone, laser focused and basically talking to herself now.

"That's it for similarities. None of them went to the same school, none of the same extra-curricular activities or jobs, so how is he casing them?" She wrote that question down under their columns of names and similarities.

Subsequently, she moved over to the local map they had tacked up yesterday. "Okay, moving on to the next bit of facts we know."

She started placing colored pins into different locations. Red pins stuck in the location of where the bodies were discovered. Then, Cris made a big circle in the approximate area where the abductions most likely happened and put a blue pin in the center of those.

Going back to the whiteboard, she drew a big line across the bottom underneath all their names. Below that line, under each corresponding name, she wrote the date and estimated time of the abductions, when the body was found, and estimated time of death from Wyatt's reports. With the exception of Delilah, she only had the date and estimated time of the abduction, so far.

Cris was acutely aware of Beau and Campbell in the room talking and even Chief Williams coming in and out. But she was focused and not breaking concentration. On the small space remaining at the side of the whiteboard, she added in red marker: Chloroform; used to subdue for the abduction and potentially before the strangulation. Not enough to knock them out, only enough to make them too weak to fight back, meaning he lives or is holding them close by the abduction sites. She drew a line under that and added under Lillianna and Annabelle: Ligature Strangulation. No sexual abuse, no skin or debris under finger nails. No defensive marks or indications of any kind.

Cris was broken from the map board trance she was in by Beau's voice suddenly becoming more prominent in her ear.

"Steele, if we can get a profile, or even some information, ready to go out to the public by 3:00, I can get us into the TV station so it will begin airing at the 4:00 news, and continue to all the rest of the broadcasts."

Cris shook the haze off. "Book it, we will come up with as much as we can by then!"

"Yes, Ma'am!" Beau walked out of the room as he was dialing his cell phone.

Now that her spell was broken, Cris smelled Pizza. She thought she heard Chief Williams had come in at some point in the early afternoon with pizzas for them to share. Her nose and stomach were now giving her confirmation. As she grabbed two slices and slapped them on a plate, Beau was already walking back in.

"We're all set for 3:00."

Cris had already taken a bite and with a mouthful of pizza, she gave a greasy thumbs up. "Great, thanks, Beau."

Beau smiled. "No problem."

Campbell was leaning against the table holding the pizza. "I'm sorry if the pizza's cold. You looked like an artist deeply lost in the creativity of a piece. We didn't dare disturb you and interrupt your flow."

Cris swallowed and spoke before taking another large bite. "Thanks, I appreciate it. I was totally zoned out and in a good flow, if you guys had broken it, it probably would've taken me twice as long to get all that down."

"I know, I've seen you in action before, I know how you work. It's good to see it's still there."

Cris snapped back at that one. "Why wouldn't it be still there?"

Campbell looked at Beau out of the corner of her eye, but Cris noticed it. She also noticed Campbell answered more quietly and slowly.

"Well, you've been through a lot lately, and all that would have affected many people. I'm just happy to see it obviously hasn't affected your work."

Cris could not let Campbell, or anyone else, see what lived inside of her. "Of course, it hasn't!"

She looked at her watch, 2:30. She looked over at Beau who appeared to be counting ceiling tiles or something, obviously pretending to ignore their conversation. "We should probably head over to the news station now, huh?"

Beau looked at Cris. "Yes, ma'am, it's getting to be that time."

She noticed he shuffled his feet a little. "No offense Ma'am, not that something like this happens very often around these parts, but normally Chief Williams would be the one to issue the statement to the public."

Cris was all too thankful not to be the one in front of the camera. "Well, by all means then, please have Chief issue this one as well. I'm here to help you guys solve this case, not to steal anyone's glory or step on anyone's toes." Beau looked immensely relieved.

She couldn't help but tease him. "I'm not the strict school teacher that's going to slap your knuckles with the ruler, remember?"

Beau blushed a little and she left him that way, talking to herself as she turned around. "God Bless America! I know I'm a wee bit abrasive, but I'm really not some scary, mean bitch."

Next, Cris looked over at Campbell. "Campbell, I don't care who you ride with, but I'm going to drive myself. I will follow Chief and Beau over."

Campbell glanced at Beau, then quickly looked at Cris and shrugged her shoulders non-commitally. "I'll ride with you, doesn't matter to me. These guys would probably like a break from us at this point anyway."

A part of Cris wished she knew what they were talking about while she was deep in thought on the boards, but, in all honesty, the majority of her didn't give a shit.

The four of them loaded up in their two separate vehicles and headed a little further into town to where the local news station was located. Cris looked around as she got out of her vehicle.

Going inside, they met with the reporter and quickly went into the already set up recording studio. Chief Williams stood at the small podium, while Cris, Campbell, and Beau stood just off to the side listening to the basic, shortened version.

"...We believe the suspect is hidden, then quickly subduing his victim with an inhalant as they walk by. If you have a daughter or know of any girl fitting this description, please, keep them home, or at the very least, do not let them be out alone until we have the suspect in custody. If you see anyone suspicious, please call the Jasper PD immediately!"

Chief Williams wrapped up the interview with a few more tips, pleas, and phone numbers before the reporter signaled his time was up.

Not that she was anybody, but Cris felt the need to say something as Chief walked out. "Great job, Sir. I think you got all the main points without giving away specifics of the case. You're obviously well experienced at this."

"Not really, but thanks for the vote of confidence Steele. I can only hope the public will hear it and it was enough."

Beau rested his hand on Chief's shoulder and left it there as they all walked out together. As they reached their respective vehicles, Cris looked around again.

"Campbell, if you're riding with me again, stand by." Looking over at Chief and Beau, she yelled. "Guys, I'll meet you back at the station in just a minute."

She noticed none of them moved or responded and she would have sworn she saw Campbell elbow Beau's side. *Fuck it, I don't care.*

She quickly went over to a guy sitting on a bench with a backpack next to him. He had on ripped jeans, probably used to be blue, and a faded t-shirt. His face had a beard, but it was not groomed and in desperate need of a shave. As she got closer, she noticed several tattoos on his biceps and forearms. She couldn't entirely make them out, but from a distance and quick glance, they appeared to include skulls, eagles, and the flag. She smiled, pretty sure of her original instinct. Reaching the man, she briefly talked with him and confirmed he was a Vet.

"Please, wait here, I have something for you."

Before she turned to walk away, she noticed the familiar top of a bottle sticking out of a side pouch in his backpack. Cris bit back the lump in her throat and the tears that wanted to fall as she walked back to her SUV.

She noticed everyone was still standing there watching her when she returned to the news station parking lot. She gave them all her best "bitch" face, daring them to say something as she got a plastic bag from the floor of the back seat. Without looking back, she walked with the bag, back over to the gentleman on the bench.

Handing it to him and again fighting back the tears, she hugged him hard and whispered in his ear. "Please, don't give up, keep fighting! There are still people out there who care, that is my oath I swear to you! God Bless You!"

Cris composed herself before reaching the parking lot again. She looked at the three of them just standing there watching her and put her iron shield on again.

"Are you bitches ready to go, or what?" She swirled her finger around in the air above her head, as if to say "Lets ride."

Chief Williams looked at her and smiled. "Yes, Ma'am!"

Driving back to the station, Cris was preoccupied with both the case and yet another homeless Vet. Thankfully, Campbell had the good sense to keep her mouth shut for once.

Upon return to the station, they went back to the war room and finished up a few last thoughts. It had been a long day and was getting late. Cris' brain was getting too tired to think clearly anymore, it was time to wrap things up for the day. She was pointing at the map board with multiple push pins.

"Alright, so based on the approximate abduction locations and the dump sites, we have this triangle of where the killer most likely lives, or at least holds the girls."

She turned on her heel and looked squarely at Beau. "Beau, do you have someone competent working nights who can work on sorting through all of the surveillance cameras within this triangular area from the approximate dates and times of the abductions and the drop off of the bodies?"

"I can think of a couple to choose from to put on that, yes."

"Good. They can get a copy of Wyatt's report for the approximate times of death, and they can get the times of abduction and when the call came in of discovering the bodies from the case file. I know it's a lot to cover, but it's necessary. We need to catch a serious freaking break! I don't think I need to remind anyone that we are out of time here! Based on his previous time frame, we should be getting a call by the morning from some unfortunate soul finding her body. I'm praying for the fact that there has not been another girl abducted is because Delilah is still alive."

Beau was a little wide eyed as he left the room. "Yes, Ma'am! I'll get right on it!"

Cris didn't even remember leaving the station or the drive back to the hotel. All she knew was she fell face down into her pillows and exhaustion finally overtook her. Fully clothed and all, OCD be damned, that was all she wrote.

Chapter 28

ris hopped out of the shower, the steam still swirling in the air as she grabbed her towel and wrapped it twice around her tiny 10-year-old frame. Grabbing the hand towel from its squeaky metal holder, she sloppily rubbed at the mirror trying to clear off the steamy haze. Looking in the partially streaked and partially cloudy mirror, she smiled wide, then quickly replaced it with a scowl. Ugh, big teeth, red hair, and pale skin covered in freckles. I'm so ugly, who could ever really like me?! She shook her head as she turned away from the mirror and grabbed her clothes from the lid of the hamper. Today she and Luke were going to take all the scrap wood they could find laying around and build a cabin in her back yard, then they would have their own little fort to hang out in after school. She couldn't wait to get started on it! After getting dressed and brushing her teeth, Cris quickly put all of her personal items in her drawer of the vanity, hung the towels back up and threw her dirty clothes into the laundry basket. The bathroom was all picked up, it was time to go meet Luke!

She bounded out of the bathroom into the kitchen where she found the figure of her father hunched over the table, looking hard into the half empty amber glass with ice; seducing, consoling, and conspiring with Sailor Jerry.

He suddenly looked up at Cris with glassy eyes. "Cris, hey baby! Come sit with me a minute, will you?"

As she traipsed over, she looked at the glass sweating on the table, already almost empty. Although she could tell he wasn't drunk, in the past two years, not once could she remember him drinking this early. He pushed the chair back slightly and patted his thigh, signaling for her to sit as she got closer. She sat on his lap and looked into his matching crystal blue eyes, searching.

He kissed Cris on the forehead as he wrapped his arms around her and squeezed tight.

His speech and articulation were clear as day, but his words were as dark as the dungeons in hell, and that was what scared her the most. Leaving his arms wrapped around her little body, he rested his head sideways on top of hers.

"I've been doing a lot of thinking lately. I'm really sorry I wasn't here much for the first eight years of your life."

Cris started to speak, but he put a finger on her lips as he shook his head from side to side. He kissed her again, on the temple this time.

"Please baby, this isn't easy, let me finish what I have to say." He grabbed another quick swig of courage from Sailor Jerry before he continued on.

He swallowed hard. "I'm even more sorry for my mental absence over the past two years that I have physically been here. You and your mom... you two mean everything to me."

He gave a little grunt. "Shit, you guys are what got me through all my deployments and lonely days at sea."

He swallowed up the last of his courage; the ice cubes clinked as he gingerly set the glass down. "I can't explain what happens to me, but I really want to try to make you understand, as much as possible."

Cris took a breath, getting ready to tell him it was okay, she did understand, but at her inhale of breath, he shook his red head back at her. "Please!"

Not wanting to answer and upset him, she set her head on his shoulder and looked up at him. He reached for the strength of his companion, only to find it was gone. Instead, he rested his head on top of hers.

"I live a nightmare in my head every day. Those 12 years of my life play over and over in my mind. My commander yelling in my ear, the buttons I personally pushed, the weapons I fired, the missiles I'd launched at the enemy, then seeing the faces of the innocents that got blown up in the crossfire. Going onto other ships at sea and ports with hostiles to "clear them by all means necessary" while sometimes watching my shipmates pay the ultimate price. The chain of command and government shrugging it off as "casualties of war." They weren't the ones firing the weapons, it wasn't quite that simple for me. I can't get those images out of my head, I still see them all. Then when I hear loud, booming noises, my mind goes back to being on the ship and firing those lethal weapons. I can't stop it from coming back. I don't just remember it, I relive it, I'm still there."

Cris turned slightly on her dad's lap and reached her arms around his neck, hugging him as tightly as she could. He squeezed her back so hard she thought her spine might snap.

"I'm sorry, baby! I know the toll this is taking on my friends and family. I know what this is doing to you and your mom, and it's not fair. I want to make it better, I promise I'm trying to make it better!"

Cris spoke softly by his ear. "It's okay daddy, we really do understand, and we love you!"

He gave Cris another hard squeeze and grabbing her shoulders, moved her back slightly so he was looking at her. She noticed his eyes had gone from glassy to longing. "I love you so much, you are such an amazing young lady, always remember that! When life gets tough, you're tougher, you're my girl!"

He gave a small shake of the head. "So, you're up and at 'em bright and early, what are you doing today?"

Glad to be coming back to a more normal conversation, she remembered what she was getting ready to go do and smiled. "Me and Luke are going to..."

Her dad cut her off "Luke and I."

Cris rolled her eyes. "Whatever Dad, that sounds funny. I'll write it the right way in class, but when I talk I'm gonna say it how it sounds right to me. So, anyway, we are going to gather up whatever scrap wood we can find and build a cabin out in the backyard."

He shook his head and smiled, but Cris noticed that yearning was still in his eyes. "Two things I'm gonna say to you. You keep cuttin' those eyes like that, you might find your ass in some serious trouble one day when you do it to the wrong person. And, second, you take care of that boy and treat him right. I know you guys are best friends right now, but you best keep being there for him. He's a nice young man and he's going to grow up to be a great man, I can tell. Don't fuck it up and let him go, Cris, okay?"

Cris felt her face get warm, but still couldn't help but smile. "Yes, Sir."

Her dad slid Cris off his lap and stood up. "Good. Now go have fun, build that cabin and clean up your mess when you're done. There's a bunch of wood under the back deck we'll never do anything with, go ahead and use it up too. You can use my hammer and nails in the shed, don't hurt yourself and put them back in the shed after."

He tapped her on the butt before grabbing his glass and refreshing the ice. Walking over to the counter, he picked up his companion and refilled the glass.

She saw him head over to the desk that held the stationary and office items and she noticed his eyes suddenly looked clearer than she'd seen them in the past two years.

Good, he's feeling better now he got that out. I'm glad I could be there for him. Now I don't have to worry about him and can concentrate on building the cabin with Luke.

Just before the door clicked closed, Cris could've sworn she heard him say "I love you, baby." She shook her head, assuming she was imagining it, then fully brushed it off as she looked across the field at Luke.

As she flew down the stairs, Luke looked over at her. He was standing in front of the garage next to a huge pile of wood, proud as a peacock. She was already across the field and in their driveway within seconds.

"Look what I already got from the garage! My Grammie said we could have it!"

"That's so cool! We have some at our house too, we will definitely have enough to get it all built!"

"I've got it all out, now we just need to bring it over to your house."

"We have a little garden cart at our house, we can load it up and wheel it over. Hang on, I'll go grab it." She ran over, grabbed the cart and was back just as Luke was finishing pulling the garage door down.

They couldn't fit much of the bulky wood on the wagon at one time. It took them six loads with Cris pulling the cart and Luke walking alongside with his hands-on top to help balance it. Once they got all those stacks unloaded over in the far back corner of her yard where the cabin was going to be built, they brought the cart over to her back deck and began loading those pieces up. They had four loads from under the deck. Getting all of it together in a pile, Luke and Cris looked at each other and smiled. She held her palm up and Luke gave her a hearty high five.

"Let's get the hammer and nails from the shed, my dad said we could use them."

Walking inside the shed, Luke's eyes got wide. "Wow! Your dad has a lot of stuff in here, but I've never seen a shed or garage so organized!"

Cris shrugged. "It's easier to find things that way. Put stuff back where it belongs and you won't have to search for it the next time you need it. Now, where are those... oh, here we go. Cool, he has two hammers. Can you grab the box of nails right there?"

Luke reached down on the bottom of the bench. "Got 'em."

"Alright, let's go get started!"

They walked back over to the pile of wood, Cris set the hammers down to the side of the pile. Luke followed suit, placing the nails next to the hammers.

Cris started picking up the pieces of wood and making piles. "Before we start trying to build, let's get this wood organized by size so we can see what we have and what size we can build the cabin from there."

"Good idea."

They stacked the two-by-fours together, then a bunch of wider planks, and two matching sizes of plywood. Cris assessed their supply and began seeing the pieces of wood going together like a puzzle. She was mumbling to herself, and Luke was just standing to the side watching her.

She turned and looked at Luke. "Okay, so I think the best way to start is these two pieces of plywood. They are both the same size, so I think it makes the most sense for those to be used for the roof. They are probably about four feet by four feet, so that's about the size our cabin will be, not too bad. At that size, I think we will have enough two-by-fours to use as studs and then the planks will attach to those for the walls. If we have any planks left, we can use them inside for a floor. How does that sound?"

Luke was staring at Cris, unblinking, his mouth slightly agape. "How do you know how to do this? I have no idea what to do for any of this, and you know exactly how it should all fit together."

"I've helped my dad build some small things here and there, and it's just a basic structure. So, since our cabin size is based on the size of the plywood, I think we should start by attaching the two-by-fours to the inside bottom of the plywood on all four sides and one down the center. From there we can attach the other two-by-fours along what will be the bottom. Let's just start there."

"Yes, Ma'am. I mean, okay."

Cris had already grabbed the plywood and the first two-by-four they would hammer in place. She smiled as she gave Luke one of the hammers and a nail. She put her knee on the board to hold it in place.

"Okay, Luke. Try not to let the board move as you hammer it. We will each put one on the end to hold them for now."

Luke looked a little nervous but shook his head and placed the nail and got the hammer ready to swing. Cris was just bringing the hammer down and pounded her thumb instead, as a sudden loud crack from inside the house reverberated through her body, piercing her heart as her stomach dropped.

She immediately, without thought, ran towards her house, yelling back to Luke without looking. "Stay out here!"

She didn't notice the pain or trail of blood from her thumb following her in.

Heart pounding, Cris was searching frantically as she came through the door, quickly sweeping rooms with her eyes as she passed. She ran into the room her dad used most of the time.

Before she even reached his room, the strong metallic smell assaulted her, and she struggled not to throw up.

She couldn't believe her eyes, that had started spilling tears as she ran over to him. "No, daddy, no!"

As she got closer, she saw he was holding a picture of the three of them against his chest with his left hand. Then, on the stand next to his now damaged head, she saw the two envelopes, each with its own name, one for mom and one for her. The one for her also had his dog tags draped over it. With their own special letters, just like when he was deployed, it was clear to Cris he had finally lost his battle, or won it depending on how someone looked at it, when he silenced his own demons with his trigger finger.

Shaking, crying, gagging, Cris picked up the blood-spattered phone from the nightstand and dialed 911, it rang once before she heard a female voice. "911. What's your emergency?"

Chapter 29

Cris, still mostly asleep, standing by her father's dead body and hearing that 911 operator answer, she reached over and grabbed her ringing cell phone. "Help, please! My dad, oh my God, please help me!"

"Hello? Is this Detective Steele? Hello!"

The sound of the 911 operator's voice going from female to male and calling her by her married name immediately snapped her out of her dream. Cris looked at the bright red numbers on the clock, almost blinding her now sensitive eyes, 4:14 am. *Shit! Delilah!*

Her head was still swimming too drunkenly in the reality from 17 years ago to come up with any kind of coherent and plausible excuse as to why she answered the phone like that. *Best to just ignore it and move on, story of my life.*

"Yes, this is Detective Steele."

"Oh, thank goodness, I thought I had the wrong number!"

Cris didn't reply. She also wasn't alert enough to recognize the voice, but she certainly didn't trust her voice to speak.

Apparently, her caller must have realized she was waiting for him to continue. "I'm sorry to call so early detective, but I knew you would want to know right away."

The light bulb in her head finally brightened up, just a little. *Wyatt.* "What's happened, Wyatt?"

"I think we finally caught a break! Beau called me with a list of colleagues and asked my opinion on who I thought would be best to look over specific surveillance cameras. I asked him to let me do it. It would save time, I already know most of the specifics of this case, saves time from looking it up, plus I have a pretty good idea what to be looking for." Wyatt took a quick breath. "I'm sorry, I'm rambling, too much caffeine I guess. Anyway, I've been pouring through them all night and I'm positive one of the cameras got the killer walking towards the abduction site!"

Cris sat upright on the lumpy bed. "You're friggin' kidding me!"

"No, Ma'am. I've looked at it ten times now making sure I wasn't seeing something that wasn't there. His identity is not clear, but I think if we get it to our Forensic IT guy, he can help us a little."

"Thanks, Wyatt, great job! I will get in touch with Campbell and we will be right over! Would you be able to contact Beau while I'm prodding Campbell along?"

"Of course, I'd be happy too!"

"Thanks, Wyatt. See ya soon." Cris ended the call and immediately scrolled to Campbell's number.

It was going on the fourth ring before Campbell finally picked it up with a yawn. "Hey Cris, what's wrong?"

"Time to get up and moving Kim. Wyatt just called me, it looks like we finally have a lead to follow. He found something on a surveillance video. No time for showers. Get up and dressed and meet me in the hall in 10 minutes."

"Ah, shit, 10 minutes?" She paused, but only for a second. "Fine, I'll get moving."

Cris ended the call and swung her feet to the edge of the bed to put her shoes on. Looking down, she suddenly realized she had not even changed last night. She knew she must have been so exhausted from everything over the past five days, that she fell asleep in her clothes. And her sleep had not exactly been restful. The memories came rushing back, just like she was that 10-year-old girl standing there all over again; the images assaulting her visual cortex.

She sat on the edge of the bed, doubled over, and started rocking back and forth on top of her knees, she could not stop the tears that automatically poured over. She hated reliving that day.

I'm sorry dad, I should've been there for you. I should've seen what that sudden clearness in your eyes really meant and stayed inside instead of leaving you alone. Maybe you'd still be here today, and maybe you'd even be whole. I'm so sorry daddy! I'm so sorry!

This was the first time she had this dream since losing Luke. He had always been there to get her through before. Then the sudden irony of them both dying from a gunshot to the head made Cris want to throw up. At some point, she had become lucid and aware she was still rocking on the side of the bed, staring at the carpet in front of her, unblinking and weeping unconsciously.

Cris wiped her eyes and face with the bandage on top of her forearm. "Stop it bitch! Get your ass up, dry your fucking eyes and pull your sorry ass together. You have work to do and a life to save. Get the fuck up!"

Cris looked at the clock, 4:26. *Shit!* What time had she called Campbell? 4:17, she thought. Jumping up from the bed, the springs in the old mattress creaking, she slipped into her shoes as she hustled to the bathroom. Grabbing her clothes from the backpack, she wasted no time getting them on. She transferred the items in her pockets from the clothes she wore yesterday, and into bed last night, into her clean clothes. A quick brush of the teeth then pull the hair up in a pony tail, Cris snapped the band in her hair extra tight, just to feel the pull and piss herself off a little more. She pulled a few strands of hair out of the elastic band along her centered part line and temples, and at the same time, quickly glanced at her arm in the reflection of the mirror. *There, the tentacles should help take some of the attention off my face, and no time for a clean bandage today!*

Rushing out of the bathroom, she looked at the clock again, 4:29. *Thank God Campbell usually runs late. No time to make the bed today either.* She grabbed her phone and keys and placed the do not disturb sign in the slot as she let the door click behind her. Hearing a ruckus, Cris looked to her right. Campbell was rushing out of her door, with two bags hanging off her shoulder and banging into the walls. Her long blonde hair now spiraling down in waves.

"Whoa, I've never seen your hair with waves!"

"That's because I don't wear it like this. It was wet when I put it in the bun yesterday, and since I didn't get a shower this morning, this is what I'm left with." Campbell pulled a chunk of her hair to further drive the point home. "I'll figure out something to do with it on the drive over, while I also put on my face."

Cris grinned. "Yes, please do get your face on."

"I need caffeine before I can come up with any smart-ass comments. It's too damn early for me."

"Well, I think we will be stuck with the shit at the station today. There's no coffee places open this early. That sludge oughta either wake you up or at least inspire some ingenious lines."

Campbell replied with a clipped snort as they loaded up, then spent the entire drive in silence with her face in the mirror of the sun visor. Cris was fine with that. It gave her time to attempt to chase away the shadows and darkness trying to drown her and refocus her thoughts to the case. The enormity of that challenge made her wish, for once, the drive was slightly longer.

Campbell had just finished putting her "face on" when Cris rolled into the parking space. Once the vehicle stopped, Campbell looked away from the mirror at her surroundings.

"Ugh, we're here already! I didn't even get time to do my hair yet."

"If you don't want to keep it the way it is, I guess you better grab a hair tie then and strap it back or up in some fashion."

"Just give me a sec."

Campbell reached around the back of her head and started braiding her hair. Cris just watched in awe, she couldn't even braid someone else's hair successfully, much less her own. Before she knew it, Campbell was whipping her head up, with the beautiful braid in place.

"Damn, girl, you're good at that!"

Campbell shrugged her shoulders. "It comes from years of practicing. First on your friends, then on yourself."

Cris looked over at Campbell and smirked. "Are we still talking about the braid here?"

"Shit, Steele, you're finally talking my language and I'm too caffeine deprived right now to enjoy it."

They were just about to reach the entryway when the headlights from a car pulling into a parking spot swept over them. Both girls turned around as the engine was cut. Cris instinctively placed her hand over her weapon. The driver's door flew open quickly and her grip tightened momentarily.

"Hey girls, wait! I brought you something, c'mon over and get it."

Cris let her hand drop and expelled the breath she'd been holding and loosened her stance, as Beau stood there holding two travel mugs. Both girls turned back and walked over to him.

"Dang, that was good timing! I was wondering how I was going to carry three of these in."

Cris grabbed the mug from his hands. "You brought us coffee? Thank you."

Campbell followed with a high-pitched "Aw!"

"No problem! I knew with it being so early we were all going to need some, and the stuff here really isn't made for human consumption, I swear. I made some at home right quick before I left."

Campbell looked at Beau all doe-eyed. "You are my hero right now!"

Cris rolled her eyes, and immediately she could hear her daddy's words about "cuttin' them eyes to the wrong person" and it made her smile.

"Well, thanks, Beau. It's going to be a long day, this will certainly help us get going on it."

The three of them walked in together, armed with coffee in hand they were eager to meet with Wyatt and see the surveillance video. The department was almost empty and much quieter at this time of morning. Walking back to the war room, Wyatt was already in there waiting, with the laptop on the table.

He looked over at them eagerly as they walked in. "Oh, great you're all here!"

He seemed a little amped up, but Cris figured it was a combination of shitty coffee, lack of sleep and an overabundance of adrenaline all wrapped up with one big pretty anxiety ridden bow.

Beau walked over and slapped Wyatt on the shoulder. "Man, I can't believe you've been up all night and you found something! I can't thank you enough, buddy!"

Cris stood next to Wyatt and looked over his shoulder, Beau still had his hand resting on it. "All right my royal knight, let's see what you've got!"

Wyatt pushed his glasses up his nose as he sat up ram rod straight and zoomed in on the footage.

Cris gave a huge smirk and once again was unable to bite her tongue. "Son of a bitch, fuck me like a two-dollar whore! We just might have a face!"

Chapter 30

The image and angle of the man in the video was poor at best. Cris found herself rubbing inside her pocket again as she was cursing under her breath. They had an image of his face, they were so damn close, only to be disappointed by the realization they would not be able to make a positive ID with it. She stood up straight and tried to stifle a stretch as she tried to compose her anger and frustration at the poor video quality, her lack of quality sleep certainly wasn't helping.

"So, is there anyone "techie" in this neck of the woods who can try to come up with a clearer picture or a decent composite sketch out of this image?"

Beau smiled as he shook his head. "Nope, the image on this laptop is as high tech as it gets in these here parts. And all the "techies" have not graduated beyond video gaming." Beau paused and looked over at Wyatt as he chuckled. "Okay, maybe that part seems true enough."

Beau went back to looking at Cris. "Actually, we have a state of the art forensic department and some very experienced kick ass analysts. Their department is adjoined with Wyatt's, which is also why he was good for this searching task. Wyatt spends a lot of his time in there with them. And lastly, yes, our video expert has already been called and will be here very soon."

Cris felt her cheeks get warm. She hadn't meant to offend him, she just had a way with words and it wasn't usually a good way. She also sucked at apologies and feelings, better to just shove them down and ignore that something awkward happened.

"Good. Should we head over there and wait for him then?"

Campbell was sitting on the edge of the table and made a loud slurp as she put the coffee mug to her mouth. All of them turned to look at her. Campbell's eyes looked over the mug she still held up to her mouth. She stopped drinking and held the mug in her hand.

"Sorry, I didn't think it would still be that hot. That's a damn good cup of coffee Beau, thanks."

"Glad you like it." Beau turned back to Cris again. "Sure, we can head over there. Wyatt can let us in. I'll text Chief and let him know where to find us."

Cris grabbed her coffee off the table and started heading for the door. She turned around to see the three of them still standing there talking. Campbell looked over at her and Cris took the opening.

"I'm just gonna go outside by the pond and get some fresh air."

"Okay, we'll be right there."

Standing outside, the sun had not come up yet and likewise, the heat of the day had yet to arrive. Cris began walking around the small pond, doing her best to look for snakes or any other critters in the dark grass. She had to admit, the early morning air felt good and helped clear her head and frustration a little.

"You have a hard time sitting still don't you?" Beau had quietly come up from behind.

Cris had a feeling he was trying to sneak up on her or startle her, but the poor bastard had no idea she didn't have any nerve endings left at this point. Her nervous system was always in a constant state of arousal, always in the fight mode. She didn't so much as flinch. At his arrival, Cris took it as her cue to move along and began walking towards their destination with Beau still by her side.

"I prefer to stay busy and moving, yes."

"The longer I hang around with you, the more I realize you're a very interesting person, Steele."

"Damn, it must be really boring around here. But, hey, glad I could provide you with some free psychological entertainment."

Beau shook his head and grinned as they arrived at the door. Wyatt and Campbell arrived just a few paces behind. The four of them stood in a little circle facing each other.

"I want Wyatt to go home and get some sleep. Mike, our IT genius is here and already got all the info he needs from Wyatt. Although I'm kinda throwing myself to the wolves by being with these two alone."

He thumbed his hands towards both girls, then Beau looked over at Wyatt. "Thanks for everything man, I owe you big for this one!"

The men grabbed each other's right hand in a shake and pulled each other together as they slapped the other person's shoulder with their left hands. They all gave a wave, then Wyatt walked into his lair, presumably to get his stuff together, as they continued on around the corner of the building to another door.

Cris was a little taken back when they walked into the forensics department. First, by all the advanced looking equipment in the sterile area, but mostly by Mike. She wasn't sure what she was expecting, but it certainly wasn't this. Mike must have been at least 6'2 and looked very thin and gangly. He wore cargo shorts, an unbuttoned shirt with a t-shirt underneath and sandals, and sported long black hair just barely touching his shoulders, one side tucked behind his ear, the other side hanging down freely. He looked like a cross between a rock star and a grown man living in his parent's basement playing video games all day. She couldn't help but wonder if he was part of the reason for Beau's comment just a few minutes ago.

Cris tried to close her jaw as introductions were made all the way around. Mike looked right at home as he settled into his little nook and began turning on his equipment.

"Wyatt gave me all the times and frames to look at, so I know exactly where I need to go on these feeds. It should only take me a minute to get them all pulled up and find the best image to work with."

Cris was still skeptical about the quality of the images. "So, just how much are you able to enhance these images? I assume Wyatt showed us the best quality image, and I've gotta say, it wasn't pretty."

Mike looked back from his computer haven and smiled a big white toothy grin. "With this technology, I can find and enhance a tick burrowing in on your ass cheek. You just stand by and let me work my magic."

"By all means." Cris motioned her open hands towards his electronic wonderland as she backed up slightly.

When she looked over at Beau, he was standing just off to the side smiling and nodding his head in agreement as if to say "Yeah, this guy is the shit."

Cris did as she was told, which was not the easiest for her. She stood back and watched as Mike clicked, dragged, zoomed and a bunch of other things she couldn't even begin to comprehend and kept repeating the process after looking at the image over and over. The only noise in the room was the air conditioner periodically kicking on and the click of keys from Mike's keyboard and mouse. Cris had to agree, it was like she was watching pure magic happen.

She saw Beau and Kim jump a little bit when in the deep silence Mike raised his hands up over his head and pushed the wheels of his chair back as he loudly declared "Done!"

Beau, Campbell, and Cris all leaped forward to look at the screen. There sat a slightly grainy, but entirely distinct enough image of the suspected killer.

Cris looked back wide-eyed at Mike. "This is amazing! Unbelievable!"

Beau tipped his head and smirked. "Not bad for a bunch of Lil' ol' country bumpkins, huh?!"

Cris noticed Campbell almost spit out her coffee.

Cris smiled back, suddenly in a much better mood. "Yeah, not bad at all."

Hearing the main door click shut, the four of them all turned to look and watched as Chief Williams came meandering in. He shouted across the expanse of desks and equipment.

"How are we doing? Any luck?"

Mike was leaning with his back against the wall in the corner of his area, he had one ankle over the other and his arms were crossed over his abdomen, looking as cool as a snowball before going into the hell fires of summer.

He grinned over at Chief. "I've done all I can do."

Chief had made it over to Mike's work area. "Are we able to make an ID?"

Beau shuffled to the side, making room for Chief to come to the monitor. "I think we will be from this image, Sir."

Chief looked at the screen and squinted his eyes. "Not bad! We need to run this through the system and find out who this asshole is, now!"

Mike stepped forward. "I'm going to assist the team with identifying him. They should be here soon, and I planned to get started now."

"See how quickly you can get it done. If you can't find him in the system we will have to broadcast his photo to the public for help. I really don't want to do that and take the chance of tipping him off and losing him. But, we have to end this!"

Mike sat down in his chair, already clicking the keys and working more of that magic that had Cris' head spinning. "I'm on it."

"Good." Chief turned to the three detectives. "Beau, Steele, and Campbell, go to the war room and get the computers going. I want you guys searching any past articles and cases that look like it might match these girls' characteristics. If even one hair on your body stands up, or you get one twitch in your gut, even if you don't immediately see the connection, look into it!"

Chief started turning to walk away and shouted back over his shoulder. "Any of you find something, call me immediately. I will be contacting the press to let them know of a potential broadcast of the picture for help in the meantime."

The three of them hurried back to the war room, leaving Mike and the crew that would soon be arriving, to do what they do best. Chief already had someone bring in three laptops for them each to work on, with a pen and pads of paper sitting beside each one, and they wasted no time in getting started.

Cris immediately took control of assigning the tasks. "Okay, so we aren't all searching the same thing, let's each do a certain project. Beau, it makes the most sense for you to search the case files since this is your town, there may be something that stands out to you. Look at open, closed and cold files. Use your search filters to help narrow it down, but not too specific or you could miss something."

Cris looked to Campbell who had already sat at her laptop, next to Beau's. "Kim, you search articles and databases within a 100-mile radius. Again, use some general search filters to narrow it down, but not too specific."

Cris sat down at her own laptop on the other side of Beau. "I'm going to search the local articles and databases over the past 20 years."

They had been silently scouring the systems and sites for slightly over an hour, none of them saying a word or moving. The only noise in the room was the occasional noise from the keyboards. Cris didn't think she was the only one surprised when Chief Williams came in and spoke, breaking their intense concentration on their screens. His voice booming in the otherwise quiet room.

"I just got a call from Mike. They had six of them working on that photo in all the systems nationwide, private and public, and they've got nothing. He obviously has no record. It's like he doesn't exist."

Cris sighed a little louder than she intended. That was their quickest and best hope, she knew it would only get more difficult from here. Chief looked at her a little softly, probably trying to encourage her.

"You guys keep doing your searches, you never know what may come up. As much as I don't want to, I'm going to post his profile on the local news and social media and ask the public for help. Somebody has to know him or has seen him, and hopefully, they will call before he sees it."

They were barely back to resuming their searches when the IT crew came in to set up little phone stations along the back wall. She had to give this small-town credit, they were quick and on it.

Cris could tell when the broadcasts went out by the sudden buzzing of phones. She tried hard to keep concentrating on her so far disappointing search, but it was difficult. With each call, she prayed it might be the tip or name they were looking for. From what she could hear from the one-sided conversation, she would swear it sounded like most people were just trying to get rid of their ex's. Then she heard one that might sound promising and real, the conversation had been going for more than two minutes, the longest yet. Cris stopped looking at her computer screen and searching and just listened.

"I understand. So, what is his name, Ma'am?"

She walked over to the operator who was still talking. Cris saw she had written down a name on a piece of paper. She must have seen Cris walking over because as she got close, the operator took the piece of paper and handed it to her. She took it from her hand and wasted no time getting back to her computer.

Doing a quick search of the name written down, an article immediately popped up. Cris' eyes got wide as she stared at the screen with disbelief. "Holy shit!"

Chapter 31

She couldn't believe the face she saw looking back at her. This woman matched the same characteristics as the girls who were abducted and murdered. Brown hair, hazel eyes, Caucasian, and Cris would bet money she was about 5'4 with a slim build.

"How in the hell did this not show up in all the searching we did?"

Beau looked over from his laptop. "It's difficult when you are only trying to find specific features. It's clear in this article that it was ruled a natural death, it was not big news, making it even harder to find in our search parameters."

By this time the tip line operator had hung up and walked over to them. "The caller insisted on remaining anonymous, but she said she was a former teacher and this man looked very much like a boy she had in her class. She always wondered about his mother's death and didn't really believe it was a heart attack. She said he was odd and she could sense his evilness, her words, so when she heard his mother had died she had all kinds of red flags going off in her head."

Cris read the rest of the article and read out loud the parts she found interesting. "Her 16-year-old son found her and called it in."

She paused briefly. "If that teacher is right, it could explain why the girls he's taking now are 16, his age at his first kill."

Cris clicked a few more keys, searching further. A few scrolls down the page and she stopped as she raised her pointer finger up.

"Ah! There were allegations and investigations by the Department of Social Services and Child Protective Services for abuse of her son. They were never founded and the child was never removed. He was a minor so his name would not have come up in a search. The only mention of him appears as the living relative in his mother's death."

Campbell leaned over Cris' shoulder looking too. "Sounds like a decent motive to kill his mother to me."

Scratching his chin, Beau chimed in. "I agree, but it still doesn't explain why he's taking these girls and killing them now."

Chief Williams was standing just outside their group. "So, this looks like our guy?"

Cris turned and looked Chief hard in the eyes. "Judging by the features of his mother and the history, yes, Sir."

"I agree. I'm going to get his face off all news and social networks. We can only hope he didn't see it and we still might have the upper hand."

Cris looked back to her screen, already clicking keys and getting to work. "We will start searching for an address to get the warrant going in the meantime."

Cris slammed her fist on the table. "There's nothing. It's like he's a phantom. How is that possible? No employment, driver's license, car registration, credit report? That just doesn't happen this day and age."

Campbell further agreed with her previous statement. "Sounds like he's definitely our guy. Nobody that's innocent would go to such lengths to be completely off the grid."

Cris was staring at her screen, thinking. She spoke low, talking more to herself than anyone else. "Let's try this. I will find you, you low life piece of shit."

Cris quickly clicked more keys. "I'll be the daughter of a whore! Look at this address in comparison to the circle we made, it's right in the middle, where our blue pin is."

Beau was standing and looking between Cris' screen and the push pins on the board. "Holy hell! This has got to be it! How did you find it?"

Cris smiled back at Beau and Campbell, who appeared to be standing right on top of poor Beau. "This house is in his dead mother's name."

Beau was already spinning on his heel. "Let's go get that address to Chief and get a warrant going."

Cris was now up and following Beau, with Campbell trying hard to stay near his side. Walking briskly towards Chief's office, she was again surprised by the speed and organization as the crew came in to start packing up the makeshift call station they had so recently set up.

It was a short walk and Chief was in his office when they arrived. "I just shut everything down that was broadcasting his photo. Did you guys get anywhere on the address?"

Beau stepped in further so they could all fit into the small office. "Yes, Sir. We got the address." Beau handed him the piece of paper. "Just need you to call in that warrant."

Chief looked back at the three of them, but a little harder at Cris. "You're sure on this?"

Cris immediately held her head high and spoke up. "Yes, Sir."

"Okay. Go get suited up, the warrant will be ready in five minutes."

Beau nodded his head at Chief and walked out the door. Campbell and Cris followed, but as soon as they were out of Chief's office she grabbed Beau by the arm.

"How can he produce a warrant so quickly? It is a legit warrant we will be getting right?"

It was Beau's turn to smile. "Yup. It helps when the judge is your brother."

Cris smirked back. "Nice."

Campbell started looking around the office. "So where do we get our vests and gear?"

Beau pointed as he started walking. "Right over here."

They walked the short distance to a closed, locked door, behind which was a room not much bigger than a closet, but it held everything they would need. As they got dressed they discussed the plan of action. They would take their two vehicles and park the next street over and approach from the back street.

Cris looked at Beau. "With the warrant, Chief will have back up there for us too, right?"

Beau slyly smirked over at her again. "Oh, yes. He will provide back up."

Ready to go, they hurried out the door towards their own respective vehicles, except for Campbell opting to ride with Beau this time.

Although the sun was out, the asphalt was wet and the smell of the ozone was unmistakable. Evidently, it had just rained and Cris slowly watched as snake like smoke lazily danced up towards the sky. She was temporarily mesmerized, but then she shook her head, and hoped it wasn't an omen.

Within minutes they arrived at the scene and parked at their previously discussed destination. Cris was amazed and impressed to look over and see the SWAT team getting out of their vehicles and gearing up with weapons and helmets sporting cameras.

Beau and Campbell had walked over to Cris. Looking over at Beau, Cris pointed towards the SWAT team. "I'm beginning to think you guys are just pretending to be some quiet little country town."

Beau grinned. "I'm not saying otherwise. So, SWAT already has the warrant. They will disperse and position themselves surrounding the property. Three of them will go to the front door, and we will be right behind them. Once they go in, either welcomed or by force, we will follow and secure the house as we look for Delilah. Do you guys understand? Once we start moving in, there will be no verbal communication."

Campbell nodded. "Got it."

Cris re-checked her gear. "Understood."

Beau looked over at the SWAT team and gave one nod and a thumbs up. All together in unison they crouched down and began silently walking their boots towards the address. Arriving at the backside of the house, parts of the teams hid around it, some took their position right next to the door, more stayed back along each side and a final group of six, including Steele, Campbell, and Beau, all headed for the front.

Just as planned, the three SWAT were at the door, one directly in front and one on each side. Directly behind them were Campbell on the left, Cris in the middle and Beau on the right. Cris could feel her adrenaline fully rushing through her veins now. She was ready.

The SWAT guy right in front of her held up three fingers and counted them down. Upon reaching one, he banged on the old door. Wasting no time, he busted it in. Cris took the opportunity, and the lead, and crouched low as she squeezed in front of the SWAT team member.

Everything happened so quickly and seemingly silently. The suspect must have heard them and immediately tried to flee. Cris saw the figure of a man who looked like the one in the surveillance video heading towards the back door. When he saw it was surrounded and the SWAT team had begun to enter that way as well, he turned back around towards her.

Seeing he had a pistol in his hand, Cris raised hers and got in position trying to dig in with her heels. She could see the wild in his eyes as he fired at her before her stance was firm. She felt the burning of her skull as she fell to the ground.

Everything was blurry and going in slow motion. It was silent except the loud ringing in her ears. *Why the hell is it so silent?* She saw the SWAT team tackling him and Campbell looked like she was running over to her and Campbell's mouth looked like it was screaming but there was no noise coming out of it and everything was so slow and fuzzy. She saw more SWAT walking out of a room with a girl who looked a lot like the other girls they had been finding. *It must be Delilah.* Cris felt herself smile before it all went black.

Chapter 32

Cris squinted her eyes. She would swear that person walking towards her was Luke. There was no way, it just wasn't logical, but her heart started pounding and she picked up the pace nevertheless. As the figure loomed closer and became clearer, Cris' stomach started churning. There was no mistaking that crooked smile, it was Luke's signature smile and she had never seen another one quite like it.

"Holy Mary, Mother of God! No way!"

She took off at a run towards him. He was running towards her now too, arms outstretched. They clashed together, hard. Arms wrapped fully around each other, squeezing for all they were worth. She could feel her body shaking and the tears pouring down her cheeks. For once she didn't care.

Cris pulled back grabbed both sides of his head and looked Luke in those kind green eyes. "Look at you, my whole, beautiful, Steele Appeal. I'm so sorry I didn't tell you enough I loved you. I'm sorry I was seemingly cold and unemotional. Please tell me you know how much I love you, I promise I will be better at showing you more from now on...."

Luke pushed her hair back behind her ears. "Shh, it's okay baby. I know how much you love me, and I know why you carry your protective shield. But I also know what's really in your heart, the kind, caring and compassionate person you are when you think no one is looking."

He wiped the falling tears from Cris' eyes, pulled her head forward and kissed her on the forehead, then held her there for a minute with his temple on her forehead. She wrapped her arms around his waist. God how she had missed the feel of him in her arms. She inhaled his scent like a drug. She couldn't believe they were back together, then pulled back and looked at him confused. She remembered going in that house and the gun shot. She felt the side of her head, there was no injury. The realization hit her and her eyes went wide.

Luke kissed her hard while holding her hands. He slowly released her lips and even more slowly released her hands until their lingering fingertips disconnected as he began walking away. "It's not your time baby. Go. Find someone new to share your raillery and sense of humor with. Move on with your life. You've got a world to save down there. Go kick some ass, just like the old days on the playground..."

Luke's crooked smile was already fading out of sight and Cris had dropped to her knees, crying and reaching for him.

"... I love you, baby, carry on with your life down there, I'll be waiting for you up here. Don't worry, your dad and I are standing watch." And just like that, the sight of him was gone and in its place she was assaulted with obnoxiously loud alarms.

Cris opened her eyes to see Chief Bolton standing next to her. Although her reality seemed to have changed, that blasting alarm still beeped on. She felt a bandage wrapped around her head and a slight headache, but not too bad. She looked up and saw the IV dripping presumably pain meds and understood why her head didn't hurt so bad. The alarm suddenly stopped and Cris saw a nurse with strands of gray in her hair come into view from the back of her bed. Her thoughts were still fuzzy, and she was disoriented, but she was determined to focus.

The nurse leaned over the bed slightly. "Welcome back young lady, you gave us quite the fright. How are you feeling?"

Cris licked her parched lips. "Top notch."

The nurse smiled and squeezed Cris' arm as she stood to talk to Chief. "Her heart rate is coming back down now. We will continue to monitor it, but I think it was just a spike, maybe a bad dream or something. Let me know if you need anything else."

Chief looked at Cris as he spoke so quietly it was barely audible. "A bad dream. That certainly wouldn't surprise me. Thank you, Ma'am."

Cris knew it wasn't a dream, it was real. She smelled Luke. Held him, felt his kiss. She didn't bother trying to explain it, they wouldn't believe her anyway. They would probably think she was delirious. Looking back at Chief, who was now sitting down in the chair by her bed, she could see the thankfulness written all over his face.

"Damn you, Cris, you had me worried."

"Sorry, Sir. I assure you, it was not my intention when I woke up this morning..." Cris paused thinking. "...or whatever morning I last woke up."

"Yesterday. You're lucky to be alive right now, the bullet grazed your skull. Had you moved to the other side, it wouldn't have been the same story."

Cris tried her best to smirk. "Skill, Sir. Not luck. All skill."

"Glad to see you still have your sense of humor, although you might notice, I'm not laughing. Between the bandage on your head and the one on your arm, that looks mighty close to the artery according to the hospital I might add, I have to ask if you have a death wish? What in the actual fuck were you thinking? Going in head strong through that door ahead of the SWAT team? I'm worried about you Steele, I cannot lose you."

Cris felt that extra caring again, she didn't think he would feel or say the same to the rest of the team. It felt like he was saying he couldn't lose her as a person, not as an employee.

She pushed the thought aside as quickly as it came and responded the only way she knew how. "Ah, don't sell the team short. Bryan could step in for me."

Bolton raised his voice. "This is not the time for your fucking antics, Steele."

He took a breath and spoke much more calmly, almost pleadingly. "I need you to assure me you're not out trying to get yourself killed. Please."

Cris gave him a stare down and narrowed her eyes, her voice deep, clipped and crystal clear. "I do not have a death wish. I know what waits on the other side. It is warm and glorious, and I am not ready to see it again until I have seen that mother fucker fry for taking that away from me." She gave a brief pause. "Sir."

"Would you mind telling me what happened to your forearm? The doctors said it was deep and should have had stitches. Thankfully you kept it clean and the bandage tight enough that it shouldn't scar too bad. They did clean it up more and put some liquid glue on it. I couldn't answer to them how it happened though since you wouldn't tell anyone."

Cris sighed. "That's because it's kind of embarrassing. I expect you to take it to your grave if I tell you."

Chief smiled. "Shit, Cris. That bad? You have my word, I will not repeat it."

"I was organizing my silver wear drawer, I had a knife in my hand and stepped back and slipped on Stormy's ball. The knife gashed me on the trip down."

"That's it? I was waiting for some good juicy deep dark secret or something."

"It was klutzy of me. I'm not normally a clumsy person."

"It's okay to be human Cris, we all are. But, don't worry. I won't let anyone else know you're not superhuman."

Cris shrugged but didn't say anything. Not thinking, out of habit she put her hand up to her head to push back her hair, then stopped at feeling the bandage.

"It might be awhile before you pull your hair up in a pony tail again. They did the best they could, but the contact area was slightly burnt and open. They had to shave around it to get it clean and stapled. If you leave your hair down, it shouldn't be too noticeable."

"Well, in the meantime I guess it will just add to my superhuman persona then, right?" They both gave a chuckle.

Cris suddenly remembered why she was even there. "Delilah! Did they find Delilah alive?"

"Yes, Super Steele. You had the right address and got your man. Campbell and Beau interviewed Delilah after she was safe at home with her family. Our job here is done."

"Was she physically harmed?"

"No. He had her secured in a room, but she was not physically harmed. According to her, he thought she was his mother. He kept asking her why she didn't love him, that he tried so hard to be a good boy for her but she still hated him. We're convinced she made it a day longer than the other girls because she realized he was disturbed and played along with him the best she could."

"Wow! Good for her, she kept herself alive!"

"For sure. It was 10 years ago that he murdered his mother and the anniversary somehow snapped him. Although the fact that he killed her and lived with everything still in her name indicates he was already well on his way to the break. Either way, somehow in his contorted mind he was mixing his 16-year-old murdering self with these 16-year-old girls. So even though they are younger than his age now and couldn't possibly be his mother, his convoluted mind twisted it. No doubt he will plead insanity, but with 3 murders, including his mother, I don't see this small-town judge being too compassionate."

Cris thought about Chief Williams and how he instantly had a warrant and SWAT team at his disposal from said judge. "No, I don't either."

Cris scooched herself up a little higher in the bed and thought more about Delilah. "Damn, that girl has some survival instincts and tenacity."

She noticed Chief looked slightly confused and realized he couldn't read her thoughts. "Delilah. She should go into our line of work, sounds like she has the mind that works the same way. You never know, maybe someday we'll see her on a team in Sun County."

Chief smiled. "Yeah, I guess you never know. She may have found her calling with this whole ordeal. Speaking of which, there was some banter between Beau and Campbell about Beau, Wyatt or Mike transferring someday, or Campbell transferring up here someday. They were only half joking, at least I think, and I don't know these other people, so I wasn't really paying attention, but since you got to know them, I thought you might get a kick out of it."

Cris thought of that and laughed softly. "I don't see them leaving this area, and we both know Kim wouldn't actually leave the comforts of the island and be that far from the ocean. Although, if Beau came down it would give Bryan a break from the Campbell drool train. So, yes, thanks for sharing, I did get a kick out of it."

"Good. Well, I bet you'll be happy to get back and see Stormy. Bryan says she's doing great, but you know they always miss their mommas."

"Yes, I will be very happy to get back home and resume a normal life, whatever that even means. I know I promised Bryan I wouldn't ask him, but has he made any headway on Luke's case?"

Cris noticed Chief shifted in his chair. He straightened his glasses and cleared his throat. "Well, he was going to talk to you about that when you got back. We sat down together, like we usually do, and went over all the facts and evidence, which as you know, wasn't much. Since I know his conclusion, and we agree on it, I might as well tell you and save Pete the potential backlash."

Cris sat up as straight as her IV would allow her, she could feel her heart beating harder. *Keep it down, calm yourself. You don't need to set the alarms off again and get stuck here, you need to get home.*

Chief shook his head. "There's no easy way, so I'm just gonna say it. Based on the limited evidence we have and the zero help from interviews, the investigation indicates Luke's death was an accidental shooting by an amateur hunter, that just happened to get a very unlucky shot. So, yes, we still have a murderer to find who left the scene, but it was not a premeditated homicide, it was most likely an involuntary manslaughter."

She couldn't believe what she was hearing, and she fought back her tears and emotions with every fiber in her body. "My husband was shot in the fucking head, no way in hell it wasn't intentional."

"Well then, who did it? Give me some names? Who would have anything against him or something to gain from his death?"

Cris clenched her jaw. "I don't know, but I sure as hell intend to find out."

She thought of it from the something to gain angle and wondered why an image of Pete immediately came to her mind.

Chapter 33

Bolton wheeled Cris out to his SUV, despite her insistence on walking out herself. She was sitting in the wheelchair as he opened the back door to put in the small bag containing her meager belongings from the hospital. She noticed her backpack also sitting on the seat and a few of her plastic bags for the Vets on the passenger side floor. She didn't say anything as he closed the back door and opened the front one for her. Chief held his hand out and grabbed under her forearm as she stood and his other arm around her waist to help keep her stable. She wanted to tell him she could do it on her own and didn't need his help, but she knew he would do it anyway and also she didn't have the energy to expend on something so futile. The nurse turned away with the empty wheelchair as Chief closed her door.

Cris let Chief get buckled and put his vehicle in gear before she looked in the back seat, pretending to notice for the first time. "I see you've already got my baggage back there."

"Yes. Campbell drove your vehicle back down since I was going to be here with you. We both gathered your belongings from the hotel, I'm sure we got it all."

"I see she also felt the need to include my plastic bags of supplies."

"Campbell told me how you hand the bags out to homeless Veterans. She thought you might want some for the trip back down in case we stopped along the way for food or something and you saw the need."

"That was nice of her to share." Cris tried to sound sincere, but she knew the sarcasm was evident.

Chief glanced over at her. "You know, if it wasn't for your injury I would probably smack you upside the head. It's okay to let your shield down a little bit. And quite honestly, the fact you do hand those out to them doesn't surprise me at all. I know you are caring and you try to help others and enjoy it, you are the proverbial "give someone the shirt off your back" kind of girl. Even if you try not to let anyone see."

Wasn't that almost exactly what Luke had just said to me? That's just bizarre! Cris couldn't help but look up at the sky and choke back the tears. *I promise you, Luke, I will find your murderer if it's the last friggin thing I do!*

When Cris didn't respond to Chief, he looked over at her. "Rest, Cris. You've been through a lot in just the past week alone." He gave her a quick pat on the thigh and returned his attention to driving, ending any further conversation for a while.

Cris again felt that extra caring from him and she was sure, as amazing as he was, Chief was not so introspective of the rest of his staff like this. But she didn't want to say anything, especially after the last time when he told her he had some knowledge about her childhood. Besides the fact it was awkward, more importantly, she was now laser focused on Luke's case.

She laid her head back on the headrest and pretended to just be quiet and resting, enjoying the ride, but her mind was going a million miles an hour. She couldn't wait to get back home to her own private war room she had set up in her office. She was going to find this killer on her own, hunting accident or not, which she knew was bullshit. She was going to bring this guy down hard!

Cris' head started to hurt and her eyes were feeling gritty from watching the scenery pass by the window. She decided to close them to stop all the sensations. She didn't realize she had fallen asleep until she actually woke up. Looking out the windshield, she realized they weren't far from home.

"Feel a little better now? I know I always do after a nap, as rare as they are."

"I didn't even realize I was tired and I certainly didn't think I would have fallen asleep."

Cris' head felt itchy and she, again, forgot it had a bandage on it until she went to scratch it.

"You know, I've come to the conclusion, I seriously think I'm jinxed for head shots. Between me, Luke, my d..." She caught herself and gave a quick cough to try and cover. "I think I'm a magnet and maybe I should become a hermit for everyone else's safety."

Chief snorted. "I think you'd go stir crazy after the first day. Better keep your day job, Steele. I think we'll all take our chances."

Cris started thinking about some of the things Chief said recently, her mind starting to work. It felt like she was trying to put pieces of a puzzle together, but she couldn't quite put her finger on why. *"Let's just say I have some knowledge about your childhood and leave it at that. I have compassion for you, I can't help that. I feel the need to protect you, whether you need it or not." "I'm worried about you Steele, I cannot lose you. You've been through a lot in just the past week alone."*

Thoughts, memories, gestures, and words from the past year, but especially the past week, swirled through her head. *"Just the past week alone"* made her feel like Chief actually meant and left unspoken was *"your whole life"*. She didn't want to know, but yet, the nagging voice in her head would not stop.

"Chief, I'm not sure how much detail you know about my childhood. I don't know what's included in the hiring records, but I can't help but wonder if your concern over me having a death wish is in part because of that." Cris didn't finish the sentence with her thought of *like father, like daughter?*

"I don't get any personal background information from your file, I'm not privy to that kind of information. My knowledge does not come from your records, Cris. But, I have to admit, you're right, maybe a small part of my concern over a death wish does."

Chief thought for a moment and she let him do it without interrupting, she could tell he was thinking about either what he wanted to say, or if he wanted to say it.

"Let me ask you something, Cris. Did you ever wonder how you got this job so quickly, especially being fresh out of school?"

She was taken back by the question. She certainly hadn't seen that coming and was wondering where this conversation was suddenly going.

"Actually, no, I didn't. I guess I just kinda assumed it was my excellent grades and hands on training combined with a low applicant pool."

"There were dozens of well-experienced applicants who put in for this position. Many with years of experience and glowing reviews from their current divisions."

"I don't understand then, Sir."

"I knew you were finishing up with grad school and were almost ready to graduate. What I didn't know, but was secretly elated when I found out, was you would apply for a job on Shine Island, come back to Luke's hometown. When I saw your name with all the other applicants... Well, let's just say you don't know the strings I had to pull to get you hired over those other, even more, well-qualified applicants."

Cris was beginning to wonder if she was delirious after all because she could not make any sense of what was coming out of Chief's mouth.

"I'm gonna be honest here Chief, I am so confused and getting a little creeped out. I was thinking you had knowledge of my childhood by somehow hearing it from someone else, although I wouldn't know who. I have so many questions, but first of all, how did you know me before I applied for the job? No, wait, and why were you watching me? Why did you get me the job? How did you know Luke and this is his hometown?"

Chief held his hand up and cut her off. "This is all wrong. I shouldn't have said anything, at least not at this time, but I can't lie any better than you can. First..."

Chief was cut off by his phone ringing, he glanced down at his screen and sighed. "Shit. Hang on."

Cris noticed they were already turning onto her street. Her head was spinning both from the injury and the information overload, or question overload was more like it. She vaguely heard Chief talking on his phone, but she did realize the conversation was over quickly.

Chief looked at Cris. "I'm gonna drop you home quick, Pete will meet you there with Stormy. Your keys are in your bag from the hospital. I've gotta fire to put out back at the station, I've gotta get back there now. Sorry, Cris, I promise we will finish this conversation later."

"You bet your ass we will."

She tried to sound strong as they pulled into her driveway, even though she felt anything but. Looking at the empty house, green light still burning on the porch, she quietly released a sigh as she opened her door and got out.

Chapter 34

Chief had just finished getting the last of the bags out of the back when Pete pulled in. Stormy sitting in the passenger seat of his truck, her whole body moving with excitement as she saw her mommy and her home. Pete came rushing over to the side of the SUV where Cris and Chief were standing.

"Go ahead, Chief, get back to the station. I'll help Cris get her bags in."

"Thanks, Bryan. I appreciate it." Chief looked over at her. "Steele, I'll catch up with you later."

Cris mumbled under her breath. "Yes, you certainly will."

Pete started walking to his truck as Chief pulled out, he yelled back to Cris. "Hang on, I'm going to grab Stormy. You can love on her while I gather your bags."

Before she could respond about the bag carrying, Stormy came bounding over and jumped up on her. Her heart immediately melted and the bizarre conversation she had just been having with Chief faded away. She sat on her front lawn so Stormy didn't knock her down. She felt so much lighter with Stormy by her side. This dog was their baby, and she still couldn't help but feel like a part of Luke was living on through her.

Pete came over and joined them on the lawn, looked at them and smiled. "Aw, the simple joys a dog can bring. I know I've enjoyed spending these last few days with her. She's so happy to see you."

He spoke a little quieter. "And so am I. Although, I have to say, between your arm and your head you look the worse for wear. I thought you were kidding when you said you got a little scratch on your arm. Damn, Cris."

Cris tried to speak through Stormy twirling around her, sniffing and licking her.

"They're both a long way from my heart, I'll survive. Thank you for taking care of her for me Pete, it was really nice to know I didn't have to worry about her." Cris decided to ignore the other part he said about her arm and being happy to see her.

As Stormy started to calm down slightly, she focused on sniffing Cris' bandaged head, suddenly seeming concerned. "It's okay, Storm. Momma's okay. Things are gonna start calming down now girl, I'm gonna stop coming home smelling like blood."

Pete chuckled. "That would be nice, sounds like a good goal after this past week! Campbell filled me in, whether I wanted her to or not. It sounds like it was a pretty eventful couple of days."

"Yeah, sorry, I have no control over that girl. I should probably send the Jasper PD a sympathy card for having to put up with us."

Pete smirked. "I'm sure the two of you spiced things up a bit up there for those country boys."

"I was actually pleasantly surprised and quite impressed with a lot of their technology and equipment. It was kinda like a hidden gem or something."

"Well, we are all certainly glad to have you back. I'm not sure about Campbell, but you for sure." Pete gave a little laugh.

Cris didn't respond to his comment and again looked up to the empty house. "Speaking of which, I guess it's time to get back to reality."

Pete stood up. "You okay to handle Stormy? If so, I'll grab your bags."

Cris kept a hold of Stormy's leash as she stood. She saw stars and things swirled briefly, but she tried not to let on.

"Yes, I can handle this wild beast. Huh, girl?!" She gave Stormy a pet on the head and moved on to scratch her ears.

They walked up the porch steps together. Upon reaching the door, Cris remembered her house keys were in the hospital bag.

"Oh, you actually have my house keys in one of those bags."

"That's okay, I'll just use mine, it's easier than digging yours out." Pete quickly pulled out his key ring, unlocked and held the door open for Cris and Stormy.

Cris took Stormy's leash off, and she took off tearing through the house. "Guess she's glad to be home."

Pete set the bags down just inside the door. "I'm sure she is. She was very content at my place, but there's no place like home."

Pete gently placed his hand on Cris' shoulder. "I'm going to go grab her stuff from the truck. I'll be right back in."

Cris picked up the bags from the floor and carried them to the couch and began unpacking them. Once she set the supply bags for the Vets aside, she was only left with her backpack and hospital bag. She walked back to the bedroom with her backpack. Going into the closet, she placed her dirty clothes in the basket, and only gave a quick glance at Luke's dirty clothes still sitting there that she refused to move. She heard the front door shut and knew Pete had come back in. She shook her head as she shut off the light and left the closet, closing the door, and Luke's clothes, behind her.

She finished emptying the bag in the bathroom where she quickly put away her toiletries. Going out to hang the empty backpack in the coat closet, she noticed Pete putting Stormy's things back in place and was staring at the closed door to the office as he passed it.

Shit, I forgot about the office! I hope he didn't go in while I was away and see my own war room I've got going on for Luke. Nothing I can do about it now if he did. She wondered if he caught her staring at him, staring at the door. She straightened her shoulders as best as she could muster and kept walking.

She turned just slightly and yelled back to Pete. "I'm going to go check the mail quick, I'll be right back."

"Okay."

Cris took the short walk out to her mailbox and wondered why she had told Pete she was coming out to check the mail. It wasn't like it was his business, he wasn't Luke. Then, she realized it was a habit she had with Luke she wasn't even aware of. She grabbed the stack of mail from the mailbox alongside the road. She was hoping none of her neighbors were out as she tried to hurry back in. With all the police activity last weekend, her outburst, and now being all bandaged up, they must really wonder what the hell was going on.

She walked back in to see Stormy playing and jumping all over Pete. Hearing Stormy's bark and Pete's laugh automatically made Cris smile, whether she wanted it to or not. Pete must have heard her come back in even through Stormy's antics because he looked over at her.

"Hey, Cris, I was thinking. What did you have planned for dinner? All the food you have is frozen. I've got nothing going on. If you're up for some company, I thought maybe we could order in?"

Cris hadn't thought about dinner, she really didn't have much of an appetite. Even more, she didn't know how she felt about Pete staying for dinner. She was torn with her emotions with him right now. She couldn't help but still be suspicious of him, even if she had no solid evidence to be other than a gut feeling. The fact he hadn't found Luke's murderer, in her book also made it logical to further warrant her suspicion. At the same time, he was still Pete who was always so nice to her and always so good with Stormy. Luke's death had definitely come between them, at least to her, and she really didn't know if she was being logical or not.

She noticed Pete had come to the entryway of the dining room. Trying to avoid eye contact and answer the question right away, she looked over at the breakfast bar. She saw a piece of paper laying there and grabbed it. No matter how much she didn't want to, she couldn't hold back the smile as she read Pete's bill for his cleaning services. She glanced at Pete as she shook her head and snickered.

Setting the "bill" back down, Cris picked up the mail again and turned to set it on the table. *I'll deal with this later, right now I guess I have to see how I'm going to deal with Pete.* When she set the mail down, she saw a piece of paper folded in half sitting in the middle of it. She knew she left the table completely cleaned off before she left.

She turned to look at Pete as she pointed to the paper. "Is this yours too? Did you leave that there?"

Pete walked over towards the table, looking as he shook his head no. "Nothing I brought in. It was probably something you left there before you left."

"No. I know I have a head injury, but I am positive the table was clear."

Cris picked up the plain white paper and opened it, reading it to herself. The message inside was typed on a computer in a large font:

You are a sick coward bitch! You throw your husband in front of you to take the bullet instead of yourself. I will make sure I get you alone next time and I will not miss! Sweet dreams bitch!

In her peripheral vision, Cris vaguely saw Pete come rushing over as she gave a whimper, put her right hand over her mouth and slowly dropped to her knees.

Be on the lookout in late 2018 for the follow up:
Burying Steele

About the Author

H.B. Tyler resides on Hilton Head Island and can be found on occasion seeking inspiration, or sanity, in the crash of the ocean waves (which may or may not be accompanied by a liquid amber companion). H.B. is married with two extraordinary and mismatched boys, as well as one neurotic dog; which always guarantees to keep life busy, interesting and entertaining.

Keep up with H.B.

www.HBTyler.com

Facebook.com/Author H.B. Tyler

Snail Mail correspondence to:
H.B. Tyler
PO Box 22125
Hilton Head Island, SC 29925

www.ingramcontent.com/pod-product-compliance
Lightning Source LLC
Chambersburg PA
CBHW071511110726
47908CB00003B/804